IMAGE *destroyer*

LILY ALEXANDER

Image Destroyer

Copyright © 2022 by Lily Alexander

All rights reserved.

No part of this book may be reproduced in any form or by any electronic or mechanical means, including information storage and retrieval systems, without written permission from the author, except for the use of brief quotations in a book review.

This book is a work of fiction. Names, characters, businesses, places, events, locales, and incidents are either the products of the author's imagination or used in a fictitious manner. Any resemblance to actual persons, living or dead, or actual events is purely coincidental.

ISBN: 978-1-958933-00-8 (Ebook)
ISBN: 978-1-958933-01-5 (Paperback)

Cover Design: Kate Farlow, Y'all. That Graphic.
Interior Design: Stephanie Anderson, Alt 19 Creative
Edited by: Abby at Abby Content Editing
Proofreading by: H. C. Bentley

IMAGE SERIES:
Image Adjuster
Image Protector
Image Destroyer

HOLLYWOOD CONNECTIONS SERIES:
Winter Bloom
Spring Breeze
Summer Storm
The Fragile Duet
(coming 2022/2023)

*This one is for my husband, who was both
impatient for this story to be written and helped
make it better every step of the way.*

*Thank you for not letting me give up on this one, even
when I thought I was failing at telling this story.*
< 3

AUTHOR'S *Note*

This book contains mention of SA (any instances took place before this story's timeline and there is no graphic description of the acts), has themes of parental manipulation and much of the story takes place in a rehabilitation facility. This book is not dark, but please read with caution if these things are a risk to your mental wellbeing.

If you need more detail on specific items this book may contain, please reach out to me via email and I'll be happy to give you more information!

CHAPTER
One

"SEE? WE MADE it. You were upset about nothing, Jerry." Olivia's tone was flippant, but her attorney looked less than amused as he glared at her before getting out of the car. He slammed the door, making her jump.

She hesitated for a moment, thinking he might come around to open her door, but he stopped at the trunk instead.

"Fine. I'll get it myself." Olivia pulled the handle and climbed out, blinking against the brightness of the sun.

"You weren't even *packed* when I showed up this morning, Olivia," Jerry groused as he unloaded her bags.

"And it still worked out. That's all I'm saying. For the record, I wasn't packed because I wasn't planning on coming."

As she adjusted her sunglasses and pulled her purse strap over her shoulder, her attorney turned bright red, his rage palpable as he smoothed his tie down.

"We've been over this, more than once. It's this or jail. Which do you prefer?"

She tsked with her tongue, waving a hand to dismiss his overly serious tone. "I think you're being a little over-dramatic."

"I assure you, I am most certainly not." He fastened the button on his suit jacket and slammed the trunk, leaving her luggage on the ground next to the car.

"What about my bags?"

"I'm sure someone will be along in a moment to help with the bags."

He guided her toward the front door with a hand on her shoulder, as though he didn't trust her to walk inside by herself.

"I'm *going*, Jerry. What am I going to do, walk home? Since it took over an hour to get here, that seems unlikely."

"I'm not taking any chances with you after how this morning has gone."

They entered what appeared to be a beachside mansion, the air conditioning wrapping around them like a cool cloud the moment the door opened.

Instead of a grand foyer, there was a business-like lobby, complete with a reception window. Olivia had been expecting an open space with high ceilings, not a doctor's office-type lobby with old magazines on a table and uncomfortable chairs. It was wholly disorienting.

"Welcome to Sunrise, how can I help you?" The receptionist asked, smiling at them from behind her counter.

"Olivia Black, checking in," Jerry said curtly, glancing over at her.

Olivia replaced the scowl on her face with a tight smile.

"Of course. We've been expecting you. Someone will be right with you." The pretty receptionist touched her headset, answering a call after acknowledging them.

A door on the far side of the room opened seconds later, revealing a middle-aged woman in tidy purple scrubs.

"Hello, Olivia. If you'll come right this way?"

Jerry positioned Olivia in front of him, giving her a little push as she followed the woman through the door. They were led into an open living room area full of ultra-modern plastic tables and chairs. Not a sharp edge to be found; everything molded as one piece. Olivia wondered if this was a design choice or a safety decision. She decided it was probably both.

"Please, have a seat. If you'll give me a moment, I'll let Pauline know you're here."

"Thank you," Jerry said.

"Why are you being so nice? I don't even need to be here," Olivia grumbled under her breath once the nurse walked out of earshot.

Jerry made a frustrated noise in his throat, tossing a sharp glare at her as he gestured to the closest chair. "Sit."

"I'm fine. We were just in the car for like forever."

"Olivia. *Sit.*"

Annoyed she felt compelled to obey him due to the severe tone he was using on her, Olivia plunked herself down in a bright red chair.

"It's this or jail. I'm not sure how else to say it so the information gets through your head. Do you understand how deep the shit you're in is? It's so bad they required me to escort you in. You were not trusted to do it yourself, and for good reason." The disdain in his eyes reminded Olivia of being scolded by her father.

The shoe fit, honestly. Her attorney was at least as old as her dad, but thankfully more attentive.

"I'm a full-grown adult, you know. I don't need a chaperone. Besides, Mom said she'd find a way to spring me early. It's not a big deal."

Jerry's jaw muscles popped as he ground his teeth together. Olivia knew she was treading on thin ice with him. He was more forgiving than he should be with her, but she would be headed to his black list if she didn't quit giving him such a hard time.

He'd been faithful as her attorney for years, even through times when she was incredibly needy or problematic. She appreciated him, even if she didn't act that way all the time. Also, she paid him extraordinarily well for the privilege, so it seemed like a fair trade.

"Funny, because the court order in my briefcase says differently. I'm not aware of many adults who misbehave like toddlers in need of a nap quite the way you do, Olivia. Perhaps I should have just let you end up in jail."

Olivia shifted uncomfortably on the hard chair in the sterile feeling room.

The smooth plastic seat reminded her of the chairs elementary schools used. She scoffed at the thought, realizing it was probably intentional. The people running this rehab probably acted as if all the residents were volatile children. She'd been spoken to in quiet tones by two separate people since they arrived, which felt like enough evidence to make such a claim.

Everyone kept saying how awful her situation was, but they were all blowing things out of proportion. People did much worse things than blackmail or post revenge porn or follow their ex around, especially in Hollywood. They didn't *all* go to jail.

"I guess," she huffed, realizing he'd probably been aiming his pointed glare at her for quite some time, waiting for a response.

Her stoic attorney was nonplussed by her attitude, but it wasn't something she could just turn off. Nothing had gone her way for months now, and she was in an exceptionally bad mood.

"Sixty days, Olivia. Two months. Pretend you're on an acting retreat or something. Use the time to better yourself, or something." Mouth pinched, he gestured with his hands in illustration. "I know you don't want to be here, but it is required by the state of California." He raised an eyebrow.

"Unless you'd rather take your chances in jail? There would be no privileges. No celebrity cell. General population, zero chance of getting out early for good behavior."

Olivia groaned. It was all so *unreasonable*. "I hear you. I swear I do. I've been here for nearly a whole hour already and I've played along fine. You and I both know I don't belong here."

He made a noise in his throat that made her eye twitch.

"So you keep saying, but you're incorrect. You *do* need to be here. The judge presiding over your court case says you do. The state of California says you do. I'd bet the people who pressed charges against you would whole-heartedly agree with the judge, not *you*. Make it work. You can plot your rise from the ashes once you've been thoroughly rehabilitated. Also, you've been here fifteen minutes and interacted with precisely nobody. Get a *grip*, Olivia." He barked the words with finality, but she was just getting started.

She pinned him with a glare. "I'm not some fucking *junkie*! Anyone who has to drive in Los Angeles on a regular basis could be labeled as needing help with anger management."

He leaned forward on the table, meeting her gaze and asserting authority over the top of it. "You stalked Maxwell for months! Showed up multiple places you shouldn't have been. Sent a drone to take pictures of him and his new girlfriend. You *stalked* him. You're a spoiled, selfish brat and while that may be your mother's fault, it's time you took ownership. Nobody owes you shit and nobody cares who you are. You're nothing more than a familiar face who pops up sometimes in the background of a show from time to time. Mostly you're just a girl who got famous doing porn and stayed famous for behaving badly."

Eyes popping wide, Olivia growled at her attorney, excuses for what she'd done dancing on the tip of her tongue. He'd never spoken so harshly to her in their decades of working together.

"How dare y—"

"I see I've *finally* gotten your attention," he interrupted the rant she was fueling up for. "You participated in blackmail, which resulted in someone getting paid to post revenge porn. You stalked your ex. You broke into someone's apartment. All *illegal*. You were convicted and sentenced. You have been mandated to either get some help or get locked up. This is not open for debate." He shook his head fiercely, fists tight on the tabletop and a vein throbbing in his temple. "My personal opinion about it is irrelevant. You have to prove to the world at large you've turned yourself around, not me. I don't give a single shit what you do in your free time or to make money except when it gets you in trouble and results in me working overtime. Make. This. *Work.*" With a resounding thump, he slammed his briefcase on the table to punctuate his words.

"No need to get so excited, Jerry. I wouldn't want you to have a heart attack." As she stood, Olivia turned a pitiful face at him she felt was sure to melt his currently cold, logical heart. Snark, as usual, shielded her embarrassment.

"I'm not new at this, you know. Your sad little girl act won't work on me. Get your shit together and take the therapy. Or you *will* go to jail. It's a term of your parole. Mind your p's and q's. Understand?" His expression softened the tiniest bit as she continued to stare at him. "Christ, you're annoying, kid. I can't figure out why I deal with you most days."

"Because you love me, Jerry."

"Yeah, yeah." He sighed, straightening his jacket as he got to his feet.

Olivia took his capitulation as a small win as she watched an official looking woman cross the room toward them. She was wearing a tailored pantsuit in navy, her hair in a classy twist. The clipboard in her hands and lanyard with an array of keys not only killed the chic look she was going for, but also gave away her position.

"Hi there!" the woman interrupted, a welcoming smile on her face. She extended a hand to Jerry, then to Olivia. "I'm Pauline, I'm the director here at Sunrise. You must be Olivia?"

"Yes." She gave nothing further, and the director gave the tiniest flinch at the lack of social nicety offered.

"Lovely to meet you. We've got a few items to take care of as far as paperwork and formalities, then we'll get you paired up with a more experienced resident for a tour of the campus. Sound okay?"

"Sure." Olivia's cheerful tone belied her absolute boredom at the thought of it all. She was horrified they still did the buddy system like it was high school and she was the new transfer student.

"We can get this all settled pretty quickly." Pauline gestured at the same table they'd previously been sitting at, sharing copies of the agreement contract with them. "I just need a few signatures, and have some points of clarification to go over in case there are any questions."

Olivia's eyes glazed over as Pauline detailed the list of do's and don'ts. It was a detailed, *long* list of restrictions. She looked up at one point to find Jerry glaring a hole through her skull.

"Wait, this says I'm supposed to surrender my phone? And my laptop?" Olivia tried to manage her tone of voice, but wasn't successful. Her horror resonated around the large room.

"Yes, it's mandatory. Those items will be kept for you in a safe place until you either earn privileges or graduate out. If you need to access your contacts list, or say, get a password, we can assist you. We allow two thirty-minute check-ins per resident per week. You will be given access to our computers and phones. We do understand some business has to be taken care of while you're here, but for a fully immersive experience, we limit it as much as we can. All communications are monitored for your safety and success. Emergencies are different, of course."

Straightening her back, Olivia used the pen Pauline provided to sign her name at the bottom of a handful of forms. She didn't have any rebuttal to the explanation that wouldn't get her scolded by Jerry. Stomach churning, she pushed the completed documents across the table and dug her phone from her purse, sliding it to Pauline as well. It felt like a limb being removed when Pauline slid the device into her pocket.

"Wonderful. We truly hope you benefit from and enjoy your stay with us, no matter what circumstances may have brought you here."

Pauline stood, Jerry and Olivia following a moment after. As she signaled to another staff member through her phone, Jerry grabbed at his briefcase.

"Are we all set here?" he asked formally.

"Oh. Yes, we should be."

"Thank you for your help, Pauline. I'll be in touch, Olivia. Behave yourself."

Olivia's nose wrinkled at the scolding.

"I'll do my best," she answered tightly, teeth clenched to keep in the swear words wanting to escape.

He walked back the direction they'd come in, leaving her at the cheap plastic table with the director without so much as a backward glance.

Rage bubbled under her skin, but she tempered it with a cool smile as a handsome man entered the room.

Her smile faltered when she realized she recognized his face.

CHAPTER
Two

THE FAMILIAR MAN crossed the room casually, hands tucked into his pockets.

Ollie Parkinson.

Fit, handsome. Trouble with a capital T. He was a B-list actor like her, though he'd had a fall from grace he was still recovering from. He was basically the poster child for how badly growing up as a spoiled child star can go. It didn't help that he had a history of getting overly handsy with female costars, among other things.

He was also someone she'd hooked up with at a club, once upon a time.

"Wonderful timing, Oliver. Thanks for coming. Would you mind showing Olivia around, please? She'll be staying in the Juniper suite."

"Sure, Pauline." His face was impassive as he replied, but Olivia could feel some faint recognition as his eyes passed over her face.

The director's eyes darted between the two of them. "Wait. Do you two already know one another?"

"We've met," Olivia said, but to her surprise, Ollie answered the opposite.

"Oh." Pauline's eyebrows pulled together as she glanced between them.

"It's been… a while," Olivia added. The night had certainly been memorable for her, but it would seem he didn't have the same recollection she did.

Ollie frowned, slanting his bright aqua eyes in her direction as if trying to place the when and where.

Olivia fought hard to keep her expression blank as she wondered how much he remembered about their night together. It appeared as though he didn't recall her at all, which was a blow to her ego, if nothing else.

"I see. Is there any problem? Do you feel uncomfortable being with an acquaintance?"

"I don't." Ollie rocked back on his heels, tossing a lock of sandy hair out of his eyes with a flip of his head. It was shorter on the sides than it had been the last time she'd seen him. Still long enough to get in his face on top, but barely.

"Olivia?"

"No," she said, tearing her eyes from him before she could get caught up staring. "We're fine."

"Alright." She glanced skeptically between them for a long moment. "Olivia, it was a pleasure to meet you. All my contact information is listed in the brochure along with your daily schedule. Please don't hesitate to reach out if you need something."

"My luggage—"

"No need to worry, your personal belongings will all be waiting for you in your room. We had someone take them over already, after they were checked. If you don't mind, I'll need to see your purse as well." Olivia begrudgingly handed over her purse. Pauline pushed around the contents, satisfied the tubes of lipstick were actually lipstick and nothing was disguised contraband before handing it back. "Thank you. We know it's awkward."

Olivia felt foolish for not having considered the possibility her things would be searched. It was possible Jerry had mentioned it and she'd ignored what he was saying. It made perfect sense though, they'd want to be sure nobody was bringing in things they weren't supposed to. She still felt uncomfortable how her belongings had been pawed through. She hated to think someone could just open her laptop or phone and go snooping, even though it wasn't likely to happen.

Pauline left, the pair of them still standing awkwardly next to the table.

"Ready for the grand tour? It's a pretty nice pl—"

"We don't have to do the polite, friendly thing."

His eyebrows rose, but he didn't argue. "Okay. Let's start with the important stuff. You hungry? There's probably snacks out in the dining room. You missed breakfast."

"I could use a drink."

Ollie snorted. "Not a chance of finding any hard stuff here, I'm afraid, babe."

She clucked her tongue in annoyance. "Not booze. I was talking about water."

"Ah. Well, in that case…" He grinned at her, sending a shock wave of sensation through her gut. She couldn't identify if it was revulsion or attraction, but either way, it irritated her. "I got you covered."

"Don't call me by any cute nicknames. I'm not your babe." Especially not if he couldn't even remember her.

Ollie's eyebrows climbed even higher. "Holy shit. My apologies, princess. I was just being friendly, but I swear, it won't happen again. Let's go find you some water, yeah?"

Olivia followed him out of the room, well aware he'd snuck in another stupid nickname but unprepared to battle him over it. Seeing him again had her stomach twisted up and her claws ready to come out.

The campus was a sprawling multi-million-dollar estate tucked into the bluffs above Malibu. Some ridiculously wealthy donor had supplied the land and paid for the structures to be built. There were two main buildings settled around a massive pool. Beyond the mansion-like structures were various garden games and expansive lawn area.

Olivia absently wondered how much it must cost to water the acreage of green every day.

"Group therapy in the big room you started in, arts and crafts is upstairs." He gestured to rooms as they passed them.

"But this is my favorite place on campus." He stopped outside the dining room, which looked a lot like an upscale restaurant.

He strode over to a glass-fronted cooler full of assorted drinks and grabbed out two bottles of water.

Olivia accepted one, cracking it open as they exited the main building through some heavy glass-lined French doors.

"The pool is open eight to ten, though most of the time we're too busy to use it, except on our rest days."

"Rest days?"

Ollie's aqua gaze met hers as they crossed the expansive stone patio around the pool. There were chairs and sofas with fire pits in multiple sitting areas. There was also an area built out with a gourmet outdoor kitchen. It was all done in peach and tan flagstone, with a few grays mixed in. It was a stark contrast to the deep green of the lawn and the nearly black natural bluffs of the area.

Olivia used her hand to shade her eyes from the bright sun. She caught some sparkles off of the water in the pool and smiled. She had a feeling her favorite spot would be right here. Not that she planned to get comfortable, but it would be nice to have somewhere to go unwind.

"We get one full day a week to ourselves. One other day, therapy sessions are limited to one or two depending on your program, so it's almost like a weekend."

"Mmm." She needed to take a closer look at the torture schedule they'd made up for her.

The ocean crashed on the rocky shore a short walk across the highway and down a sharp slope from the front gate of the compound. Olivia suppressed a groan, picturing herself sprawled out on a lounge chair near the surf with a fruity cocktail, complete with a paper umbrella.

As much as she was trying to stay neutral where Ollie was concerned, he wasn't filling the quiet space between them with pointless chatter, which she appreciated, and he was being helpful.

"The gazebo thing is the yoga pavilion. There are sports of all kinds back there, too." He pointed across the grassy expanse.

Olivia spotted a third building at a reasonable distance across the yard. Ollie explained that it was used for staff housing. All the buildings were designed to look and act as self-contained mansions with a central living space and a fully functional gourmet kitchen.

He directed them back to the building where her suite was.

Instead of a regular front door, there were industrial style glass double doors mirroring the ones on the back side of the main building. They opened into an expansive great room, where a living room space flowed into an open kitchen and dining room. There was a bank of countertop off to the side of the living room with chairs slid under it, like a desk.

He saw her looking and said, "That's the information station. They only turn on the Wi-Fi and cell service on designated evenings. They bring over a big bin full of computers and tablets and phones. Someone will be standing over your shoulder pretty much the whole time watching, but you can check your stuff."

Olivia scowled. "Great."

Ollie gestured down a hall on the first floor before starting up the wide flight of stairs. "My room is down there. There's only five—well, six with you, I guess—of us in this building right now."

"Slow season?" She quipped.

Ollie's mouth twitched. "Something like that. The main house is for... lower profile guests. Cheaper, too."

Guests.

Olivia was amused by the word. While she was certainly paying for the privilege of occupying a room, she was by no means a voluntary guest.

"This would be you." Ollie opened the door to a room marked with a small wreath made from juniper branches. She pulled off one of the small blue berries, crushing it between her fingers and releasing the bright pine scent.

"That's what they make gin out of," Ollie said offhandedly, the ghost of a grimace crossing his face.

"I know," Olivia replied, scowling at him. She and gin hadn't spoken a single word since that night. She couldn't help wondering if he'd mentioned it because gin was her drink of choice back then.

He blinked at her icy tone, offering her the tiniest of chagrined smiles, but said nothing. With the wave of an arm, he gestured for her to go inside while he remained in the hall.

Front and center in the large bedroom was a plush queen-sized bed. The room had windows on three sides and was brightly lit from the late-morning California sun.

"Looks alright." By all accounts, it was a luxurious suite, but Olivia didn't want to throw out high praise for what amounted to a cell. A nice one, maybe, but still a cage she didn't want to be in.

"They take pretty stellar care of us here. The showers are always hot, the food kicks ass and the beds sleep well."

"Good to know, but I don't plan on staying."

Ollie nodded, but his mouth hitched up on one side. "None of us do, right? If you need anything, I'm in the Orange Blossom room. Main floor, down the hall like I said."

"I won't."

"Right. See you around, Princess."

He left without a backward glance, and Olivia wasn't sure how to feel about that. She was used to getting the final word. Never mind the fact they had quite a few unspoken things between them.

She took a moment to admire the amazing view her room had of the ocean in the suddenly too-quiet room.

There was a folder with her name on it atop the small desk. She flipped through it, finding another copy of her schedule as well as little brochures on all of the things she'd been signed up for.

She pulled out the sample schedule and groaned.

Times / placement of all sessions may vary
Breakfast
Group Therapy
Arts and Music
Lunch
Individual Counseling
Meditation / Yoga
Dinner
Free Time

"Oh, my God. Every day?" Olivia's skin crawled. It was *so much* therapy. Smiling and pretending and putting on a show all day long, six days a week.

Jerry's suggestion filtered through her mind. He hadn't been far off base suggesting she treat it as an acting retreat. If nothing else, this would definitely be a test of her acting skills.

It was nearly lunchtime according to the schedule, her stomach alerting her of the fact with a rumble she was relieved had waited to show up until she was alone.

After a quick detour into the spa-quality bathroom to freshen up, she decided to walk back over to the dining room to see if all the praise for the food was accurate or overblown.

Ollie was not far behind her, but thankfully, he was preoccupied with another resident who was very enthusiastically telling him a story complete with wild hand gestures.

Olivia squinted against the bright sunlight as she stepped back outside and crossed the center courtyard. It certainly wouldn't take much for her to pretend she was at a resort based on the accommodations.

She confidently strode into the main building and toward the dining room. A staff member lingering near the door directed her to a table set for four. She was worried she might be forced to mingle with people she didn't want to know or speak to, but in the end, she was left seated alone.

A single-page menu was provided, with two choices for each course, similar to the prix fixe menus at any of the upscale restaurants she'd been to. She made her selections after a bit of debate. There was nothing suitable for the diet plan she'd followed for most of her life, but Olivia decided she didn't really care. If she was going to have to gut her way through this experience, she could at least enjoy the food.

As she was served at her solitary table, she watched how the other groups interacted. Her normal desire to be the center of attention was conspicuously absent. She mostly wanted to disappear into the background and be as invisible as possible so she could go home. Until she figured out a way to get around the court order and skip out, she'd have to play the game, which required figuring out both the rules and the other players.

After she'd finished the indulgent meal, she wandered around the campus on her own, taking advantage of having an empty schedule for the remainder of her first day. She decided it wouldn't be too hard to make the most of her free time if she put a little bit of planning into it.

The pool beckoned her every time she caught a shimmer coming off of the teal water out of the corner of her eye. She'd have her bikini on and the sun's rays soaking into her skin as soon as she could manage.

The grassy area went on for acres, and as Olivia walked the pristine, diagonally cut lawn, she found croquet, tennis, bocce and even badminton. While well hidden, she could see the nearly invisible fences keeping unwanted guests out... and paying guests in.

Out of things to see and assured of the 'security' of the facility, she walked the path back to her building. She didn't want to go so far as to unpack as if she was planning to stay, but she also didn't want to raise suspicion that she was planning to leave.

Besides, when Jerry had shown up to fetch her from the house, his barking had compelled her to haphazardly toss things into her luggage. She honestly wasn't even sure what all she'd packed, but she was sure all of it was just crammed in there as a crumpled ball. Leaving everything wrinkled didn't sound appealing either.

After rationalizing it would also be far easier to do her skincare routine if she organized her product on the counter, she spent an hour placing her things in the room.

Her panic packing had resulted in two bathing suits, at least, and plenty of t-shirts to go along with workout leggings. As she piled things into the dresser, she realized she'd never know if something she packed had gone missing during the search.

After she was done, she paced, wishing she had access to her computer or phone. Adjusting to being completely disconnected, aside from her two designated half hour check-ins every week, was going to be the hardest part.

Olivia flopped onto the surprisingly plush bed, plotting her next move. She had to survive long enough to leave. Until then, she would just have to play along.

Three

THE MORNING AFTER Olivia's arrival, Pauline came into the dining room to make an announcement during breakfast.

While Olivia could get behind the tactic of trapping people while they ate as a guaranteed way to spread information you needed them to hear, she at the very least needed caffeine before getting surprises. Thankfully, she'd already gotten her food from the buffet and there was a full carafe of dark roast on the table.

Olivia mixed sugar and cream into her cup as the perky director addressed the group.

"As you may or may not know, here at Sunrise we try to maintain a relatively small resident pool." Her lanyard, heavy with keys, jangled as she turned side to side, making sure to address the entire group. Olivia scanned the dining room, counting twelve residents including herself. "We also strive to keep the ratios of new residents and those nearly through the program as equal as possible so we can have what is effectively a mentor-mentee pair system for the residents who stay longer than thirty days." There were some groans, and Pauline held up her hand. "I know, I know. Sounds awful, but I swear time and again it's proven helpful. There is no opting out of this, but if you and your mentor absolutely are not a match, we can look into alternatives. I want to be clear, switching is a rare and extreme circumstance. We highly recommend taking advantage of the helping hand and expertise your graduating mentor can offer." She clapped her hands, trying to silence the whispering chatter that had broken out. "We do our best to balance a mix of strengths with overall compatibility."

"What all do we do with our mentors?" One of the other new residents, a young man, asked.

Olivia recognized him from the previous day. He'd been in the dining room at dinner, but not lunch.

"Great question. They're expected to give you advice where they can. About the facility, therapy, things like that. Answer any questions you might have. We also encourage some time together doing regular things, like having meals. Some of your therapy sessions will line up. We'd suggest trading phone numbers or emails for possible future use if it's something you're both comfortable with. Basically, they're someone you can rely on outside of the staff to guide you through your journey."

"Doesn't sound so hard," someone across the room muttered.

"I'm glad you think so. We have seen this system result in pretty wonderful friendships over the years, and that's honestly one of our hopes for every pairing. I'll be calling people in to discuss their matches throughout the day, okay?" Her rhetorical question was met with some shuffling, but not much else. "Alright. Welcome to Sunrise! Enjoy your breakfast."

Pauline strode out of the dining room, leaving the residents in a sort of shock. Slowly, people started to chatter and resume eating.

Olivia's arms were tightly crossed over her chest, and had been since Pauline began explaining things. She had a sneaking suspicion she knew exactly who she'd get matched up with.

As if he'd heard her thoughts, Ollie glanced up from a table across the room. His bright eyes locked on hers, fork dangling from his fingertips as he thoughtfully chewed. It wasn't until his table mate leaned forward to get his attention that Ollie broke the connection.

The announcement left Olivia frustrated. While in theory she could understand why having access to someone who had basically completed the program was a good idea, she could also see the arrangement being a complete pain in her ass.

She continued eating her breakfast, sad the hash browns were now barely warm and her egg yolk had congealed on the plate. Cutting her losses, she picked a fruit danish from the small basket on the table and refilled her coffee cup from the metal carafe.

Her whole body tensed as she watched Ollie saunter out the door of the dining room, his eyes once again locked on hers. Tension knotted her shoulders as he laughed. There was no way to tell if he was laughing at her or at something his companion had said.

Was he pretending not to remember her? Had she just been another groupie he'd screwed in the VIP room? Those kinds of questions got caught in Olivia's train of thought, repeating themselves and leaving her frustrated.

Olivia grabbed a napkin and took the pastry with her to her first art therapy session. The pleasant taste got her through trying to sketch a basket of fruit, one minuscule flaky bite at a time.

Right after she scribbled through the lopsided apple in frustration, Pauline poked her head into the room.

"Olivia? Could I please borrow you for a moment?"

As Olivia got to her feet, breakfast turned to lead in her gut, her stomach churning as she followed Pauline down the hall to an office. There was no reason for it to feel as though she'd been called into the principal's office, but that's exactly what it seemed like.

"Sorry to interrupt your session," Pauline said, dropping into the chair behind a rich cherry desk.

"It's fine. Drawing isn't really my strong suit." She perched on the edge of the seat, fingernails picking at the hem on her shirt.

Pauline laced her fingers together on the desktop. "I'm afraid art is not my talent, either." She peered at Olivia with intensity. "I don't want to beat around the bush or waste your time. I've asked Oliver to be your mentor."

Olivia gritted her teeth at the confirmation.

Oblivious to the lava churning in Olivia's gut, Pauline continued. "I feel he would be a perfect match for you. Well, at least as perfect as we see here at Sunrise. You already have a lot in common, and I feel as though you're starting from a similar place in your journeys."

Olivia restrained herself from swearing. "I had a feeling you'd mention him."

"Oh? Am I so predictable?" Pauline chuckled. "Do you have any objections? Do you feel uncomfortable being paired with someone you know from your outside life? In most circumstances, we'd actively try to avoid it, but it came across as though you were more like acquaintances than anything else."

Olivia could think of a few points of discomfort, but it was nothing she couldn't deal with. "Nothing in particular. I really don't know him very well at all, so..." She kept the caveat that he'd spent some time inside her body to herself.

"Lovely. Well, I'm glad the pairing works out. Is there anything else I can help you with while I've got you?"

"Unless you can release me early for good behavior, no, I don't think so." Olivia was joking... mostly. Her heart leaped as the words left her lips. She might have fainted on the spot if it were so simple.

Pauline gave a tense chuckle that told Olivia she wasn't the first to make a similar joke. It appeared the director was no longer amused by it, either. So much for flying under the radar.

"I'm glad you're settling in. Let's get you back to your session."

Pauline got to her feet and led Olivia from the office and back down the hall. To Olivia's relief, art therapy was already breaking up, and she was headed into a free period.

"Thank you for your time." Pauline turned her attention to someone else, leaving Olivia standing there with a new problem to solve.

She decided it was best handled with a cold drink and some sunshine, so she headed to the pool to debate this turn of events.

Unfortunately, she wasn't the only one who had that idea. Ollie was sitting on the edge with his feet in the water when she got out on the deck.

Too stubborn to leave, she sat down across the pool from him and dipped her own toes while pretending to ignore him.

"How was your meeting with Pauline?" he asked.

"Fine, I guess. I'm sure you already know what she had to say."

He flicked some water across the pool with his fingers. "I accepted you as my mentee, Princess. It's not like we're getting hitched. Besides, it's not a terrible match. We've got some things in common."

The only response she gave was to stare at him over

the top of her sunglasses. He clearly didn't know the half of it, and the reminder left her irritated.

He sighed. "Look. Believe it or not, I get it. We don't have to be friends, but it could be a bonus perk. It's only for thirty days. Your first month and my last. We'll survive it. Everyone does."

"I honestly don't plan to be here that long," she snipped. "What is it exactly you think we have in common?" She asked the question, knowing her intentional goading to find out what he recalled about their night together gave her fifty/fifty odds of ending up with her feelings hurt.

"Well, we do work in the same industry. Plus, we have the same name. I think that's mostly what it boils down to for Pauline, to be honest. The work thing I mean, not the name. The name thing is just an unlucky coincidence." His quip left her with a mild desire to smile, but she stifled it. He'd made an overture about how lovely her name was the night at the club, too. "Anyway, we've had similar experiences because of what we do, even if we're here for very different reasons."

"Go on," she invited him to continue, one eyebrow arched high.

"Olivia Black, actress. Got her start in commercials and soap operas as a child, graduated to bit parts in films with some more commercials mixed in as a teen. Some… *adult* film work, more minor mainstream film and also some TV roles here and there." He tilted his head as though gauging her reaction. "How'd I do, Princess? For what it's worth, that could also be my filmography. We've followed similar career paths. It's what we have in common. Like you said before, we've even met." He focused in on her face, eyes roaming over her features as though still trying to puzzle out the details of their previous introduction.

"Sounds like you did your homework. Nice to see my IMDB page is getting a workout occasionally." Sarcasm coated her words, disguising the disappointment over the fact he didn't recall anything more about her other than what he could find online.

Ollie pulled his legs out of the pool, twisting sideways before he climbed smoothly to his feet.

"So, you accepted?"

"It didn't feel as though I had real choice. You seemed like the lesser evil, so I went with it. The devil you know versus the devil you don't. You understand, I'm sure." Her tone was bland, but she chose her words specifically to needle him.

Chagrined, he gave a shrug and lopsided grin. "I've heard something similar before. More than once, actually. Looks like we're in this together for a while. I'll see you around, Princess."

He didn't spare her another glance as he went into the resident building.

Olivia sat with her feet in the teal water, kicking her frustration out as the sun beat down on her skin. She didn't move until it was time to leave for her first round of group therapy.

CHAPTER *Four*

THE SMALL CIRCLE of smooth plastic chairs in the center of the large living room made her cringe, but she took an available seat. She avoided the red one she'd sat in when she first arrived in favor of one in green.

Olivia hated those chairs.

A petite brunette quieted the group down a few minutes after the official start time.

"Welcome, everyone. I'm Dr. Annie Clay for those of you new to the program. A few quick things. While it is mandatory for you to attend group sessions, participation is voluntary. We do, however, encourage it. Active participation can be super valuable for both you and the staff as we guide you along your healing journey. It should be said upfront that we don't follow the traditional twelve steps model for this program, but the ideology is similar. Are there any questions before we get started?" She clasped her hands together, an inviting smile on her mouth. "Great. Today's topic is apologizing. One of the first steps into true recovery is making amends with those you have hurt or wronged…"

The perky, well-spoken therapist was the embodiment of everything Olivia hated about therapy.

Not that she had much experience; she'd just never felt the need to go. She didn't have problems with drugs or alcohol. No mysterious trauma she needed to heal. On the contrary, her traumas were all very well known, and she stuffed them deep down like any other normal adult. Sure, she'd had her fair share of seeing red moments where she might have overreacted, but it wasn't something that happened often. Also, she'd made some bad decisions when it came to men, but who hadn't?

The only problem was her ex's new girlfriend had to go and press charges over the revenge porn and blackmail debacle, so here she was.

As her fingernails dug into her palms, her eyes met the aqua ones of the man across from her in the circle of chairs. Unable to stop herself, she glared at him. Her knee-jerk reactions with attractive men were either to glare or to flirt, and she certainly wasn't going to flirt with him right now. Been there, done that. Besides, she was still hurt he didn't remember her.

While he undoubtedly had been drinking that night, they'd both been enthusiastic about their encounter. She might have been more so than him, if she was being honest.

She'd had a crush on him for quite a while, leading up to their chance meeting at a club downtown. Sneaking into his VIP area had been easy enough because she had been young and beautiful. She'd been so proud she was able to get into his orbit and be his choice, if only for the evening.

"Olivia?" A gentle voice interrupted her train of thought. "Is there something you'd care to share today? Maybe you could introduce yourself to the group?" The pretty therapist smiled at her, and Olivia felt the urge to claw the woman's eyes out of her skull. Intentionally folding her hands in her lap, she forced her face to relax.

"Um, yeah, I guess. I'm Olivia. I just got here yesterday. As for sharing… no, thanks."

The therapist's calm expression sagged a bit, but she recovered quickly. "Maybe next session, once you've gotten a little more settled in."

Olivia forced a pretend smile she hoped came across the same as if she'd flipped Dr. Feel Good—the nickname felt accurate—the bird.

It was obvious as Dr. Clay moved around the circle Olivia wasn't the only new resident, nor the only person who wanted to keep their business to themselves. One by one, everyone introduced themselves, but only a couple of people announced their issues, or listed off who they needed to apologize to and why. The therapist smiled encouragingly the entire time, keeping the conversation on track with kind words while making little notes on a pad in her lap.

It annoyed Olivia to no end.

Adding insult to injury, her ass fell asleep only four people in and she had to keep changing her positions in the horrible chair.

After the painfully long feelings-sharing session finally ended, Ollie approached her before she could slip out of the room.

"Hey. I…" He stopped and shook his head, changing whatever it was he'd been about to say. "You settling in okay?"

"Yep, I'm fine," she snapped, not trying one bit to mask her impatience.

"Look, I know you don't want to do any part of this. I've been here for several weeks, and I can tell you with certainty it gets easier." He was being genuine, and for some reason this was worse than him being rude.

"Okay. Thanks, I guess."

He ran a hand through his sandy hair. There was no denying he was handsome.

"You want to grab something to eat? Maybe we can… start over?" Ollie deployed what should have been a charming, lopsided grin.

What exactly he wanted to start over could have been any number of things. The uncertainty was driving her crazy, but she didn't know how to go about quizzing him on his memory. Seeing him again had brought up a ton of old feelings, which threw her off center, but she was fairly certain he wasn't propositioning her.

"No, thanks," Olivia said, pushing her way past him and out into the hallway as every possible scenario of them eating together flashed through her brain, including one where he ravished her on the tabletop.

"If you need anything…" he trailed off behind her.

"I won't," she repeated, glancing over her shoulder as her feet carried her quickly down the hall toward her room.

She had to get it together. She was here to do as little time as possible and get the hell out, not make friends with the likes of Ollie Parkinson, regardless of their history.

HER FINAL SESSION for the day was yoga.

When she got to the wooden structure in the grassy area beyond the residence buildings, she groaned.

Of course *he'd* be there.

Ollie was up on the platform, stretching on a blue yoga mat, looking like he was posing for a magazine spread. His fit body moved through some very bendy positions in a form-fitting tank and shorts.

Olivia scolded the part of her brain reacting positively to the sight.

"Are you stalking me?" She spat the words, rolling out her mat with a snap.

He gave a chuckle, but it lacked actual amusement. "I've been here for weeks already. If anything, you're following me around, Princess."

"Keep dreaming." The bitterness in her tone had already given way to simple sarcasm. She hated how he was a weak spot for her when she wanted to stay mad.

"It's okay to make a friend while you're here. Just so you know."

Olivia snapped her head in his direction. "Oh? Do you want to be my friend?" She batted her eyes, turning on what she thought of as her bombshell voice, words heavy with sarcasm.

Ollie's features stuttered as he took in the change, but his smile returned quickly. "Hey, that's pretty good. You ever consider acting?"

Olivia scowled at him. "I'm only here because it's on my schedule. We don't have to talk."

"If you say so." He shook his head, taking his position at the top of his mat as the instructor walked across the platform.

Before she could respond, they'd moved into a warmup. As they moved through poses, she tried to keep her attention on the instructor, but found herself glancing over at Ollie instead.

She was not only annoyed she couldn't quit looking, but also at him for being more adept at the yoga poses than she was.

By the time she'd tried and failed to clear her mind during the short guided meditation after the yoga session, she was highly irritable and starving.

Olivia had made it off the platform and partway across the grass when she heard the taunting voice behind her. She didn't dare turn around, but she imagined he was standing there, waving obnoxiously.

"See you around, Princess!"

She gritted her teeth and moved her legs faster, frustrated how she suddenly wanted nothing more than to spar with the infuriating man.

So instead of waving back, she raised up one arm, giving him the finger.

His laugh chased her all the way back to her room.

CHAPTER *Five*

WHEN OLIVIA CAME down the stairs from her room the next morning, Ollie was waiting for her on one of the plush sofas down in the common living room area.

"Yeah, we don't have to do this," she groused. "It's way too early."

"The dining room situation usually gets shaken up a bit when they start the mentor part. Besides, it's just breakfast." He held the door open for her, the cool morning air refreshing as they stepped outside.

As always, the pool called to her with a glimmer off the water. Olivia hoped she'd have time for a swim after lunch.

"Fine. I'm not chatty early in the morning, though."

"Noted. That actually works out, because I planned to do most of the talking."

"Can't wait," she huffed.

He opened the door for the main building and allowed her to lead the way into the dining room.

The servers brought around carafes of juice and coffee, plus the baskets of assorted pastries. Olivia was quick to notice Ollie had been correct, and nearly none of the tables had their normal patrons. Everyone was paired with their mentor or mentee, some as groups of four.

"Interesting, right? It's almost like I've been through this before," Ollie teased.

Olivia wasn't yet caffeinated enough to banter with him, so she busied her hands with pouring herself a cup of coffee and pulled out one of the tiny croissants from the basket on the table.

Ollie pushed his chair back, gesturing at the buffet at the far end of the room.

"You coming?"

"I'm going to drink this first."

He went toward the warming tables full of meats before stopping to get both a custom omelet and some fresh waffles. Olivia watched the room as she sipped at the lovely dark roast they served.

The little pastry was enough to cushion the acidic bite of her morning caffeine, but she'd need to make some other selections or face the wrath of indigestion. When Ollie returned, she took her turn, selecting some of the fruit to go with her eggs.

Ollie was digging in with enthusiasm when she got back to the table. Olivia shoved away the twinge of amusement at the sight of him shoveling bacon into his mouth, giving him a questioning stare as she dropped into her seat again instead.

"I'm going to miss the food here so freaking bad," he muttered over his mouthful.

"I can see that," she replied blandly, daintily cutting her veggie omelet into smaller bites before dusting them with salsa.

"So… I thought maybe it would be nice to get to know one another a bit better."

Olivia muttered over her eggs, "You know me better than a lot of people do."

Ollie stared at her over the rim of a juice glass. "I'm not sure what to say to that. Seems a little sad, to be honest."

She cocked one eyebrow, but said nothing. She'd have to clue him in sooner or later if he never remembered, but she liked to see him squirm over it too much.

"Fine," she sighed. "What do I need to know about you TMZ hasn't already covered?" He didn't need to know she'd spent nearly half of her allotted computer time scouring the internet for up-to-date news about him the night before. It had been years since their evening together, and she'd apparently missed quite a lot.

Ollie blotted his mouth with a napkin, a chagrined chuckle rumbling out of him. His eyes were bright as they looked at her, and Olivia remembered quickly how easily taken she'd been by his charm in the first place.

He held out a hand. Olivia stared at it before reaching out as well. His hand wrapped around hers in a warm, firm grip and he gave it a gentle shake.

"I'm Ollie. Pleased to meet you."

"You're ridiculous." Olivia sighed, annoyance warring with a twinge of amusement.

"No, I'm Ollie."

"Fine. You're Ollie. You tell dad jokes, which is weird and kind of sad. I'm Olivia. Happy?"

"Sure." He released her hand and resumed eating. "Nice to meet you… again. I'd ask what brought you here, but I already know. So maybe you could ask me instead?" He encouraged her to ask with a puppy-dog expression on his face. "We should probably talk about the last time we met at some point, too."

"Why are you so sure I don't already know why you're here?" She asked. He just blinked at her in response, a grin creeping onto his mouth. "Fine, why are you here, Oliver?"

"Please, call me Ollie. I'm here thanks to the patriarchy, deeply ingrained misogyny and some terrible life choices, mostly."

Olivia's eyebrows drew together as she frowned at him. "Sorry?"

He waved his hand as though focusing on what he'd just said wasn't needed. Like he hadn't tossed out a profound statement about the world and simply wanted to move right along.

"I'm here because there's approximately ninety percent likelihood I sexually harassed nearly every woman I ever came into contact with from the age of, eh," he tilted his head to the side, one eye squinted as he considered.

"Seventeen or so. Assaulted quite a few of them believing I was entitled to their bodies by virtue of who I was, what I did, and the fact they were in possession of a vagina in my presence. My management did one hell of a mental wash on me from the time I was a kid, but that's honestly only part of what went *really* fucking wrong with me."

"Oh. I—" Olivia was too stunned for words as she tried to process the information he was throwing out so casually. His demeanor had grown serious, which further stunned her into silence.

He didn't seem to notice or care about her brief interruption. He was on a roll and clearly wanted to get it all out in one shot.

"I did all the drugs, took all the bad advice, and committed terrible acts for *years*. I'm a shit human being most days, but was especially awful before I realized everything I was doing was fundamentally wrong. There's nothing I can do to redeem myself for what terrible shit I've already done. But I can be better from today forward, so today is what I'm focusing on. *That*'s why I'm here. My life to this point is a mountainous series of regrets. I'm here so I can be better."

Olivia was beyond stunned by his overwhelmingly honest admission. Her fork clattered noisily to her plate as it slipped from her fingertips. She tossed a glance around the room to see if anyone else had overheard. Nobody was bothered, which was an odd relief. Collecting herself, she picked up the fallen utensil and reached for her glass of juice before responding.

"I'm not sure what to say."

"It's a lot." He pushed his plate away. "But you need to know what you're up against. If you're not comfortable with me at this table, or with me, especially alone—at any point—just say so. You're safe with me, I can swear to it, but my track record isn't great. I'm more than aware. You won't hurt my feelings."

Olivia's forehead wrinkled as she frowned. "I don't feel unsafe with you." She never had. The guilt etched into his face went straight to her chest, igniting an emotion she wasn't used to having.

Empathy.

He blew out a large breath, deflating a bit since he'd dumped all the information he'd been keeping bottled up on the table between them.

"Do you have any questions? I'm happy to answer them if I can."

"You were never charged with anything serious that I saw. So what actually happened?"

"Well… I miraculously grew a brain, I guess. I had a shot to reclaim my acting career, but I did something stupid instead and threw it away. It took a very large man dangling my ass over a steep canyon to shake some sense into me. A well-aimed stiletto heel helped too." He rubbed his fingertips over his forehead as though trying to feel for a previous injury.

"But you were never in legal trouble?" Olivia was desperately trying to balance in her head what he might have done to what she had done and coming up short. Surely he'd been in trouble at some point for those things if there were as many and as serious as he was claiming.

"I wouldn't say I was always in the clear, but my management was excellent at covering things up and paying people off. I managed to stay out of jail and the spotlight." He didn't look happy about it, though.

"So, you're here because of what you did? Like me?"

Ollie cradled his coffee cup between his hands. "I doubt it's the same as you. Tell me about why you're here."

She hesitated, refilling her own cup and finishing off her fruit before explaining. "I did something I shouldn't have. I'm sure you heard about it."

Ollie nodded. "I did. But I'd prefer to hear your version, not just what they talked about on the gossip sites."

Olivia sighed. She'd had to claim her mistakes out loud more in the last few days than in the whole time since the actual event had happened. "I helped someone blackmail an actress. They said it fell under revenge porn. We broke into her apartment, too, though that part was mostly David. A guy I knew from… early in my career," she explained. She wasn't ashamed of the time she'd done adult films, but mentioning it always managed to become the focus of the conversation. "I showed up some places where my ex was, trying to get his attention after we broke up. It honestly all seemed reasonable at the time. But I guess it was wrong."

"You guess?" Ollie tilted his head, eyebrows raised.

"Fine, it was wrong. Happy?" She snipped. "I don't need to be here, though. I'm not dangerous. I'm not an addict. I wouldn't say she totally deserved what happened to her. I would probably do things differently if I had another chance."

"Oh? No addictions? But you're at Sunrise."

"Nope. I'm fine."

"Hmm. Interesting."

"How so? Do you feel uncomfortable?" She turned his words on him before taking a sip of her coffee. Her earlier empathy had evaporated under the weight of her default setting. Agitation.

Ollie made a noise somewhere between a laugh and a snort. "No, you don't make me uncomfortable. You might irritate me, Princess, but I'm betting it's intentional."

"Hilarious." She glared at him, but he was unaffected by the laser beams in her eyes. "There's gotta be something that happened to make you show up here."

Ollie shrugged again. "No big secret. I needed help, so I signed myself in."

Her heart stuttered as she processed his words. "You're here… on purpose?" The words were harsh as they flew out of her mouth. She couldn't believe what he'd said. Surely he was kidding? Nobody would sign up for rehab voluntarily. She'd been ordered here for their alleged specialization in her *issues*. So far, the specialty seemed to be catering to her celebrity status and costing a fortune. There were plenty of other choices he could have gone with.

Ollie nodded, a blush staining his cheeks. He had a habit of leaning forward with his elbows on his thighs or the table when he wasn't actively eating, his shoulders slumped as though he were trying to make himself smaller.

"I need to be here, Princess." He raised an eyebrow suggestively, implying she did as well, but not saying it out loud. "It wasn't my idea, but I have to admit it's been good for me. I was going down a bad road, one likely to end in either death or jail. I was a shit human regularly doing awful things. Whether you want to or not, you can relate."

Olivia was processing everything he was telling her as quickly as she could, but the math wasn't coming out right. "Whose idea was it? If not yours?"

"My father's, actually. I was spiraling. I weaned myself off all substances about a year ago. I liked pills. Booze. Anything that made me either not feel anything or feel everything all at once, just depended on the day. I never used a needle, though. I only briefly experimented with cocaine. I wasn't a fan of how it made me feel and hated the way it burned in my face. But pills? I could get lost for weeks. And I did. For years." He paused, gaze going distant for a moment as though a memory had surfaced at his mention of drugs. "Anyway. It took some time after getting sober to really get clarity on things. After my head was right, I got the genius idea to contact the tabloids and put out a call for anyone I'd done wrong to come forward and press charges. I was one hundred percent ready to throw myself on the sword. My dad stopped me, though.

We found this place." He swallowed thickly. "I'd still do it, though. I deserve it. I did so many unforgivable things. I don't want to minimize what happened in any way. My actions for most of my life were self-serving and incredibly damaging to others. I was—*am*—an addict and don't ever want to go back to being trapped by my addictions."

"That's…" she couldn't find an appropriate word. The gravity of his expression when he was serious was immense. It made her feel awkward and strangely exposed. She changed the subject to shift the energy. "No offense, but how are you paying for this? You weren't a major player in the best of times. You did a lot of the same things I did, right? Straight to video movies, guest spots on TV, or when you got lucky, a small recurring role. Some background film parts, commercials…"

Ollie chuckled wryly. "You're not wrong. I had some savings from when I was a kid. I made pretty decent money before I outgrew my teens. My dad was incredible at investing for me. Thank God, too, or I'd be more than broke. I spent a fortune on partying over the years. He was terrible at giving life advice most of the time, but smart with money."

"What's that like?" Olivia cracked a wide grin before she could catch herself. Her parents were both notoriously bad with money and they'd passed the unfortunate trait down to her.

"Really nice, actually." His lopsided grin warmed her chest. "So here I am. I'm not as nervous about going out into the real world again as I expected to be. This has been a… refreshing change of pace."

Olivia snorted. "You sound like a walking poster boy for Sunrise. Maybe you can do their commercials."

"Very funny. But actually, that would be a good gig. Maybe I'll talk to Pauline. I'll let you know if I need a co-star." He winked at her.

She tossed a croissant at him, earning a laugh.

"Do you seriously enjoy the routine?" The thought was horrifying to her.

He shrugged. "The therapy has all been healthy for me, the rooms are luxurious and I've never eaten better in my life. This has been like a vacation, even with all the mandatory psychoanalysis."

"You're bizarre."

"Yeah, absolutely."

A familiar itch began right below Olivia's shoulder blades. "I can't wait to get out of here. I'm not dangerous. If I have to repeat any more cheesy self-affirmations, I'm going to throw up."

Ollie barked a laugh. "Look at you, right on the verge of actually participating."

"Looks like we're both just here until we don't have to be anymore."

Ollie's face fell. "Work the program, Princess. It's good for you. Besides, you're paying out the ass. Might as well make it worth your while, right?"

She sighed, slumping back into the seat. "I guess."

Their friendly conversation came to a close with Ollie looking wistful. She could tell he was trying to help, but for whatever reason, she couldn't allow herself to accept things at face value, not even from him.

Maybe especially not from him.

CHAPTER
Six

OLIVIA SPENT AS much of her free time over the weekend as she could by the poolside.

None of the other residents seemed to care one bit about the pool, which was a downright shame. It was massive to start, the water was at the perfect temperature and crystal clear. The pool also had a lovely rock waterfall at one end.

She'd been stunned to find everyone piled onto the plush sofas in the living room, watching a movie on the giant flat-panel TV on her way out the door Saturday morning. To be fair, they all looked exhausted, but watching a screen wasn't her idea of fun when there was an alternative as tempting as the pool.

There was a selection of floating chairs in one of the storage lockers next to the house, so she tossed her towel over a chair and pulled out a bright pink one to use.

As she pushed off of the side of the pool atop her floaty, her worries lessened as though they were balloons she'd let go to drift into the sky.

"See?" She muttered to herself as she adjusted her sunglasses. "I just needed some time at the pool."

She sunned herself atop the pink inflatable long enough she was worried about getting burned. Olivia slid off into the water, the gentle waves a cool balm against her heated skin as she bobbed in a spot deep enough she had to dance on her tip-toes to touch the bottom.

The floaty wandered to the far end of the pool near the waterfall as she treaded water. Enjoying the sensation of being weightless, she closed her eyes.

"Having fun?" Ollie's voice carried across the patio.

He'd come out of the doors near the dining room, crossing toward her at a relaxed pace. He had his hands in his pockets and a grin on his mouth.

"Yes, actually. It's criminal how little use the pool gets." She adjusted her sunglasses.

"Mind if I join you?"

"It's a big pool." She maintained her standoffish attitude with him despite a mild twisty sensation in her stomach and chest when she looked at him. The most detestable thing about attraction is it has absolutely no respect for your wishes.

Mad at him for being hot and herself for noticing, Olivia glared at him over the top of her shades, but he was undeterred.

"I'll be right back, I just have to grab my trunks."

"Wonderful." Her tone was dry, but he chuckled all the way through the doors.

He was back in a few short minutes, missing a shirt altogether, but decked out in bright tropical trunks with a towel over his arm.

Olivia had to swallow over a dry throat and swim to the shallow end to cover up how she was staring at him.

To her dismay, instead of jumping in, he decided to walk down the wide, shallow steps in the end of the pool she'd fled to.

"This is nice," he said, sitting casually on the third step. Only his bottom half was submerged. He offered a tube of sunscreen to her. "Would you mind? I can help you reapply too, if you're comfortable with me doing so. You're turning pink."

"Sure."

Olivia watched his expression for any kind of flirty playfulness, but he was dead serious.

She filled her palm with the dense lotion and generously applied to his heavily freckled shoulders and back. He was well muscled, which she'd known, but she was still surprised at how well toned his body was out of clothing.

"Turn around." He drew a circle with his finger in the air. She turned, his hands deftly applying the heavy sun cream on her shoulders. He'd been right too, she was already burning. His hands rubbing her shoulders sent sparks of awareness about the sunburn as well as her neglected hormones.

"Your tattoo…" he trailed off, but his fingertips gently traced the outline of the small butterfly on her left shoulder.

"What about it?" She asked.

"It looks really familiar, I recognize it. But…" She could see him shake his head out of the corner of her eye.

Olivia snorted, though her heart had leapt at the potential recognition. "Standard issue basic bitch butterfly shoulder tattoo in purple. I'd bet half of the girls my age have one exactly like it. We all marched to the nearest tattoo shop when we turned eighteen, I'm pretty sure. I'd bet you've come across one or two at least, before."

"Maybe."

"Thanks," she muttered when he finished.

"Same." He tossed the tube into a chair, standing up before gracefully diving into the water.

He did a few long laps through the deep end, minding his own business and giving her plenty of space. His expression was distant and pensive, but it was hard to tell what he was thinking behind his sunglasses.

Olivia was stunned. It was not common for a man to join her in a pool, where she was wearing next to nothing, help her apply sunscreen, then ignore her. It was nothing he hadn't seen a thousand times before, probably, but still.

Internally, she battled between wanting to throw a tantrum to get his attention and being grateful he was doing basically what her bad attitude had implied she wanted.

Her emotional swings were confusing, even to her. The more time she spent away from her regular life, the less confident she felt in her reactions to things.

After another twenty minutes, she knew she'd regret much more time in the sun, so she decided to get out and go take a shower, perhaps even nap before the mandatory group therapy session.

As she exited the pool, Ollie called after her, "This was nice. We should do it again some time."

Olivia wrapped herself in a towel, confusion multiplying on itself. Whether he was being serious or was in some way making an innuendo about their past was a mystery.

To be safe, she answered, "Sure."

Olivia went into the residence building, the perplexing interaction replaying the whole time she was in the shower.

As she reapplied her makeup, she decided it didn't matter if he was being sarcastic or genuine. If he wanted to use the pool, it was his right as a resident, same as her. Next time, she might take a little extra time applying his sunscreen, though.

"OLIVIA? IS THERE anything you'd care to share today?"

"No, thanks."

The woman was relentless.

Every single session she turned her kind smile on and asked if Olivia wanted to share. Every single session

Olivia declined, but she was beginning to think maybe her one-on-ones would be far less painful if she shared something in group instead of keeping her mouth shut.

She'd quickly discovered some of her fellow guests had one issue they liked to talk about over and over again. At least the time they took up let her pass on sharing anything herself without too much pushback.

"What about you, Oliver? Anything to share with the group today?"

"Uh, sure." Ollie shifted in the uncomfortable plastic seat, glancing at Olivia before turning his full attention back to the doctor. "We had a short excursion into town yesterday. I was worried being out in public would be weird, but it was really great. Nobody recognized me, which isn't unusual here, but I had built it up in my head the paparazzi would be waiting at the grocery store or something, ready with accusations or questions."

"How did that make you feel?" She asked, pencil and notebook ready to go. "Not having things play out the way you'd worried about?"

Ollie cracked a slight grin. "I was relieved. But weirdly still a little sad they weren't there. It's so dumb."

The doctor beamed at him. "Not at all. Your profession has trained you to be wary of those interactions, but still crave the validation they give you. It's not all that odd at all. It's part of the promise of fame. You have to get the attention to keep the status, but the attention often isn't kind or desirable."

"Yeah, sounds about right."

It did.

Olivia absolutely hated when Dr. Clay was so insightful. It made it much harder to hate her.

"Thank you for sharing. Is there anything you'd like to talk through or are you okay?"

"I think I'm alright, thanks."

"Very good. Josh? What about you? How was your trip into town?"

Olivia listened to the handful of people who'd gotten to go on the field trip talk about their feelings about it. Half of her wanted to scream about how it was just the damned grocery store. And the other half of her was insanely jealous they'd gotten to leave campus, no matter how boring their destination was. Wandering aisles had never been one of her favorite things to do, but right now, it sounded downright dreamy.

"Anyone else?" The doctor paused, waiting to see if anyone would speak up. Nobody did, so she clapped her hands once to signify the session was over. "Thanks to everyone who shared today, and I'll see most of you for your individuals tomorrow."

A quiet round of applause went out before the sound of chairs scraping the tile floor took over.

Ollie wandered over, hands in his pockets. Olivia was beginning to see it as a pattern and wondered if it was intentional. Some kind of mental game—a forced *keep your hands to yourself* kind of thing.

"Are you hungry? I hear it's surf and turf today."

Olivia fronted a bit of an attitude with him, but didn't really put any heart behind it. As much as she'd wanted to hate Ollie Parkinson, he'd managed to get under her skin just as easily as the food he was tempting her with over the last few days.

"Why Oliver, are you asking me on a date?" She teased.

"If I were asking you on a date, Olivia, there wouldn't be any question." Her blood thrummed in her veins. He'd never used such a tone on her before and it… it was something else. "No, I'm not asking you on a date, but I would very much like it if you'd accompany me to dinner in the dining room."

"Sure, you can take me to dinner." She fidgeted with her shirt as they made their way down the hall to the dining room. "You sure you can afford it?"

Ollie laughed, the sound echoing in the large space. "As long as you don't complain about the service, I think we'll be fine."

"What makes you think I'm someone who complains?" He pinned her with a knowing look. She wasn't always a complainer, but it had happened often enough.

Being away from her mother—not to mention the hours of therapy she was enduring—were allowing some much needed, though wholly unwanted self-introspection. The longer she spent at Sunrise, the more she recognized traits in herself she didn't like. It was an odd, disembodied experience to begin to see yourself from the outside. Even stranger to discover so many of the things you thought were part of your personality were really a character you built to perform while out in public. Like it or not, Olivia had come to realize the therapy was working, though probably not for the reasons she'd been sent to get it.

"Ugh, fine. I complain. But in my defense, they usually deserve it. Satisfied?"

His smirk was downright sexy. He was handsome, which wasn't news, but he was also funny. Genuine. Things Olivia's body appreciated, even if she didn't want it to.

"Not even close." He winked, a thrill running through her body at his playful words.

She wanted to strike back with some clever and sexy banter, but what spilled out was, "I believe you. I know what it looks like."

Ollie blinked, stunned for the briefest of moments, but then he laughed. The sentiment was vague enough he probably had taken it as a general statement, not one about him specifically.

As they talked over their meal, laughing and generally enjoying one another's company, Olivia realized this might be what the beginning of a healthy, normal friendship looked like. She stored the idea in her mental file as something she and Dr. Clay could talk about. No doubt the good doctor would be thrilled.

If she was being honest with herself, she was pretty stoked to have someone she could be herself around. Someone who understood what kind of things the Hollywood celebrity machine did to people.

She'd thought her crush on Ollie Parkinson had died long ago, but something about his easy charm lowered her defenses.

"What's it like, being able to go into town?" She asked.

"Weird," he said, not missing a beat before taking another bite of his food. "Malibu is already a strange, insular kind of place. People are accustomed to seeing celebrities here too, since they have lots of them as residents at least part of the time. Add to that a handful of people who have been isolated at rehab for a while and even the grocery store is a whole experience. I was never so excited to buy useless shit and junk food."

"Living the dream." Olivia sighed.

Ollie snorted. "Which reminds me… when we go back, I have something for you in my room."

"Something for me?" There was no way to disguise her surprise.

"Don't get too excited, nothing serious. But I saw something while we were out and thought you could use it."

"Okay."

Olivia was strung tight for the rest of the meal, trying to guess at what he'd picked up for her. Even chef Jean-Pierre's tiramisu couldn't hold her attention the way it normally did. By the time they finally crossed the patio, she had completely stressed herself out with the anticipation.

He opened the door of his room, dipping inside before briefly reappearing with a small bag.

"It's not much, and I'm sure it's not what you would usually use, but maybe it'll help."

Olivia opened the bag to find a container of nail polish remover, some cotton pads and a bottle of bright pink nail lacquer.

It wouldn't do anything to fix the widening gap in her acrylics, but it was one of the sweetest gifts she'd ever been offered.

Emotion swamped her, and she struggled to vocalize her appreciation, "Oh. Wow."

He blushed a wonderful pink shade. "I've seen you picking at them and you won't get privileges for quite a while yet. I just thought…" he shrugged.

"No, this is great." She smiled at him, heart thumping in her chest. "Really."

"I'm glad you like it. See you in the morning?"

"Of course." On impulse, she went up on her toes and kissed him on the cheek. His stubble was rough on her lips, but she wasn't bothered.

"Oh." His eyes were wide when she pulled away.

"Goodnight, Ollie."

He raised his hand in a brief wave before closing the door.

Olivia stood there, focused on the little white bag for much longer than she should have. When she finally wandered up to her room, she immediately got to work removing the chipped purple polish on her nails, replacing it with a pink she never would have chosen for herself, but was thrilled to have been given, nevertheless.

CHAPTER
Seven

OLIVIA SLOGGED THROUGH the start of her second week on what little remained of her ability to fake a smile.

She now knew all of the other resident's names, and everyone knew hers, but she still sat at her table alone for meals unless Ollie joined her, which was about half the time. She wondered if she had missed some kind of memo around the etiquette of being sociable with other residents. Not that she wanted the added stress of trying to make or keep friends, but she also didn't want to be left out.

It frustrated her to no end she couldn't pick a side. The need to be the focus of others' attention was a loud voice she'd managed to silence for the first week, and now she was struggling to balance it with her desire to blend into the background so she wasn't labeled as a troublemaker.

On the days she got to use the computer, she'd inevitably find a dozen or more emails from her mom about possible auditions. Not surprisingly, there was never any discussion about how she was doing, though there were reminders to be sure she was following her nutrition plan and keeping up with her workouts.

More than once, Olivia had reminded her mother how she obviously couldn't make it to auditions in Los Angeles for the foreseeable future. The answer she'd gotten back was:

I'm working on it. You have to trust me. We'll get you back to making money in no time.

While this was what Olivia hoped for, she was doubtful it was reality. And the focus on money, while normal for her mother, was the least of her concerns.

Her mother would also have an aneurism if she saw how Olivia was eating. Every time the image of her mother's face—purple with rage over Olivia enjoying a pastry—crossed her mind, she smiled. It had been years since she'd been allowed to enjoy food without punishing her body with exercise. Turning off the automatic calorie counter in her brain was a separate issue, one she was battling with occasionally, but for the most part, she was just enjoying the novelty of being 'off plan'.

Her mother had very pointedly declared shortly after the sentencing hearing how she wouldn't be seen at a rehab facility, no matter how expensive. As Olivia had told Jerry, her mom had gone so far as to promise she'd find a way to get her out early. She'd ranted on and on about how her daughter didn't belong there, and showing up to check her in basically equated to support for the sentencing.

Olivia didn't agree with the last part, but there was no changing her mother's mind about anything once she fixated on it. The same trait had gotten Olivia into many auditions, but was also what had led to nearly every argument between the two of them.

Olivia tried to remember the last time her mom had actually *mothered* her. The last time she'd expressed worry over anything not having to do with Olivia's appearance, diet or pay. Anything at all not directly related to money.

As she stared out her window at the ocean, she came up blank.

When had her parents become her managers and nothing more? Could her dad, who rarely even spoke to her at all, be called even that?

Insides churning with emotion, she slammed her hands on the bed and got to her feet. She couldn't sit still any longer, it was leading her down all the wrong rabbit holes in her mind.

She dashed down the stairs and out the doors into the sunny courtyard, crossing quickly so she could grab a drink from the dining room before heading to her individual counseling session with Dr. Clay.

As she turned the corner, she slammed into another body, her forehead hitting something made of bone. She stepped back and overcorrected, landing flat on her ass in the hallway. As if this wasn't bad enough, something splashed all over her bare legs.

"Holy shit, Princess. Where's the fire?"

Rubbing her forehead with one hand, she looked up to find Ollie gingerly probing his chin, an open can of sparkling water crushed in his hand.

"You should watch where you're going," she complained.

"Me? You're the one sprinting around blind corners, babe. I was just minding my own business here." He stepped to the side and tossed the ruined drink into one of the many discreet trash cans lining the halls disguised as plant stands. Ollie wiped his palms on his jeans before offering her a hand. "Are you alright? Let me help you up."

"I'm fine," she groused.

He pulled Olivia to her feet, leaning in to inspect her forehead once she was vertical. His fingertips were warm on her skin as he traced the tender area that had taken the most impact. The hand he'd used to pull her up with still loosely held her fingers. She did everything in her power to ignore the shiver his soft touches gave her.

"I think you'll live, but you might want to get some ice. There's a little bump already." He frowned as he breathed in, as though something about her scent offended him.

"Perfect," she muttered. Begrudgingly, she added, "How's your chin?"

His lips curved upward. "I'm fine, thanks for asking. You late for something?"

"No. I wanted to get a drink before going to see Dr. Clay. I'd have preferred it in a bottle though, not all over me."

"Somewhere in there is a joke about me knowing the fastest way to get you wet," Ollie teased.

Olivia's mouth dropped open, and she wanted to laugh, but he didn't wait long enough for it to happen. Instead, he shook his head as though mortified he'd said the words out loud, expression pulled tight as he finally dropped her hand.

"Sorry, old habit. Maybe I'll suggest to Pauline they put some mirrors on these corners. That's a pretty color on you, by the way." He gestured toward her hand.

They stood there for an awkward moment, Olivia's heart pounding behind her ribs. She wanted to be irritated, but it hadn't been his fault. Not entirely. She was still too busy mulling over his compliment.

"I need to clean up."

"Yeah, of course." Color rose into Ollie's cheeks, the embarrassment making him even more adorable than he already was.

Olivia grunted in frustration, reminding herself there was nothing cute about him, or this situation.

"See you around, Princess."

"Quit calling me that," she grumbled half-heartedly as they did a quick dance, both of them trying to leave in the same direction at once. "I told you before, no stupid nicknames."

Ollie stepped toward the wall, allowing her to pass. "You did." The expression on his face was anything but repentant.

She muttered to herself as she went into the dining room to get her drink, swiping one of the cloth napkins to clean herself up with.

As a reward for not being as bitchy as she could have been and as a further middle finger to her diet, she grabbed a cookie off of the waiting tray before continuing down the hall to Dr. Clay's office, unsure how to deal with the torrent of confused emotions swirling inside her.

On her way down the hall, she realized he hadn't apologized for using the nickname, nor had he agreed to stop using it.

"WOULD YOU CARE to talk about what brought you to Sunrise, Olivia?" Dr. Clay was clearly tired of Olivia's lack of participation and half-answers in their previous sessions. Instead of waiting for her to open up, she'd started prompting her at the beginning of their sessions.

Olivia shifted around on the blue-pinstripe couch. It reminded her of the solid white pieces her mother had chosen for the sitting room of her childhood home. The cushions were a little too stiff to be truly comfortable, and the fabric just this side of scratchy. Olivia remembered being horrified at the price when they were delivered, but her mother had shrugged it off, claiming they were appropriate for company, which was specifically why she'd chosen them.

Olivia hated those couches and that room, nearly as much as the horrible plastic chairs in the group therapy space.

"What do you want to know?" She asked. Maybe if the perky doctor gave her something specific, they could both get what they needed out of this painful interaction.

"Whatever you'd be comfortable to sharing, Olivia. I feel as though whatever led up to that particular behavior may be at the core of some of the larger experiences in your life lately. It seems important. Wouldn't you agree?"

"I'm not really sure what else there is to say about it. Everyone here knows what happened, I'm not sure what needs to be discussed." Her tone was too sharp. Olivia knew immediately she'd misstepped. Dr. Clay raised an eyebrow. Gentling her words, Olivia continued, "Fine. I did something I shouldn't have and got caught. If I had to do it over, I probably wouldn't do things the same way." Not all of them, anyway.

Thankfully, Dr. Clay switched gears.

"I understand. Is there anything you *would* like to talk about?"

The open-ended questions drove Olivia up the wall even more than the direct ones did.

"Not in particular."

Dr. Clay placed her pen and notepad on the table next to her, lacing her fingers together once her hands were free.

"I have to be honest, Olivia, I'm becoming concerned with the speed of our progress. If we have any hope of getting you ready to graduate the program by the time you're expected to leave, these sessions need to go very differently than they have to this point."

Her gut twisted, and she fought off a snarky retort.

"I'm not sure what to say, doc. I've only been here a week. What is it I should be doing?"

"If I can be completely frank? Anything. Anything at all." Dr. Clay got to her feet and crossed the small room, pausing in front of her wall of bookshelves.

Olivia had the feeling she was getting a glimpse at the Dr. Clay who hid behind the pretty, unaffected smile. This was the woman behind the curtain, the one who heard all the horrible shit, day after day. This was the woman who processed all the trauma handed to her, then gave the people it belonged to a pretty package to hold it in while they carried it to the dumpster.

"Until you figure out what it is you're here for, I can't help you. Until you decide I'm safe to talk to, you can't make any progress." She turned, face pinched. "If it's about me personally, there are other members of the staff who can take you on for individual therapy. We understand not every therapist is a suitable fit for every patient."

She apologized, more than well versed in conceding to the person in power. She'd batted her eyes at a fair number of directors to get out of being fired over the years.

"I don't think it's you. I just don't belong here."

The doctor nodded thoughtfully, arms crossed as she

returned to her chair. She lowered herself down into it carefully.

"Well regardless, something has to give. You were sent to us for a reason. If you won't open up, we can't help. If we can't help, you won't be rehabilitated in time for your release back into the real world." She used finger quotes for 'real world' as though she didn't believe there was such a thing. "There are consequences if you don't graduate, right?"

Olivia shrugged. "They said if I don't complete the program, I go to jail."

"Yes, that's my understanding too. I don't want to see such a terrible thing happen. It's my job to help you. Let's find a way that works for us both so I can do it, okay?"

"I get it." Olivia's thoughts spun. Trying to figure out how to open up enough to get out of here but not so much the therapists knew all her business was a challenge she hadn't been expecting to need to solve.

"Wonderful. Do some thinking about how we should proceed. Either Dr. Nguyen or Dr. Wilson could easily take your case for the individual sessions if you'd like to try an alternative. Just let me know."

"It's not..." As much as Olivia was easily irritated by this woman, she didn't feel any closer to the other therapists she'd met. Like it or not, there was a level of comfort between them if only because they were most often paired up together. "I don't want to see anyone else."

Being able to say such a thing with full confidence and honesty was a testament to how far she'd already come since she arrived. Olivia thought she had Dr. Clay figured out those first few days at Sunrise. She wouldn't have given her the time of day, then. But having gotten to know her a little bit... she wasn't half bad.

"You're free to go for now. Next session, we need to really dig in, okay?"

"Alright."

Olivia wandered away from the office with a pit in her stomach. Feeling guilt over Dr. Clay doubting herself was a wholly new experience. Guilt over anything was not how she operated.

She still had to figure out what to talk about before their next session, but she'd figure something out. She always did.

OLLIE WAS MYSTERIOUSLY missing during breakfast. Olivia ate by herself, eyes constantly on the door for him, but he never showed.

Already irritable, she went through a frustrating round of art therapy where she was tasked with taking a block of clay and making it into the shape of her intentions. Whatever the hell *that* meant.

After leaning all of her weight into her hands to flatten the eight-inch cube but getting a whole lot of nowhere, she'd employed a rolling pin and eventually a mallet to help. Nothing had made much of an impact except for some dents in the material. Rage flowed from her hands as she tried to manipulate it into something—anything—other than a big, ugly block of nothing.

By the end of the hour, she was sweaty, sore and had virtually nothing to show for her efforts. To her shock,

Dr. Collins had smiled with approval on her way around the room, giving a nod.

The more Olivia thought about it, the more she wondered if the whole point was to get everyone to channel their anger into the clay until they were exhausted.

Lunch was sandwiches and salads served picnic style on the patio for a change of pace. Ollie sat with one of the other guys from their building, and Olivia made sparse small talk with one of the other ladies. She still hadn't connected with anyone, and wasn't sure if it was a good thing or a bad thing.

After lunch, she had music therapy. She couldn't help but doze through the guided session where they were all lying on the floor, focusing on how certain tones resonated through their bodies.

"Focus on your breathing. This frequency is known to help with mental clarity." Dr. Nguyen was tapping a mallet on tuning forks as she wandered around the room, carefully stepping over or around the bodies of the residents.

So far, Olivia had mainly felt the tones in her mouth. She certainly wasn't any closer to a clear mind, but the roots of her teeth ached. She wasn't sure what that meant, either. It seemed as though the entire point of her therapy sessions was to leave her tired and confused.

Lying down on cushioned mats immediately after a meal, with the drapes closed and everything quiet except for occasional ringing tones, was the perfect recipe for an accidental nap.

It also appeared to be the thing Olivia had been missing as far as meditation went. She ended more relaxed than she had been in years, odd dental discomfort aside.

She was disappointed when her music therapy was over, especially since it meant she was headed to another interrogation with Dr. Clay before finally being released to some free time before her evening session of yoga.

By the time she made her way to the wooden pavilion, she was well and truly exhausted.

"You seem particularly distracted today." Ollie's voice was a welcome interruption to her thoughts as he joined her on the yoga platform.

"Then I guess I'm in the right place," Olivia quipped, a bite in her tone.

She felt bad for snapping at him, but it had been an exceptionally difficult day. Dr. Clay had really dug in her heels during their individual session and the salad she'd eaten for lunch hadn't settled well.

He rolled out a mat that nearly matched the unique shade of his eyes.

"So true. Some good, old-fashioned poses and meditation should fix you right up." He winked at her, and if she wasn't mistaken, lingered a moment longer than he meant to while watching her do some warm-up stretches.

As the rest of the group filed in, Ollie stretched, his long legs nearly going over the edge of his mat.

The instructor arrived before she could think of anything to say in response. As they moved through the poses,

Olivia's tense muscles began to let go, her mind clearing as she focused on her breathing and intentional movements. While she still didn't put much stock into most of the things they required of the residents, she'd practiced yoga and Pilates for years, and it was a familiar part of her daily routine.

Occasionally, she'd get a whiff of Ollie's cologne and it would take her out of her clear mind space. She had to figure out how to deal with the tension slowly mounting between them. The casual touches and flirty comments were reviving all the feelings she'd thought she'd moved on from years ago.

The workout left her feeling calm and refreshed, albeit sweaty. As she lingered in child's pose, she felt the burn of his eyes on her, patiently waiting.

"I can feel you staring."

He huffed under his breath. "Sorry. I just wanted to ask the obvious. I'm assuming you're heading to dinner after this?"

Olivia opened her eyes, breath stalling in her chest at the sight of him casually using his knee as an arm-rest as he devoted his full attention to her. It was one hell of a pose.

"I'd prefer to shower first, but yes. I'm starving."

"Great. Do you want to maybe come with me?"

Enjoying the polite game, she rolled up her mat, leaving him hanging for a while as she got her things and prepared to leave.

"I suppose."

He exaggerated his relief. "Spectacular."

"Any guesses for what might be on the menu tonight?"

"Actually, yes." He rolled up his own mat, tucking it under his arm before walking with her away from the platform and back toward the residential building. "Rumor has it there's some kind of fancy steak dish with a seafood stuffing or topping. With a chicken alternative, of course."

"We have that three times a week," Olivia rolled her eyes.

"Then it's good odds the rumor is right." He winked at her.

"Fair point."

They covered the rest of the distance between the yoga studio and their building in silence.

"I need at least thirty minutes."

"No problem. Meet me in the living room?"

"Okay."

Olivia dashed up the stairs, eager to rinse the sweat from her skin.

She set the shower to steamy and let it warm up while she gathered her clothes for dinner, scoffing at herself when she realized she was debating which outfit Ollie might prefer. In the end, she settled for some skinny jeans and a designer t-shirt that had cost entirely too much money.

Going through the motions under the spray, she lathered, rinsed and repeated before drying off and running through her skincare routine. By the time she was pampered and dressed, nearly forty minutes had passed.

When she got down to the shared living area, Ollie was already waiting, flipping through a magazine.

"Have you been waiting long?"

"Nah, just a few minutes. You look nice. Ready?"

Trying not to preen under his compliment, she moved straight to answering his question. "Starved."

"Let's get you fed."

He offered an arm and after a moment of shocked hesitation, she linked hers through it.

After they were seated, he took a deep breath, discomfort clear in his tight features.

"Listen, I wanted to tell you I think you're pretty great. And I can tell you're starting to try. It's good. You're doing good. I mean… good job." He blushed, clearly flustered, but adorable as he delivered the compliment.

She didn't know how to respond, still feeling incredibly awkward when genuine praise was offered.

"I know this mentor situation isn't something you would have chosen, but I want to do the job well. For both of us. I just thought you should know."

"That's nice of you to say. Honestly, you're doing fine," she reassured him.

"Thanks." Ollie blushed, and he looked as uncomfortable as she felt, so Olivia changed the subject. She didn't have much to share, so she decided to tell him about one of the possibilities her mother had emailed about. If she was being honest with herself, it was the one she was most interested in.

"A reality show?" He asked, looking skeptical.

"Yeah," she enthused. "Sounds fun, actually. Stressful, but fun. I think it won't be much different from this place, to be honest."

Ollie laughed. "Less therapy options, though."

"Likely. Thank God." She paused as the waiter left their plates. "Would you look at that? Steak with seafood topping, as promised."

Ollie grinned back at her. "Ten points to me and whoever started the rumor, I guess, for being right. About the show. It's… exciting, Olivia. I hope you get it, if you want it. When would it start? A couple of months from now, obviously?"

She beamed as she took a bite of mashed potatoes. Talking about it out loud, with someone who understood how big of a deal it was, had her getting more and more excited about the prospect. "I'm not sure if I'm going to take it yet or not, but it's a reasonable deal. I'm definitely considering it. It would start soon," she said vaguely. It would start well before her stay at Sunrise was slated to end if her mother's information was correct.

She cut her steak carefully, battling with the onslaught of emotions ricocheting through her body. She knew how he'd react if she told him the whole truth. Carefully talking around it also felt wrong, somehow.

"Pauline is likely going to ask you how you feel about the mentorship soon." He turned serious, looking up from his plate as he dropped the words. "She likes to do periodic check-ins on both sides. They're supposed to be a surprise, but she's not very stealthy."

"Oh." Olivia wasn't sure where he was headed.

"Would you care to enlighten me about what you plan to tell her?" He prompted.

Olivia shifted around in her chair. The truth was, she hadn't wanted to admit he was a good mentor, but he was.

"You first," she deflected.

He shrugged, stabbing a piece of steak with his fork. "I'm fine with our arrangement. I wish you'd put a little more effort into working the program, but I feel as though you're finally making some progress."

The simple statement shouldn't have felt nearly as flattering as it did. "Thanks. I'm okay with how it's going. I haven't wanted to strangle you yet or anything. Not really."

"I appreciate the vote of confidence, Princess."

She clucked her tongue, head falling to the side in exasperation. "Don't fish for compliments. I'm not miserable. You say smart things sometimes."

Ollie hissed a laugh, a noise that came from somewhere deep in his chest. "Well, with such a glowing endorsement, how could I possibly disagree? And I don't want anything from you, Princess. Except maybe for you to try a little harder so you graduate." There was a flirty twinkle in his eye as he took her in. Her blood warmed at the idea of him actually caring whether or not she did well with the program.

By the time dinner was over, they'd talked about a number of things she hadn't discussed with anybody except maybe Maxwell, or her mom. Olivia found herself thoroughly enjoying Ollie's company, and unless she was reading him all wrong, he felt the same way. She could almost forget there were ten other people in the room with them, and all of them were there for some form of rehabilitation.

In fact, it almost felt like a date. Which was dangerous, if anything, though Olivia enjoyed the brief surge of joy the idea gave her.

After dinner, as they crossed the pool deck back to their building, his fingers brushed hers. The surge of endorphins she got from the tiny touch was ridiculously disproportionate, but she didn't care.

Like a gentleman, he walked her up to her door.

"Thanks for dinner. I…" he stopped in the middle of his sentence and blushed, shaking his head. "Have a great night, Princess. See you in the morning."

"Wait," Olivia blurted the word, not ready for him to leave. "Dinner was nice. I thought…" she trailed the word off, plucking up her courage. She leaned into his space, pressing her lips to his.

She could feel his surprise, tension in his mouth giving way to a gasp of surprise. For a brief moment, he kissed her back, a groan of pleasure rumbling through his chest as their mouths melded softly into one another.

Abruptly, he pulled back, shock widening his bright eyes. He looked up to the ceiling, and Olivia realized for the first time there might be cameras.

"We can't," he breathed. "*I* can't. It's not… it's not that I'm not attracted to you, Princess, it's just… fuck, it's complicated. I'm sorry."

Olivia nodded tightly, a sticky, dark emotion rushing in as blood warmed her cheeks. It took a moment, but she recognized the feeling.

It was guilt.

She knew why he was at Sunrise, and she still hadn't told him about the last time they'd 'met'. The impulse to kiss him was probably one of the things rehab should be teaching her to manage better.

"It's okay. My fault. I…" She shook her head. Olivia reached behind her, manipulating the doorknob so she could back into her room.

He grabbed her free hand, lifting the knuckles to his lips. "I'll see you tomorrow."

The sincerity in his eyes dampened the mortification she was feeling. There was something there. Something powerful. It stole her breath, forcing her to nod in agreement to whatever he was saying without words.

CHAPTER
Nine

OLIVIA CONSIDERED AVOIDING Ollie at breakfast, but he was too quick for her. When she got downstairs, he was already waiting for her in the living room.

"About last ni—" he started.

"Nope."

"No?" He asked, confusion on his face as he hustled to follow her. Olivia pushed the front doors open and strode with purpose across the deck toward the dining room.

"No, not until coffee. Maybe not even then."

"Fine, coffee first."

She glared over her shoulder at him and he conceded, hands up in surrender.

He made his plate and sat there, slowly chewing and staring at her while she processed her first cup of coffee with a pastry. The sadist in her enjoyed his torture, prolonging the inevitable as long as she could. She eventually got up to go to the buffet, but she took her sweet time collecting some food.

"How about now?" He asked when she got settled with her plate and a fresh cup of coffee.

"I suppose."

He sagged, letting out a breath. "I wanted to explain. Apologize. Both."

Olivia raised an eyebrow. "You don't have to."

"But I do. See, we're not strictly forbidden to fraternize with other residents, but for someone like me, it's definitely not encouraged. I'd bet it's a similar situation for you and honestly… I shouldn't. Not yet. But it's not anything to do with you in particular. I like you, Princess. I just don't want you to misunderstand—"

"I get it," she said abruptly, interrupting him. "This is… messy. You don't have to explain." Her tone came across cooler than she'd meant it to. Ollie flinched from her neutral words, sitting back in his chair as though trying to get some distance between them. "We're fine." She leaned toward him, forcing some warmth into the words.

"Okay," he said the word in a drawn-out way that left it sounding like a question.

"I mean it," Olivia said, reaching tentatively across the table to cover his fidgety hand with hers.

After a moment, he gave a weak smile.

"Pink really is a great color on you, Princess."

Olivia shook her head, frustrated he was able to get

under her skin as easily as he did, but enjoying the burst of dopamine his attention gave her.

THEY WERE NEAR one another most of the day, and the tension between them was still more than evident. By the time they brought around the bucket full of tech, she was ready to crawl out of her skin. She was extra sensitive, jumpy, and on a hair trigger for anger.

She'd even snapped at Dr. Clay again in individuals, and had to scramble to explain why she was so on edge. She blamed PMS before realizing she might be giving an honest answer.

"Hey, can I have your email? I'll send you my info if you want it," Ollie suggested.

"Sure." She recited it for him automatically as she scrolled through her social media feed. There were multiple references to Maxwell and Nora, so she clicked on one of the article links.

Ollie paused over her shoulder, looking at the gossip site's headline.

"You maybe shouldn't look at that," he said carefully, watching her reaction as he slid into the chair next to hers—pulling it closer than it normally would have been—after swiping a tablet off the counter.

Olivia scrolled up, then down again, looking through the images of Maxwell with Nora in various photos, all of which communicated their adoration for one another and focused on the way he couldn't seem to help but touch her, even when they were doing something like eating at a little outdoor cafe.

"They look… happy," she muttered, blinking furiously to chase a rush of hot tears away. She had come to terms with the reality that Maxwell wasn't coming back to her, so the flood of emotion was confusing.

She'd made a total fool of herself in front of God and the paparazzi one day outside a coffee shop trying to chase Nora off. She'd flung herself at Maxwell, pretending they were still together, among other things. It hadn't worked, obviously, and the gossip sites had gotten some great air-time out of making her look completely unhinged. That day had been the start of her plotting to strike out at Nora, no matter the cost.

"Looks like it."

"Nora Chase can't possibly be all sunshine and roses," she huffed, crossing her arms. She could feel frustration setting in and began to mentally chant some of the affir-mations Dr. Nguyen had them recite during the art and music therapy sessions. Even with as little time as she'd spent on campus, some things had started to stick.

"I honestly couldn't say. I met her on the *Destiny Falls* set once, I made an ass of myself actually. Acted exactly like the kind of dick I'm trying to stop being. I came to my senses pretty quickly and apologized. She actually seemed very sweet."

Olivia made a gagging noise. "I don't really care." Hot emotion churned through her body. As a distraction, she fidgeted with her nails while reading through the brief article.

His head tilted to the side, and his eyes glassed over, previously playful mouth pulled tight. After a long moment, he shook himself out of whatever thoughtful reverie he'd fallen into. "Why did you break up, anyway?" His eyes widened, as though he'd just realized what he was asking her. "If you don't mind my asking. It's okay if you don't want to answer."

Olivia pulled a face, bile sour in her mouth. She knew she'd been wrong to sleep with James, but doing so in a house she shared with Maxwell was particularly stupid. He'd tempted her with the promise of every one of her biggest dreams coming true. A dream role in a blockbuster, all the fame and fortune she'd been chasing for years. Sleeping with him to seal the deal had been the fastest, easiest way to get what she wanted. It wasn't until it was over and Maxwell was long gone that true regret set in and she realized she'd traded everything for a job she wasn't even invited to read for.

"I slept with someone else. He came home and found us. It wasn't pretty."

"And?"

"And *what*?" Olivia spat. "That's it. I cheated, so we were done. Along came needy little Nora Chase to ruin *everything*."

His mouth pinched, but he remained quiet. Olivia began to itch. She could hear all the unspoken accusations. On the heels of what had happened between them last night, she knew the insinuation that she was still upset about it probably stung.

"Just say it. Whatever it is, I've heard it before. You won't hurt my feelings."

"I don't know what to say, to be honest. You said all of that out loud and didn't even flinch. I'm trying to see how she's the problem in this scenario."

Olivia growled, jumping to her feet. Pacing was helpful when she was trying to work out a problem or have a conversation that wasn't particularly pleasant.

"If she'd never come along, I could have won him back, *obviously*."

"If you say so. But she did, and they're together now. Like, *together,* together. They seem happy. They might even be co-habitating, by the looks of where the picture was taken."

"They *seem* happy, sure. But there's always a crack."

"Sounds as if you have experience."

Olivia tossed her hands up in the air. "I didn't think we were discussing me right now, but sure. I've found the weak link in some relationships and exploited it to get something I wanted. Sex is a powerful motivator when you're young and hot."

It was Ollie's turn to look as though he'd tasted something sour.

"Don't be so judgmental," she accused. "Like you haven't done terrible things. Neither of us has any room to be a judgy asshole."

Ollie took a deep breath, eventually nodding. "You're right. But I've started to process why all the shitty things I did were wrong. Have you?"

The accusation sat there between them, cold and volatile.

"Isn't that why I'm here?"

He barked a short laugh. "Actually, yes, it is. But you didn't answer my question. I've watched you fake your way through therapy since you got here, so no, I don't think you have. And I'm not sure what Nora Chase has to do with any of it, to be honest. Listen—"

"No. I don't want to listen. She's the reason I'm in this place. I don't want to talk about her." She clicked the button to close out the window on the computer, the images gone but still burned into her mind.

"This isn't even about Nora. Do you realize that? This is about *you*. You're here because of the things *you* did."

She gasped, one hand snapping out to slap him. He caught her wrist in his palm, mouth tight as his surprise morphed into anger.

"How dare you!" She snapped.

"How dare *I*?" Ollie got to his feet, Olivia taking a step back as he towered over her. "It's not nice to hit people." He grated. "The sooner you come to grips with the fact you need to be here, the easier it's going to be for all of us."

"Except I don't—"

His shoulders sagged as he released her hand and peered deep into her eyes. "You *do*. No anger issues, right? You just tried to hit me. I thought I'd managed to crack a little bit into whatever shell you keep so damn tight around you, but I guess not. Maybe you really are *this* person and nothing more."

"I didn't—" Emotions collided messily, giving her a flash of heat followed by ice in her veins. She was out of control, and she absolutely hated the wobbly feeling it gave her.

Ollie continued, "You're here because you did something unforgivable to Nora, thinking it would get Maxwell to come back to you… after you did something equally unforgivable to him. All of that just made him realize he dodged a bullet. You understand what you did was as horrible as it was illegal, right?" He paused, his intense gaze looking right through her. The empathy he was showing to her even as he fought with her made her itchy. "Trust me, Olivia, I know all about unforgivable. I should be punished every day for the rest of my life for the things I've done. I should have gone to jail. I would still willingly go if any of those women pressed charges, to be honest. I deserve it. The worst part is they would have to come forward because I don't remember a lot of it. But you claim you committed those horrible acts in the name of love? After you cheated on him. For what, a job? Even if it was for *the* job, the one that would have made you a superstar, it doesn't even make sense. Did you even like him?"

Confusion swirled hot and greasy in her stomach. The urge to scream denial of his claims was strong, but the sting of truth lit up her flesh everywhere his words landed.

"Of course I did!"

"Then why did you sleep with his friend? If you were so happy, so in love, why do that?" Ollie's tone was even, and his volume had never risen. His resolute calmness somehow infuriated her more.

Olivia flailed her hands, the rage pounding through her blood hot and bitter. She glanced across the room, mortified there might be onlookers, but nobody was paying them any bit of attention. She had no doubt they were listening, but they were all very purposely not watching, at least not while she was looking.

"Because he was *there*, okay?" She hissed. "Is that what you want to hear? He was hot and interested in me, and a rich, big-shot lawyer. I thought..." she stopped, the words she was about to say backing up into her throat, choking her. Her anger cooled with the revelation. "I thought if anything ever happened between Maxwell and I, he'd be a perfect second choice. Sleeping with him seemed like a good way to seal the deal. Plus, he was offering me the chance at a job I wanted more than I've ever wanted anything in my life. He said he could get me a reading, and I believed him."

Ollie nodded, watching her as she processed the admission. "You fucked a man you didn't really know or like to secure a backup plan you only needed *because* you fucked that man. Do I have it right? No judgement. Seriously. I only want to be sure I understand. And that you do too."

"I…" Olivia's body sagged. She didn't like hearing the words in her mind let alone out loud. That hadn't been how she looked at things at the time. He was just a guy. They'd been talking, and one thing led to another, and they ended up having sex. Maxwell had come home. The way his whole face had transformed from open and warm to cold and closed off was something she'd never forget. Even afterwards, she'd discounted her own betrayal. She'd brushed it totally under the rug for a while, but the hurt was raw there. She'd put herself in his proximity for weeks, trying to make him see how much he missed her. Her intentionally dramatic scene at a coffee shop one day had been a ploy to chase Nora off, but no such luck. Instead, she'd looked like an overly dramatic ex making a scene when it hit the gossip sites. She'd played the part perfectly without even intending to. "I didn't mean…" she stopped again, words failing.

"We never mean to. But we do it. It's in our nature as addicts. We can't help but hurt the ones we love because we rarely live beyond the moment. We are impulsive and destructive. It's why we're *here*." Ollie pointed aggressively at the floor.

Shock rolled through Olivia's body. Self-introspection was clearly not her strong suit. She never worried about other people or their feelings. She hated every single moment of this.

"Participate in therapy, Princess. If you don't, you're doomed to be this person forever and nobody likes her very much. Including you, I'm guessing."

"That's…" Olivia wanted to protest, but she couldn't find the words. He wasn't wrong. It was infuriating.

Ollie crossed his arms as he continued, "As far as the rest of it… I'm not really a relationship guy and I'm *definitely* not the person you should be talking to about those kinds of things."

She snickered. "Isn't that the damn truth?"

Bringing up their past was something Olivia couldn't manage to avoid doing. It still rankled deep how he didn't remember her, and it was a well-ingrained habit to poke at someone's sore spot until they reacted. The icing on this particular cake was the fact she knew he wanted to kiss her again, but probably still wouldn't.

Ollie squinted at her. "Look, you clearly remember way more about how we met than I do. If I'm being completely honest, there are entire *years* I don't remember. I was drunk constantly. Taking lots of pills. It's nothing personal. But you've been holding it over my head with little snarky comments since you got here, so why don't you come right out and tell me what's on your mind, *Princess*?"

Olivia snatched the tablet out of his hands, efficiently scrolling to a website archive she'd found. It had a picture of them from that night, among thousands of others. A younger version of the both of them trapped in a faded image looked back from the screen.

She was beaming at the camera, slumped under the arm he'd put around her shoulders. They were sitting in a round booth in the VIP section of the club. A few guys were at a distance on her other side, members of his entourage. The table was littered with drinks in all stages of fullness, crumpled up napkins, and traces of a suspicious looking powder.

Olivia thrust the tablet back at him.

Ollie turned a sickly shade of white as he took in the image. Without a word, he calmly turned and walked out the front door.

CHAPTER
Ten

OLIVIA WAS TOO stunned to move for a moment, in complete disbelief that he'd up and left.

One of the helpers had seen him go as well, but didn't follow him. He'd leaned over enough to see where he'd gone with the tablet, but clearly wasn't concerned.

She hated to sacrifice her limited tech time, but their conversation wasn't done. After a quick moment of indecision, she went outside to find him.

Ollie was in her favorite little seating area off to the side of the pool, one hand fisting his hair as he scrolled around on the tablet with the other.

"It was a long time ago."

Ollie looked up at her, still stunned.

"I *knew* you were familiar. But I…" He frowned again, staring at the screen as though it held some kind of secret. "I'm sorry, Princess. I just don't remember much. There are things, like the smell of your perfume. The damned butterfly on your back. But…" He shook his head. "I… I did a lot of things I don't remember. Things I'm not proud of. I have so many regrets about those years. There were a lot of women…" He grimaced, setting the tablet onto the table between them before dropping his head into his hands, palms pressed into his eyes.

Olivia sat on one of the love-seats across from him, reaching for the tablet. After one more look at the image, she exited the site and turned it off.

"I think it might be the only picture," she said, still impressed it existed at all.

"How on earth did you find it?"

"Pure luck. I was looking for something else and fell down a rabbit hole. This website goes on for days. The number of images they have of private events and celebrities is crazy."

Ollie nodded dazedly. The stress around his mouth dug at her. As much as she'd hoped he'd recall on his own and was kind of enjoying having a grudge to hold over him, she hated to see him this distraught.

"Do you want me to tell you what I remember?" She asked.

He looked out over the pool, clenching his jaw while he decided. Finally, he nodded. "Sure. Maybe it will help me."

"It was about… three years ago. I was twenty-two and fresh off my first real movie gig. I bribed the guy at the door of the club and snuck into the area you were in.

I convinced you to let me have a drink with you by giving you an eyeful of cleavage and batting my eyes." Olivia was kidding, mostly, though she had actually done those things. Ollie wasn't in any mood to laugh about it quite yet, however. He remained stone faced, so she stopped trying to make jokes.

Ollie's eyebrows drew together. "Was I already drunk?"

"You were a little tipsy, but you were coherent. No slurring or stumbling, or anything like that. We danced a few times, held a conversation… at least as much of a conversation as you can have when the music is so loud. You honestly seemed fine." Olivia's mind spun back to the memory she'd replayed a million times.

The way his hands felt on her waist as the two of them melded into a puddle of sweaty lust on the dance floor. His breath on her neck as he leaned close to speak into her ear. The way he'd made her feel once they'd kicked everyone out of the booth and shut the curtain. The way he'd folded his body over hers from behind as she knelt on the seat of the booth.

Nothing about their encounter had struck her as off, but now she wondered how reliable her perspective on it had been.

He shook his head. "I was probably pretty loaded. Pills ran my whole life then. It's possible I was completely out of my skull, but only looked like I had been drinking. I got really great at functioning when I was blasted. What happened after that?" He asked, tone shifting slightly as though he were bracing for further impact from her words.

"I had a few drinks—"

"Gin and tonic. With lime?" he suggested, eyebrows creased as though the memory surfacing was painful.

"Yes, exactly. But I wasn't drunk either. I was annoyed because it tasted like they were mixing my drinks super light. We danced some more. You kicked everyone out of the room and had your guys close the curtain…"

She was starting to understand why he was so freaked out. It wasn't she was simply forgettable as one of many girls he slept with, it was that he didn't have any memories of the night at all.

Ollie stared at her, eyes wide. "Did I… did you want to—"

Olivia tensed. "Nothing happened that I didn't want. Enthusiastically and wholeheartedly. I swear it." The words were firm, enhanced by the shake of her head.

He watched her carefully for a long moment before he finally nodded. He seemed to breathe fully for the first time since they'd come outside.

"Okay. Okay." He repeated the word a few times, swiping angrily at his eyes, which were leaking tears.

"Ollie, I didn't realize…" Olivia's chest compressed with guilt. He was still struggling to get a handle on his emotions. She sagged, understanding dawning that it was probably the same thing he'd been feeling since he started trying to get help.

"No, no. It's not your fault."

"It's not yours either." He stared at her, as though those words were difficult to process. "It's not," she repeated.

Olivia reached into one of the dorm-sized refrigerators and grabbed a sparkling water. Ollie shook his head when she offered him one as well.

They sat there in silence, the sound of the sprinklers white noise in the background. Olivia was sweating despite the cool breeze the evening had brought, a new torrent of emotion swirling in her gut.

She'd wanted to be angry he didn't remember, if only because the event was so important to her. She hadn't considered that there might be other circumstances around *why* he didn't remember.

"Am I… one of your regrets?"

"Yes." He quickly raised a hand, seeing her eyes widen.

Her chest had immediately compressed at the simple word, bile rising quickly into her throat. While she also had innumerable feelings about their interlude, regret wasn't one of them.

"Not for the reason you think," he rushed to add. "I don't regret that it was you. I regret how I don't remember it. I regret who *I* was when it happened—that I was him at all, to be honest. I'm so sorry." His apology was quiet, but heavy with sincerity. "For not remembering. And for being *him* when it happened. I'm sure you didn't deserve such a thing. You couldn't. Nobody does."

Olivia sat back in the seat, uncomfortable with the heavy emotions, but unsure how to manage them without seeming fake. Instead, she gave him the honest truth.

"It's honestly one of my best memories."

"I…" Ollie cleared his throat, struggling to look her in the eye. "I need to take this back inside." He lifted up the tablet. "And I should probably… go talk to someone."

"Oh. Okay."

He nodded and left her outside, emotions going completely haywire. She waited a few minutes before following him in. The helper allowed her to sit at one of the computers and take the rest of her time, which she hadn't been expecting, but was grateful for nonetheless.

Her focus was terrible as she scrolled through her messages, her mind on Ollie's reaction.

She sifted through the countless spam items, where she found the promised email from him with all of his personal contact information. Her chest squeezed. She now had everything but his home address while he only had her email. After a moment of hesitation, she replied with her phone number. It was a suggestion for the mentor situation, she knew that, but it had been a long time since she traded information directly with someone and it felt extra personal after the conversation they'd just had.

After clearing out the junk, she found a number of messages from her mother.

There were a bunch of upcoming audition notices as usual, but one email left her blinking in shock. Her mother was pushing for the reality show at every opportunity, and the promised dollar amount made Olivia's eyes pop. So far, there'd been no mention of it, but her mom had finally managed to get an offer from the producer. If the number was real, it would more than cover the fine and court fees she'd had to pay for her part in the blackmail situation. Plus her stay at rehab. And Jerry's fees. With a decent amount leftover, even.

A crack had finally appeared in the exit door, and the timing couldn't have been better.

CHAPTER
Eleven

OLIVIA WISHED SHE could go back to the level of awkwardness between her and Ollie after she'd kissed him in the hallway.

It had been a light teaser of tension compared to the stiff interactions they were dealing with after what she couldn't help thinking of as *the big reveal*.

She went to breakfast the next morning, already rehearsing what she might say to him. Possible conversations had been running through her head since she went back up to her room. None of the variations led her to much more than *sorry I didn't tell you sooner, I'm a bitch and liked hanging it over your head because I was upset you didn't remember*, which didn't feel altogether helpful.

When she got over to the dining room, he was already sitting with a couple of the guys he was friendly with. He glanced up, making eye contact before ducking his head.

Olivia held her shoulders back and went to her normal table by herself, not willing to let her ego take a further hit. If he needed some time to work through what he'd learned, that was fine.

She made her coffee, ate her breakfast, and went along with her day, resolved to understanding he would talk to her when he was ready to.

As it turned out, he wasn't ready until after dinner. Group therapy and yoga were their only sessions together during the day, though he was suspiciously absent during lunch. He watched her warily from across the circle during group therapy, ducking his head as he had that morning whenever she made eye contact. During yoga, he set up his mat clear across the platform.

By the time yoga was over, Olivia was starting to feel some agitation at how deftly he was avoiding her. She worried what she'd told him about their past had pushed him so far away he might not come back. It seemed silly but true. They'd only been in proximity to one another for a couple short weeks, but she genuinely liked him and didn't want to lose what it felt like they were growing between them.

She spent dinner watching him interact with the same table of guys as before. This time, however, he'd taken a seat with his back to her, so at least the awkward eye contact wasn't an issue.

Olivia ate her food plus dessert, anxiety building the whole time about who might get up to leave first.

She was about to scream, her body was so knotted up about things.

In the end, she was the one to leave first. She pulled herself up straight and forced her eyes to stay on the door instead of looking his way. Even if he didn't want to go back to building a friendship, he was still her mentor and they had things they had to do together. She wasn't sure she could handle the emotional stress of continuing to feel the way she had for the day.

"So ridiculous," she grumbled to herself, once she was out on the pool deck. She exhaled, taking large strides toward the residence building.

"Olivia, hey. Wait." Ollie's voice rang out from behind her, bringing her feet to a stop right by the seating area where the bombs had fallen.

She turned around, intentionally blanking her expression. "Yeah?"

He stopped several feet away from her, looking abashed as he stuffed his hands into his pockets. "I'm not avoiding you."

"Oh?" Olivia propped a hand on her hip, head cocked to the side as though daring him to lie again.

"Ok, maybe I am. But only because I'm not sure what to say to you. Can we sit? Just for a minute." He gestured to the furniture.

"I guess." Olivia knew her tone was petulant, but she couldn't help it.

Ollie grabbed a couple of drinks and sat across from

her, their positions an exact match for the night before. The energy between them was still distorted, an odd current that made Olivia's skin itch.

He made a few false starts at conversation while the sun made its final descent over the ocean, leaving them with a cool evening breeze.

"I had a couple of emergency sessions with Dr. Collins."

"Not Dr. Clay?"

He shook his head. "I thought it best to get some distance for this particular issue since she's helping you, too. I didn't give specifics, I just needed some perspective so I could manage what I was feeling. Everything felt a little out of control after we talked…"

The fact that he'd thought to speak to a different counselor because she was close to Dr. Clay blew Olivia's mind. The simple gesture was so above and beyond she wasn't even sure how to quantify it.

"I get it," Olivia said. "It's not a big deal."

"Except it is. But she gave me some strategies to manage it and I'll be fine. I just was so… surprised by what you told me. And disappointed in myself."

"It was a long time ago," Olivia repeated, unsure of what else to say.

"Please don't misunderstand, I'm thankful you told me. It was honestly a last straw situation. Mostly because I *like* you, Olivia. And I hate that I don't remember being intimate with you. It makes me feel… wrong. For being interested in you now. Like I haven't earned the right or something."

Olivia found herself blushing, the sensation once again running riot under her skin. Nervousness made her hands and feet prickle. She hadn't wanted a friendship the way she did with Ollie for a very long time. If she was being honest with herself, she hadn't allowed herself an actual friend in many, many years. She's gotten too caught up in how transactional relationships could be in Hollywood and developed a knack for leaving before she got hurt.

Even though it meant hurting the other person first.

"I like you too," she admitted, the blush burning in her cheeks. She wanted to tell him how thoughtful he was. How he was one of the best people she'd ever met. How he didn't have to be sorry about anything, but she'd started to worry she might be the one who had taken advantage of him the night they were together. Instead, she asked, "I'm sure Dr. Collins set you straight?"

He cracked a smile and nodded. "She did. In no uncertain terms. I needed today to kind of… process it all out." He opened the seltzer, taking a deep drink as though he needed it for strength. "Can we… can we make a habit of this? Sitting here, talking? Even though it threw me for a serious loop the first time around, I think it's healthy to do."

Olivia shrugged. She loved this spot, so she didn't see any reason to say no. Besides, it was a pleasant way to spend an evening without any of the other residents hanging around or listening in. Plus, it got her out of her room.

"Sounds good to me."

He grinned, lightness returning to his demeanor. "After dinner in the evening? You, me, maybe some swimming?"

"Sounds great."

"Okay."

He didn't say anything else, but Olivia could swear she heard him think more apologies at her.

There didn't seem to be anything else to say, so they just sat there as the sun sank lower into the surf, sipping their seltzers and holding space with one another.

Olivia melted into the cushions of the wicker loveseat, piling the throw pillows at her back so she could recline.

They sat there long enough Olivia dozed off.

She startled awake to him standing over her, calling her name in a soft voice.

"C'mon, Butterfly. Let's go inside before you crash out."

She added the nickname to his tally, taking the hand he offered to help her stand.

Ollie gathered up their trash and dumped it in the closest recycling bin, shaking his head as he approached her.

"You ready to go up?"

"Sure."

Olivia got to her feet, drowsiness leaving her a little unsteady. They crossed the courtyard in silence, his hand brushing hers in a way that made her pulse spike.

He opened the door for her and told her goodnight from the bottom of the stairs.

"See you in the morning?" He asked.

Olivia put one foot on the bottom step. "Right here, bright and early for breakfast."

"Good night, Olivia."

"Good night, Ollie."

Exhaustion pulling at her limbs, she went through the motions of getting ready for bed once she got into her room. The bed welcomed her with open blankets, and she accepted the warm hug gratefully.

CHAPTER
Twelve

AYS FLOWED INTO one another far too easily for Olivia's liking. She'd get up, eat breakfast, go through her sessions, and go to sleep, only to start the cycle all over again.

Some nights Olivia swam, but after the decadent meals, all she wanted to do most of the time was relax. She and Ollie had taken to stretching out on the furniture every evening to discuss their day.

Olivia suspected it was a way for him to practice as her mentor while staying close to her without crossing boundaries he'd set. The tension was still there, though, lingering between them. She could feel it as an almost tangible thing. The awkwardness had improved, at the very least, but they were still working their way back to the previous level of comfort.

They hadn't spoken about the night at the club any further, but it was always there, hovering in the background of their interactions. Every now and then, she'd look up to see him studying her closely, as though still trying to revive the memory of that night. All he had to do was ask, and she'd tell him every single detail she remembered.

If she was being honest with herself, aside from yoga, it was Olivia's favorite session at Sunrise. She appreciated it mostly because she got to participate in it outside, near the pool. As an added benefit, it could be done without any overt supervision after a lovely meal. There wasn't any part of it not to love.

"Where do you live?" Ollie asked out of nowhere. They'd been discussing the evening's dessert selections a moment before, so his abrupt topic switch took her by surprise. "I mean, when you're not enjoying the pleasures this lovely place has to offer. I'm guessing you're in L.A. proper?"

Ollie misunderstood Olivia's hesitation, rushing to say, "You don't have to tell me if asking is over the line—"

"No, no." Ollie wasn't one of the bad guys. He wasn't paparazzi or someone looking to collect money. He was a friend. Or something close to one. It was just that she didn't really have a stable address to tell him about at the moment.

"My parents bought a house in Brentwood when they were newlyweds."

He whistled, cracking open the top of a berry-flavored seltzer, offering it to her. She accepted, and he opened a second for himself before resuming his position lying down. "That's an expensive part of town."

"It's on the outskirts, but yeah. They were gifted some down payment money as a wedding gift. It was still a big purchase, even then, though nothing compared to prices now. It's one of those old bungalows. Pretty unassuming from the street, small but a great yard."

"I do love the architecture of this area. There's never mistaking you're in California when you drive through any part of Los Angeles."

Her lips tipped up. "I've said the same thing for years. It's true. When I was little, it was all wood paneling, shag carpeting and colorful tile."

"Sounds charming." He was smiling at her, enjoying her descriptions.

"It was." Olivia could feel the smile melt from her face. "When I started getting paying acting jobs, Mom used a lot of the money to redo the house. Some things we definitely needed—the kitchen was truly awful, for example. Outdated brown and orange with a splash of avocado with the appliances." She shuddered dramatically. "But she turned everything ultra-modern. Black. White. Chrome. No color anywhere. I miss the charm of the old house sometimes." She met his eye to tell him a truth few people knew. "Actually, it's my house now."

He sat up, flames dancing in his eyes as he watched her from the other side of the fire table.

"Oh yeah?"

She sat forward, resting her elbows on her knees. "A few years ago, my dad got into some bad investments with his construction business. I'm pretty sure it was a Ponzi scheme, but he doesn't ever talk to me about much of anything. To keep the house from going into foreclosure they had to refinance it, but my credit was the only one still worth a damn. So the deed is actually in my name now. Which is nice since it was my money that paid for all of the upgrades even though Mom picked it all."

"Do you normally live there full time? With them? No judgement if you do, everything is crazy expensive, especially in LA."

"No. Not usually. I keep my room ready there, but I've had my own places or lived with someone for years. It depended on how my income was flowing. The last few months I was home, though."

By court order. She hated that part. She'd had a studio she'd loved for a while after Maxwell broke up with her. Outrageously priced, but it had been all hers.

He grunted, tipping his bottle up as he took a deep drink.

"I get it. I've got my own place now, but there were a lot of years I was basically renting half a bedroom or something for hundreds of dollars a month. I went back to my parents' house plenty of times over the years. I'm lucky though, they never really gave me a hard time about it."

"Yeah." Olivia didn't elaborate. The echoes of her mother's voice in the back of her mind were too loud.

Back again, Olivia? Maybe the next one will stick. Can't believe you didn't nail down one of those lawyers when you had the chance!

There would always be lots of laughter and a meaningless, half-hearted apology. Usually a claim about how she was just joking, though it never felt like a joke to Olivia because she wasn't laughing.

Something about being away and having the time to see how other people operated showed her how raw her feelings actually were about her mother's rules and jokes.

"Hey. You alright?" Ollie was staring at her, his obvious concern drawing his features tight.

"Sure. I'm just tired. I had an extra session today." It was partly true. Dr. Clay had put her through her paces during her individual session. Now that they had things to talk about, she wasn't letting up even a little bit.

"We can call it a night if you want."

"No, I'm okay. It's nice out here. Talking about home puts me in a weird place."

Ollie nodded and shifted back in his seat. He kept his eyes on her, she could feel his attention even as she lay on her back and looked up at the night sky.

"Let's talk about something else then."

"Okay."

Neither of them could come up with a suitable topic, so they sat in the quiet for a number of minutes.

"I graduate out in twelve days," Ollie said, tone soft. "Which is wild."

Olivia could barely hear the words, but she felt their shape as they sunk into her flesh.

"Are you excited?"

"Yes?"

Olivia smiled, turning her head so she could see him. "Are you sure? That sounded like a question."

He looked adorable sitting there with his hands clasped in his lap, an abashed look on his face.

"I don't mind it here, to be honest. I've made lots of progress which I'm afraid will stop or go backwards when I leave."

"Plus the food," Olivia teased.

"Oh my God. I'll miss the food so damn much. I almost broke down crying when Jean-Pierre came around to check on us at lunch the other day."

Tension broken, they both laughed.

"What'll you do after you leave?"

Ollie inhaled deeply, gaze unfocused as he looked into the flames.

"Go back to my apartment. Start looking for work, I guess. I don't know." He rubbed his hands together. "Dr. Clay has already gotten me set up with a team out in the real world so I can keep up my therapy, but there are so many variables out there. Going back to some of my old routines terrifies me."

"Yeah." Olivia wasn't sure what to say. Her whole life was already topsy turvy, and she had a sinking feeling it was only going to get worse. Especially after Ollie left campus and she was there by herself. The staff was nice enough and some of the other residents were friendly, but he was the only one she'd gotten close to, and even they weren't *that* close. She wasn't sure *what* they were.

"I've been considering looking into some kind of training for counseling…" he trailed off. "But it's probably quite a ways off. Not worth getting too excited about until it's a real possibility."

"You know it pains me to compliment you in any way," she teased, "but you'd be good at it. Maybe something with kids."

He beamed, his endearing smile coming out in full force. "Yeah? That's actually exactly what I was thinking. I could be the person I needed when I was younger. It's probably just a daydream though. I don't know the first thing about running any kind of programs for kids. And teenagers especially are kind of know-it-all assholes."

She knew he was still worried there was no true redemption for his past behavior, that for some reason, he couldn't ever truly be better. Olivia wanted to be cranky with herself for entertaining the friendship between them, but it was hard to resist his charm. He'd fully embraced *her*, after all, sharp edges included.

"I don't think anyone does until they do, Oliver."

His head snapped up at her use of his actual name. "What?"

"You're already listing out all the reasons it's a foolish plan, or why you couldn't make it work, right?"

He didn't admit it, but she could see the answer in the slight tilt of his head.

"Well, stop. Nobody comes out of the womb knowing how to run a shelter for troubled teens or an after-school program for endangered youth. Whatever you're thinking of doing, it's a worthwhile idea. You'll probably have to jump through a ton of hoops to set anything up, mostly because you live in California. Not because it's a bad idea, or it won't work. Don't count yourself out, is all I'm saying. Everyone has to learn the things they don't know before they know them."

His wide eyes blinked at her a number of times. She tried not to smile in a way that made her seem smug, but his response to her diatribe had made her proud.

"See? I'm not just a pretty face," she teased.

"I know," he said, clearing his throat as he continued to gawk at her. "That was wise, Olivia."

"You're surprised?"

"Honestly? Not really, but I don't think I've ever heard you string together quite so many words without swearing, unless you were talking about… food. Or maybe the pool."

"There's more to me than those things, like there's more to you than misogyny." She raised her eyebrow, hoping he understood she was playfully poking at his insecurities, not taking a full-fledged swipe at him.

He snorted, then laughed in earnest. "Of course there is. You're full of surprises, Princess."

Riding the wave of positive endorphins, she dipped

toward him. Just before her mouth made contact, he ducked away, sliding across the seat as he sat up straight.

"You know we can't." Ollie's aqua eyes were soft as he took in the length of her body.

"Nobody would know."

His mouth formed a tight line, and his eyebrows drew together.

"I would. I would know. Neither of us… we're not… *allowed* and I don't want it to be like that."

Olivia knew what he was saying, but what she heard as the words got twisted up inside her head was, 'I don't want you.' It was the second time he'd shut her down and defensiveness and embarrassment rode her hard, turning her shame into anger.

"You don't even remember the last time, so don't worry about it," she snipped, pride bruised yet again.

Ollie's whole demeanor changed as he processed what she'd said. Regret rushed in, but it was too late.

"That's not fair."

"I know." Olivia held her hands up in apology. "I shouldn't have said that. It was a stupid reflex."

"Trust me when I say I want… whatever this is," he gestured with an arm between the two of them. "Whenever it happens, to be for real. This place? It's not reality. It's a weird purgatory where we're play-acting being real adults. The only responsibilities here are to show up in the dining hall on time and go to therapy. It's not real life. I'm not even sure you know what you feel for me right now. Do you?

Do you trust it? Because I don't. I'm into you, Princess. I am. But I also still don't really know who you are. Am I making sense?"

His calm delivery of the words had taken most of the sting out of his rejection.

"You sure it's Purgatory and not Hell? Group therapy and one-on-ones with Dr. Feel Good seem like Hell." Olivia used humor to deflect her hurt.

"I'm sure," Ollie played along, humor in his tone. "It's not quite a vacation because of all the rules. But it's close. The rooms, the food, the pool…"

"The *therapy*, though."

"Point taken." A laugh rumbled through his chest. "But we're both shit at this whole thing. I'm re-learning how my perception skews what's actually happening as far as consent and you remember us being intimate once upon a time. Neither of those things make for a reasonable excuse to get naked while still actively in rehab."

Olivia tsked her tongue. "Who said anything about *naked*?" He skewered her with a knowing glare, daring her to deny where she was eventually headed. "Fine."

"For what it's worth, I'm glad I'm your mentor, Olivia. And I'm glad you're comfortable enough with me for the idea to cross your mind, especially considering what hap-pened between us a few years ago. It's just not something we can entertain. Not right now. No matter how much I want to."

"I hear you."

There were a few heartbeats of silence, the only noise came from the waterfall at the far end of the pool.

"I think I'm going to head up. You coming?"

Olivia nodded. "Yeah, I need to get some sleep."

"Alright. I'll see you in the morning."

"Okay."

Olivia nursed her damaged pride as she headed up the stairs, but let it go at the door to her suite, too tired to keep worrying about it, knowing deep down he was right.

He usually was.

CHAPTER

Thirteen

AT BREAKFAST A couple of mornings later, Ollie greeted her with a tense grin.

"Morning. You sleep okay?"

"Fine, thanks."

He muttered something she didn't catch before getting up to gather his food from the buffet. Olivia mixed some sugar and creamer into her coffee, trying not to be too concerned with what he'd said.

"So, I got some news last night," Ollie said, plunking himself down with a plate full of pancakes.

"Yeah?"

"They're bringing back my character on *Destiny Falls* for a couple of episodes. So, when I go home, I'll have at least a week's worth of work ahead of me."

Olivia's heart stuttered in her chest. It was a relief he had similar news to her reality show decision. It made it easier to bring it up.

"Yeah? That's great. I mean, it is if you're excited about it."

He focused on cutting his pancakes into smaller bites, features blank as he worked. Olivia sipped at her coffee, waiting for him to respond.

"I… am? I know I was just saying how terrified I was to go back in front of the camera, but it feels like closure. I already know the cast and crew, so this seems like the best-case scenario."

"Well, I hate to steal your thunder, but same."

"You're taking a show?" Ollie's stunned expression did not at all match up to how Olivia had pictured him reacting.

She'd found a long-winded message from her mom and the paperwork for a reality show in her email the night before. It felt wrong not getting Jerry's eyes on it to check things over, but she knew he'd flip out at the mere sugges-tion because it meant leaving Sunrise almost immediately.

Olivia had given her electronic signature and sent it back, simultaneously thrilled and terrified over making such an impulsive choice. Sleep had been elusive as she wavered between relief over finding her way out and worry she'd made the wrong decision. Her mom had promised everything was taken care of, and she was trying to trust her.

"I sent back the contract last night. It starts filming right away, basically. Isn't it exciting?" She mimed clap-ping, exaggerating her expression to show her enthusiasm.

He slumped back into his chair, crossing his arms. "Sure, it's exciting, but if you don't finish your sixty-day cycle, you go to jail, right? I don't understand. How does taking the show get you out of that?"

Olivia's skin began to itch. The same thing had left her worried, despite her mom's assurances. "I'm sure they found a way. There's always an exception, right?" Her casual shrug made him sit up straight. "My mom said she had someone working on that part."

"Olivia, be serious. Do you even hear yourself? There are *no* exceptions when it comes to this. It's part of your probation. If you take this show, if you leave this campus, you *will* be arrested. Thrown in jail. Real jail. Like, a tiny concrete cell with metal bars and no forgiveness for people like us. Someone like you..." He shook his head, horror etching his features.

"Someone like me, *what*?" Her emotions began to careen out of control and no amount of breathing exercises were going to help her. Panic that she'd made the wrong choice barely out voiced stress over misreading the closeness between the two of them yet again. "I'm not weak, Oliver. I'm not as soft as everyone seems to think I am."

"Jesus Christ." He ran his hands through his hair almost violently, dropping his fork onto his plate loud enough someone at a neighboring table looked over. "You're insane if you can twist this situation around to suit you. You don't need this cushy Malibu rehab, you need an actual psych eval." His whisper-yell was harsh, the words grating through his throat.

"Fuck you, Ollie. This is my chance! *The* chance! You

know better than anyone what this means! Why are you so hellbent I shouldn't take it?" She shrank back from the glare he was giving her. "You *know* what this kind of opportunity means to an actress like me."

"Of *course* I know what it means." He lowered his tone, arms dropping from his hair to the table. His aqua gaze suddenly held pity, and it was worse than the rage. "I couldn't give a single damn about a comeback right now, Olivia. Not for myself and not for you. A comeback is the absolute last thing on my mind. It *should* be the last thing on yours. I don't want you to go to *jail*. Don't you understand? It's dangerous. You *will* get hurt. What's the point? All you have to do is to finish out your time here before you look for jobs."

Olivia pouted, arms crossed. "You know as well as I do that isn't how this works. If you get an offer, you take it. If you don't, they move on. They won't wait for me to be done here. They'll just pick someone else."

"*So let them pick someone else.*" He was begging now. His warm hands folded over hers, his body perched on the edge of the seat so he could be as close to her as possible.

"I can't." She breathed the words desperately, willing him to understand how she needed the money, the fresh start... all the things the opportunity could possibly offer her.

Ollie blinked slowly, dropping his chin to his chest. "You're throwing it all away, Olivia. Everything you've done the last few weeks. Don't you feel different? You seem different. But I can't help you through this if you won't help yourself."

"That's exactly it, I do feel different. I'm fine! The therapy worked, and now I'm moving on with my life. Isn't that what you're supposed to do?"

He released her hands, shaking his head harshly side to side. His lip curled up, disdain in the way he was looking at her. True panic set in, her heart galloping so hard behind her ribs that she could feel it clogging her throat. Her one anchor, her one friend… and he was looking at her as if she was something disgusting he'd stepped in. Worse, it felt like he was saying goodbye.

"Ollie, come on, it's not that serious—"

"Except it *is*. And you refuse to believe it." He stood again, tossing his napkin onto the table. "Some things you have to learn the hard way. I'm starting to think you might actually need to learn everything that way."

He stared her down for a long moment before turning to leave.

Tears formed in Olivia's eyes, hot and shameful. She tried to blink them away, knowing what it would look like. The last thing she wanted was for him to think she was turning on the waterworks to gain his sympathy.

"Ollie…"

"I can't help you," he repeated. "I've tried to be here for you, Olivia. But you're making a mistake."

He walked with purpose to the open door, striding through it without a backward glance. Despite the warmth of the room, Olivia felt chilled. A quick glance around the room confirmed everyone in the dining room had seen their argument. She tossed her shoulders back, daring someone to gossip about it in her presence.

She now truly doubted the decision she'd made, but had her heels dug in so far she couldn't change her mind.

"I can do this," she said to herself. "I can. It'll be fine. Totally fine." The words rang hollow in her ears.

Ollie was supposed to be the easy conversation. The one that buoyed her confidence in the situation and told her she was doing the right thing.

Resolve shaken, she headed back to her room to pack. She was taking control of her own future and getting the hell out of rehab.

PAULINE LOOKED PANICKED as she followed Olivia out the front doors a couple of days later.

"You know what will happen, Olivia, please, reconsider!"

Olivia found the ride-share car her mother had ordered for her waiting right out front.

"I swear I'll tell them you did everything you could, Pauline. You won't be in trouble over this."

"I'm not worried about trouble. But I have to report you leaving, Olivia. There's no way out of it. It's mandatory."

"I know." She paused before dropping into the back seat. "It'll be okay." It had to be.

Pauline looked dejected as she put the phone to her ear and made the call.

"Drive," she ordered the man behind the wheel.

As they pulled away from the lush estate that was Sunrise Rehab, Olivia battled two very conflicting emotions. Her heart sank at the same time it tried to be buoyant. She was proud of herself for making a choice. Any choice. She was hopeful it was the right one, that things would work out even while she worried she was doing the wrong thing.

Her mom had promised she had the details all worked out. She had to believe it was true.

She repeated those words like a mantra as the little sedan got closer and closer to Los Angeles. This would be one of the most expensive ride-shares in history, but worth it.

The studio was aiming to film two episodes that day and into the evening, one right after the other. They'd wanted her for the second one, so she would have plenty of time to get in, have her makeup done and get on set unless traffic held them up.

Olivia's phone brightened and began to vibrate. It was Jerry.

She declined the call, unwilling to hear his scolding at the moment. There would be plenty of time for that later.

CHAPTER
Fourteen

OLIVIA FELT VIBRANT as she stepped into the soundstage.

There was nowhere she was more alive than when she was on camera. Her nerves went into overdrive, then vanished altogether as she made her way toward the makeup stations.

Handlers were posted at intervals, people with clipboards and headsets directing the cast and crew.

She paused to look at the set, a broad smile taking over her face and her blood pumping. She was excited to be there; that alone made the occasion worth noting.

The design of the show's set made it feel as though the cast were sitting inside the living room of a large house. Unlike most homes, many of the walls missing and microphones were rigged up all over the place. Plus, there were cameras stationed at every possible angle.

Olivia waited her turn to sit in one of the vacant makeup chairs and reveled in the feel of getting her hair styled and full camera-ready makeup done.

The stylist wasn't at all talkative—at least not with her. The three makeup artists were holding an animated conversation amongst themselves, but the cast may as well have been invisible.

By the time Olivia was sent to wardrobe, the surge of happy feelings was wearing off. Her phone had been pinging with alerts for messages the entire time she was getting pampered. She hated to think about how wound-up Jerry might be since she was ignoring him.

It was suspicious how nobody had introduced themselves. She'd seen no fewer than seven other actors, but not even one had so much as made eye contact with her. She'd tried to speak to one of the women when she'd been seated at the station next to her, but the hairstylist turned on the blow dryer right when she was about to say something. A sinking feeling took hold in her stomach as she left the small changing cubicle. She'd been outfitted with a fuchsia romper clearly intended to be a duplicate of one she owned. One that had ended up in paparazzi photos wearing more than once.

The director was hustling everyone into place as she walked around the corner of the set.

"Ah, Olivia. Wonderful. Here's what we need you to do." He walked her through the simple set directions, but she was left confused.

"That's it? Is this just for the first scene, or…?"

He gave her what she took to be a reassuring smile, but it didn't make her feel one bit better.

"Nope, for the whole thing. It'll be great."

Doubt swamped her as she took her place and watched as the other cast members began to interact. There were a number of thoughts racing around her mind about reality shows not being real, but she let them filter through instead of chasing them.

All too quickly, it was her turn on set.

It only took a moment in front of the camera for her to realize she was not, in fact, a special guest star. At least not like she'd thought.

There were jokes lobbed at her expense she was completely unprepared for. Commentary on her appearance and wardrobe, none of which had been her choice, but the audience wouldn't know that.

Two of the men sneered at her, getting a good eyeful of her flesh while openly talking trash about her. The adult films she'd made early in her career were mentioned, complete with a few blurred-out clips. Her digital moans echoed through the space. Fun was poked at her expense.

Her criminal record was brought up, as well as her very recent stint at rehab… and how she'd left against better judgement.

She was used as an example of what not to do. Who not to be.

As instructed, she threw a tantrum, much like she had at the coffee shop that day with Maxwell and Nora. Except this time, her heart wasn't in it. It was one hundred percent acting, perhaps one of her very best performances. Inside, she was dying the whole time.

Then, as directed, she stormed off one side of the set.

That was it. Her *big moment*.

She was a live prop. A joke.

A handler hustled her into a green room where she found her mother waiting.

"Darling! You're done so fast. Are you all finished up?"

Too stunned to do much but nod, Olivia waited for the signal that she was to de-wardrobe while her mother chattered on and on.

Once she was finally cleared to change, she swapped for her personal clothes, trying desperately to get control of her emotions.

"Did you know it would be like this, Mom?" she asked, watching as her mother sipped at champagne that was not intended for her consumption.

Her mother looked pleased as punch, sitting there on the sofa. Olivia was mortified.

"I had an inkling." She looked up, finding Olivia staring back at her. "What? You didn't?"

"No, I…" Olivia realized what an idiot she'd been. "I just thought…"

"Thought what, dear? That your *talent* was in high demand? It was. High enough you'll collect a decent check for your efforts. Well done." She waved her glass around, nearly spilling the contents over the side.

"Well done? I didn't do anything. All I did was stand there and take it. Then fake a tantrum and walk off."

Olivia sat heavily on the sofa. She was as far away from her mother as she could be, but it wasn't nearly far enough.

For the first time, Olivia got truly icky vibes from her mother. Past conversations and behaviors started to spin wildly through her memories. There'd been some discomfort and red flags before, but this was a neon sign in her face.

"It's a *job*, baby. And you did so well! You've been here, what, a couple of hours? And you're already done! The money they promised us is as good as in the bank. You did great."

Olivia stared at her mom, trying to decide if the *r's* of her words had really been as slurred as they sounded.

"I didn't do great, Mom. All I did was show up to be roasted, but I had absolutely no idea that's what was going to happen. How many of those have you had?"

"Honestly? I have no idea. Probably not more than six."

Olivia gasped. She was well and truly plastered if her guess was accurate. Six glasses made a whole bottle and then some, and they weren't serving cheap champagne.

"You should probably slow down."

"They sat me down with a glass as soon as I got here, so I got to watch the whole thing. I hate to say it, baby, but your expression when they started digging into you was priceless!" Her mom's cackle rang out and didn't stop. Not even when she noticed the horror on Olivia's face. "What's the matter with you today? Did that fancy pants rehab get you all in your feelings? You're excellent at being dramatic, flashing your ass, and showing the sass, Olivia. It's always been your talent. Don't take it personally, none of those things were what they wanted from you today." She gulped what was left of her drink, setting the empty glass on the tray sitting on the table and taking a fresh one.

"Today, they wanted a punching bag, Mom."

"Oh, please. Get over it. We'll still get your big fat check, and that's the most important part. Do you have any idea how hard I had to work to negotiate the final number?"

Olivia wanted nothing more than to get up and leave, but she had nowhere to go and no way to leave.

"Why *did* they pay me so much? It doesn't make any sense."

Her mother just waved her hand again, this time spilling half her glass onto the sofa.

"Don't look a gift horse in the mouth, baby. Just take the money and be happy about it."

The hairs on the back of her neck stood, a terrible feeling sinking into Olivia's gut.

"What are we waiting for, Mom?"

"I think the director wanted to have a quick word, but I have no idea. I'm here to support you and drink this champagne."

"Who do I need to talk to about the deal you made?"

"What deal?"

"The one where I don't go to jail even though I left rehab early, Mom. The deal you promised you took care of."

Her mother snorted. "I don't recall ever saying I made a deal for that, specifically." She stumbled over the last word, the syllables getting tangled around her slow tongue.

Blood rushed in Olivia's ears. She knew she'd read at least a handful of messages implying it, but couldn't recall if her mother had said the words outright. It was always some version of *I'm taking care of everything.*

"You said there was a deal. You said repeatedly it was taken care of."

"And there was! You got to be on TV. You're going to get paid well for it. *Very* well. There will be publicity and maybe some doors will open for you. It's a good thing, darling."

"Are you being serious?" Resignation settled into her chest. Her heart was pounding behind her ribs, the rush of adrenaline making her hands shake. The threat of going to jail became very real, all of a sudden, and she had nobody to blame but herself.

"Of course!" Her mom clucked her tongue, appraising Olivia like she'd lost her mind. Olivia felt as though she were seeing things clearly for the first time.

"I left rehab, Mom. If there was no deal, I'm breaking my probation. They're going to come and arrest me."

"Jerry will beat them here, most likely." She shrugged.

"He's coming?" Hope surged, but she knew even Jerry couldn't stop the series of events she'd set in motion. The gravity of everything she'd done and the consequences she was facing for them began to crush her.

"Probably."

"Did you talk to him?" Olivia got up, rummaging through her purse for her phone. She held it up to her ear, letting the dozen or so increasingly frantic messages from her attorney play.

He was absolutely on his way and there was no part of Olivia not cringing from the tone of his voice.

"No, I figured I'd see him when he got here."

"Mother."

"*Olivia.* When did you grow such a conscience? We've done this routine for years and it's never bothered you before. We find you a job, you act like a total diva and get some extra attention while you're doing your thing. Speaking of which, we need to find you another dating prospect. You lost your lawyer which is a damned shame, but maybe we can find you someone else."

"Nobody wants anything to do with me, Mom. Did you not see what happened? I'm a joke. This isn't going to be my stepping stone from the B-list to the A-list. This is what happens to you when your career dies. I just fell from B to D or worse. This is *bad.*"

"If you can blossom from starring in adult films disguised as sex tapes to commercials and spots on primetime, this is nothing but a bump in the road."

Olivia's mind tumbled words around like they were stuck in a cyclone. Every carefully constructed lie she'd told herself was crumbling under the weight of the truth. She was everything they'd said about her and more. She'd done terrible things to everyone she'd ever known. There was likely nobody who would help her at this point, and honestly, she didn't blame them.

She wanted nothing more than to call Ollie, but she doubted he would answer.

"Don't be upset, Olivia. You were always so beautiful, baby. So easy to convince to act a certain way. You really were the perfect little girl." The words all slid together, too many *l*'s and *r*'s mixed with the amount of champagne she'd consumed.

Her mom sighed and set down yet another empty champagne flute. Olivia's stomach pitched, acid churning uncomfortably.

"What do you mean?"

"What do I mean? You always did exactly what I told you to. You believed everything I told you. You're a good girl, Olivia. Without you, we'd be in deep shit financially. I love your father dearly, but he's shit with money. He works damn hard, but concrete simply doesn't bring in the cash you could with your hair-flipping and over-the-top dramatics. I swear, putting you in front of a camera when you were a little girl was like turning a lightbulb on. You loved it. And you never stopped."

Her mother kept talking, but there was a buzzing in Olivia's ears.

She cackled, long and loud, waving her arm around in illustration. "Even now, after all that mess, you're getting us out of a rough spot."

"What rough spot, Mom?"

"Oh sweetie," her mom said, tearing up a little and visibly swaying because of the alcohol. "You became everything I could have ever hoped. Everything I could never be. You were the best investment we ever made."

CHAPTER
Fifteen

ER MOTHER'S WORDS settled over Olivia like a cold, wet blanket.

"Mom?" The single word slipped over her lips as tears gathered in her eyes. The beat of Olivia's heart hurt, and she could barely catch her breath.

"Oh, come on, Olivia. I figured you'd come to terms with everything ages ago. We're a good team, aren't we?"

Her head swiveled back and forth as she struggled to truly grasp the bomb that had been dropped. Lies. It was all lies. She grappled with the idea that she'd been someone's retirement plan and not much more. A commodity. A caricature of herself nobody liked. Not special, or talented, deserving, beautiful… or any of the things her mother told her she was, basically her whole life.

A pretty piece of ass good for bringing in some money.

As if she finally recognized Olivia's silence wasn't shock alone, her mother clapped a hand on her shoulder.

"Oh, baby. Are you seriously surprised? I can't imagine how, but it looks like you honestly are."

"Surprised? Mom…" she swallowed the lump in her throat before continuing, "You just told me my entire existence was organized so you could get rich. Everything I believed about myself is a goddamned lie! I'm going to *jail* because of what you taught me. I hurt people! Doesn't any of it matter to you?"

Her mother laughed, and it was as though Olivia was finally seeing her clearly. Olivia realized with horror that her mother was well beyond eccentric and probably something closer to a sociopath.

"Let's not be too dramatic. You got plenty out of our arrangement."

"Except I didn't even know there *was* an arrangement, Mom!"

She waved her hand in dismissal, a sickening grin on her face. "You'll get over it, dear. It won't be too bad, if you have to stay at all!"

Olivia sagged, realizing if she'd just committed to being at rehab and done the work, she'd be out in a few weeks and all the better for it. Instead, she'd wasted so much time and energy fighting it and trying to find a workaround; at the end, she'd landed herself exactly where everyone had warned her she would. Ollie had been right all along. And she had been a complete fool. The weight of her misdeeds piled onto her chest, making it even more difficult to breathe.

"I have to go," Olivia said woodenly, snatching her purse off of the side table. "I have to go." She didn't know how or where, but she needed to get out of the green room and away from her mother.

Her mother climbed to standing from the sofa she'd sat on, nearly turning her ankle in her sky-high heels.

"Jerry will be here soon, be patient. We'll figure something out."

"There's nothing to figure out, Mom. I *believed* you. Like an idiot, I thought nothing bad would happen because you said you'd worked it out. I thought… I thought you would follow through, which is clearly stupid."

"Olivia! How dare you talk to your mother like that in this house?!"

"We're not in your *house,* Mother, we're in the green room of the reality show I just got kicked off of. After they all made fun of me so I would have a ridiculous diva-style tantrum. Did you miss that part? Your house isn't even *your* house. We all treat it like it is, but it's *my* house. It was *my* money you used to pay for it all this time, always hustling me along to the next job. Redecorating and paying for things with money *I* made."

She waved her hand again, her diamond anniversary ring twinkling in the overhead lights. A subtle shift of her eyes gave her away—she was right. Olivia added that to the pile of things she could hate her for if she could muster the energy through her shock.

"Did Dad know it was you who talked me into doing porn?"

"Olivia. Now you're being ridiculous. We don't need to have this discussion right now—"

"Did you? The man hasn't been able to look me in the eye or have a real conversation with me in *years*, Mother. Is that your fault, too?"

"Oh, *grow up.* You took a job. You were good at it. You made connections in the industry and you outgrew that particular part of your life, so who cares?"

"Me! I care. I lost my parents and any kind of grip on who I am, Mom." Tears streamed down Olivia's cheeks, the words ringing deeply true even if she'd never consciously considered them before. "Dad never speaks to me unless it's in forced, two-word sentences. You became my manager instead of my parent. Everything about our relationship became transactional. About what I could do for you."

Her mother was inspecting her fingernails instead. "This is truly exhausting, dear, I'm sure we can talk about it later."

Ice formed in Olivia's veins. Had her mother always been this cold? Had she always looked past it and accepted it as normal? The most horrifying part was she'd followed her mother's example on many occasions. Her stomach pitched and rolled, leaving her dangerously close to needing to vomit.

"Holy shit. You really don't care."

As the silence grew loud around them, Jerry stormed in, phone at his ear and tie flapping.

Olivia was reminded of the early days of dating Maxwell. She loved when he came home from the office in his full suit. Watching him loosen his tie was one of her favorite parts of the day.

The memory made her stomach curdle. She'd been beyond rotten to him too. There were no relationships in her entire life that hadn't been wholly self-motivated.

"I'm a terrible person," she muttered under her breath.

Jerry snapped his phone closed and hefted his briefcase onto the counter, snapping it open and pulling out some papers.

"Well, the good news is you'll get paid for this, but the bad news is the police are right behind me. Well fucking done."

"I'm sorry, Jerry."

His eyes snapped to her at the dejected tone of her voice. "Are you alright?"

She shook her head. "No."

Olivia's mother grunted in exasperation. "She's being *incredibly* dramatic, Jerry. She had some kind of epiphany about her lovely little life and it's disturbed her."

His face grew serious. "The reality has finally sunk in, has it?"

"I'm sorry," Olivia repeated.

"Well, nothing can be done now. This bed is made, I'm afraid. You were warned. It's all in the documentation. My hands are tied. You'll be taken into custody and held until you can get a hearing with the judge. I'll do my best, but…"

"I understand."

It was Jerry's turn to look shocked. Olivia's mother muttered under her breath as a harried production assistant dashed into the room.

"The police are on their way in," she said, speaking into her headset after delivering the news.

"Thank you," Jerry said, straightening his jacket and pinning her mother with a stern look.

Three uniformed officers filed through the door. Time went into slow motion as they called her name.

They put her in handcuffs and led her on the longest walk of shame of her life. The cold metal bit into her wrists as they took the longest route possible through the studio and out into the lot. Her heart throbbed sorely as she ducked her head, trying to hide her shame during the ample opportunities for anyone with a cell phone to get video of them taking her away.

Olivia was folded into the back seat of the patrol car and driven away with what felt like dozens of pairs of eyes watching her every move. Cast, crew, and even cameras had followed her to the car.

It was everything she deserved, but fear had her paralyzed. She would have bet a significant amount of money they were expecting more drama. Another tantrum as she fought being put in cuffs and loaded into the car. The realization made her stomach roll uncomfortably.

She'd seen enough crime shows to know what might be ahead of her. She did her best to blink away the tears.

She knew she wasn't the victim. For the first time, it was truly sinking in that she was the villain, and she probably always had been.

OLIVIA WAS PHYSICALLY present for all the goings-on as she was transported to the jail and processed, but none of it made much sense. Everything was too loud. Too bright.

Jerry was there, trying to take control and promising he'd do what he could.

She'd been at the police station before, back when she was arrested for the break-in and blackmail. She'd gone full diva at the time, going so far as to ask the officer if he knew who she was before trying to shirk the responsibility onto David. They hadn't taken any ridiculous BS from her then, either.

She was fingerprinted. Posed for her mug-shot. Her belongings were stripped from her and she was tossed in a holding cell with five other women.

As she huddled on one small section of a metal bench in the grimy holding cell, Olivia thought about every harsh word she'd heard after a bad audition, every conversation about going with the expensive materials for a remodel. She relived every time her father looked away from her or completed a conversation without a single word spoken.

She mourned the little girl who had loved her bathroom when it had been done with teal tile and pink fixtures.

The one whose dad had told her a fairy tale every single night before bed and whose mom spent hours teaching her how to do fancy hairdos and makeup. The little girl who dreamed of being a movie star.

It had all gone so wrong.

CHAPTER
Sixteen

AFTER A COUPLE of days in the holding cell, Olivia went before a judge. Jerry tried to negotiate bail or bond, but the judge wasn't feeling generous about anything. As far as he was concerned, she'd blown her opportunity by leaving rehab. Olivia got the distinct impression he was making an example out of her. He held up the original ninety-day sentence and she was processed into the county jail.

The burly guard introduced her to her new temporary home and then left. Olivia had never felt so unprepared or alone, and it was all her own fault.

Two of the four bunks were occupied.

"This one." The woman sitting on the bottom bunk on the right side of the cell gestured above her. "She doesn't care for company." She waved a hand at the woman on the top bunk across the room.

"Okay." Olivia moved to put the scratchy blanket they'd given her down on the thin mattress.

"What's your name?" her bunkmate asked.

She was a middle-aged woman with auburn hair. There was an air of 'don't fuck with this one' hanging around her to compliment her facial scars.

"Olivia."

"You a troublemaker, 'livia?"

She paused halfway up the ladder to her bunk. "No."

"Good. We're not here for trouble. I'm Mags and that's Joan."

"Hi."

The other woman had yet to speak, but Olivia didn't care enough to press her luck. She laid down on the stiff mattress and stared at the ceiling, starting a methodical sort through a metric ton of memories.

ON VISITATION DAY, two weeks after her arrival, Olivia was surprised to have her name called by the guard.

She stepped toward the bank of countertop with cut-outs for a dozen or so people to have conversations through a piece of plexiglass with holes drilled through it.

When she was seated, Jerry appeared, looking much more dour than he usually did.

"You doing alright?" Concern was etched into the lines

around his eyes, and for the first time, she realized how tired he was.

"I'm okay, all things considered. Thanks for asking."

He nodded tensely. "Good, good. I've got some contacts working to see if we can get you out any earlier. I've called in a few favors. And I can get you some money for things while you're here."

She smiled. "I appreciate your help. I'm pretty sure I'm stuck here, but it's a nice gesture."

"I was able to take your things. Your purse and your luggage. I'll keep them safe for you."

"Thanks."

She could hear faint pieces of other conversations as they both shifted awkwardly on opposite sides of the glass.

"I wasn't expecting any visitors. This is a surprise."

Jerry took a deep breath. Olivia tensed, knowing if he was stressed about whatever he was here about, it wasn't happy news.

"I wish I were here strictly for social reasons. Your parents… they're requesting you sign over the deed to the house, Olivia."

"What? No," she said, the word cold on her tongue.

His eyebrows shot up at her instantaneous, negative response. "Simple as that? Just 'no'?"

"Correct. Just no. I'm not signing over the house my money saved and remodeled to *her*."

"It's both of them making the request, but noted. I was not expecting that answer, but I'm happy to hear it."

Olivia clenched her fist. If nothing else, the last weeks had given her a healthy dose of quiet time alone with her thoughts. There were not very many bright ones when it came to her parents. Not since she was little.

"After what she did, I'm not about to give her the house, too."

Jerry nodded, sliding the briefcase off the counter and onto the floor. He steepled his fingers. "Well, if that's the case, perhaps I can help you."

"With what?"

"Since the house is yours, are you aware of the issue with the property taxes? And the outstanding fine?"

Olivia went cold. "What issue?"

"It's been unpaid for at least three years."

An array of colorful language spewed from her lips. The guard caught her eye, giving her a warning to settle down.

"It's supposed to be paid through the mortgage company. It always was before, anyway. I obviously can't do any business from here, but I could call them—"

"I can help with all of it, Olivia. But you should know we've-your father, the accountant and I-already gone through the paperwork. It was never set up that way. It was set up to be paid separately every year. And it hasn't been paid for the last three."

Olivia dropped her face into her hands. Things were getting better and better all the time.

"How much?"

"At least thirty-five thousand, but perhaps up to forty with late fees. Plus the fine on top of that. You've only made one agreed upon installment of the total."

She could feel the blood drain from her face.

"I don't have that kind of money sitting around, Jerry."

"I know."

"Neither do they, obviously. What do we do? How did the accountant not notice?"

Jerry inclined his head. "I have a theory that has to do with your mother. Would you like to hear it?"

"Sure."

"Did you happen to wonder why the police were able to get to the set so quickly? It takes time to conjure up a warrant for arrest and get all the moving parts required in motion. There was no homing beacon sent out to the local PD simply because you left Sunrise. Did it seem at all strange to you how there were cameras and crew places they wouldn't normally have been?"

Olivia thought back. She hadn't noticed anything too unusual, but she wouldn't have known.

"She was stalling, or at least it seemed like she was…"

Jerry made an agreeable noise. "Your mother had made a separate deal with the producers. She got a separate bonus for allowing them to get your arrest on film. In all honesty, the arrest appears to be the real ratings driver. Though rumor has it, they were a bit surprised by your lack of response to the situation."

Olivia shivered. "Disappointed, you mean."

Jerry didn't respond with anything more than a slight tilt of his head and a raised eyebrow.

"Oh my God. I suspected, but I didn't believe…" Her heart thudded into her stomach, betrayal bitter in her mouth. "No wonder they offered me so much money for such a little time…" She scrubbed a hand over her face, every nerve in her body screaming.

"She knew about the taxes. I would hazard a guess she was trying to fix it before anyone found out."

"Its why she pushed so hard for me to take the show."

"I'd put good money on it." Olivia shook her head, at a loss for words. He continued on, "We can probably negotiate some payments, but it will still be pretty brutal." Sympathy was evident in the soft lines around his mouth.

More often than not, Olivia was on the receiving end of a scolding from this man. But now? He appeared to be the only friend she could count on.

"What do I do, Jerry?"

"Are you attached to it?"

"The house?"

"Yes. Do you have some kind of sentimental reason to keep this particular property?"

"No. Not really. I mean, I grew up there and I probably should feel homesick or something, but I hate what she's done to it. I don't feel much of anything about it. I miss the way it was when I was a kid. What they were like." Olivia stopped herself, Jerry locking gazes with her.

"Then I suggest you sell it. You could certainly get more than enough to pay off the debt, take the rest, and start your life over. If you're feeling generous, you could give your parents what they paid for it or some other modest amount. Your father's company isn't doing badly, but it's never done well enough to keep up with your mother's lifestyle. Not without your contributions."

Olivia had never heard Jerry speak so plainly showing disdain for her parents.

"What happened, Jerry?"

"What do you mean?" He wouldn't meet her eye, so she knew he was fibbing. He adjusted his tie, then the cuffs on his jacket.

Olivia stared at him, one eyebrow raised in question. "Something clearly happened," she said after a pause.

"Of course it did, silly girl. You're in here."

Olivia's heart thudded inside her ribs. This man had been around most of her life, and took excellent care of her, even when she didn't want him to.

"That's actually kind of sweet, Jerry. But seriously, what's going on?"

"Your parents were never clients of mine, but you are. I treated them as friends, because I wanted what was best for *you*. But I cannot continue to tolerate their disgraceful behavior. When I saw the display your mother put on after you were arrested, I don't think they do, nor did they ever, in fact, have your best interests at heart. You're an adult now, Olivia. The time has come for you to act as such."

She found herself smiling at him. "You've been telling me that for years, Jerry."

"Well, I fucking mean it, girl. Sell the house. Pay the bills. Bank the rest. Gift them something if you like, or don't, it's up to you. Either way, wash your hands of them. That's my official suggestion. Otherwise, it's going to sink you all. They've been living off of you since you were a literal child. It's disgusting."

Olivia met his eye through the glass, listening to what her heart was saying before responding.

"Can you help me make all the arrangements? I'm a little stuck at the moment." She gestured to their surroundings.

"Of course. I know plenty of people who would love to take a listing in your neighborhood. We can get you top dollar, I'm sure."

"And if they put up a fight?"

Jerry shrugged. "The law is on our side, for this one. Your name is on all the paperwork. I double checked. They don't have a leg to stand on, not even with possession being nine-tenths of the law and all that."

Olivia fidgeted with a loose thread on her jumpsuit. "I'm not angry with him, Jerry. But I'm absolutely furious with her."

He nodded slowly, looking down at his hands before turning his attention back to her. "The way he's treated you isn't right, Olivia. He enabled everything she's done. Being absent and not preventing the mistreatment is no better than the things she's done."

The words landed like blows to her chest. She knew he was right, but she missed her dad. He'd disappeared when she'd needed him the most. She just wanted him to give her a hug and tell her it was going to be okay.

"Alright."

"Yes?" He confirmed, reaching for his case.

"Yes. Please proceed with finding a realtor and whatever else you need to sell my property, Jerry. Do I need to sign something? Put it in writing?"

He shook his head, making a few quick scribbles on a notepad he'd pulled from his pocket. "No, it's alright. Verbal will do this time around. Is there a dollar amount I need to keep expenses under?"

"There should be some money left from the last show in my account. I don't have a way to check it, though."

"I can check with the accountant for actual numbers. Do you have a guess at what should be left?"

"Fifteen thousand? I'm not sure."

"Even if your guess is only close, it should be more than sufficient." Jerry nodded before clearing all the information from his history.

"Do it. Thank you, Jerry."

"My pleasure, Olivia. I'm sorry to see you here."

She shrugged. "It's not so bad. The food is terrible, the bedding is awful and the clientele is questionable at best, but I can't complain. I'm not in danger that I'm aware of and I've got plenty of time to myself. I've learned quite a bit about Olivia Black over the last couple of weeks to be honest."

"I barely know you anymore, girl," Jerry said affectionately. "I'm afraid after this… I can't continue to be your attorney, Olivia. I'm retiring."

"Oh." Olivia hadn't been expecting him to say any such thing, but she understood. "I see."

"Don't think you broke me." He quirked his mouth in a sly grin. "While I can't handle divas like you anymore, my dear, I need to spend some time with my own grown kids and my grand-babies before I keel over from the stress. I am, however, sincerely glad to see you've finally moved beyond the tantrum stages."

"I really am sorry, Jerry. For all the times I put you through the wringer. It wasn't fair. I'm sorry for who I was. I let her turn me into a monster for her own personal entertainment."

Jerry's face drooped, his mouth pulling into a frown. "I'm sorry too, Olivia. Maybe if I'd used a different tack, things could have been different."

"We all have regrets. I appreciate your long years of service."

"Even when I wanted to wring your neck, it was truly my pleasure."

The powerful moment between them was interrupted by the booming voice of the guard announcing their time was up.

"I'll be back in a week or two to let you know how things are going."

"Okay. Thanks again."

Jerry was escorted out by the guard on his side of the window, and Olivia was taken back to her cell.

Her heart was sore, but she didn't dare show how upset she was. Even in her area of the cell block, weakness was easily spotted and exploited. As far as her cell mates went, things were okay, but there was no reason to push her luck.

Later, she lay back on her bunk thinking about the possibilities of how the conversation with her parents would go when they were told the house was being sold out from under them.

There would be cursing. Throwing things. Stomping feet. The silent treatment.

Olivia picked at her fingernails, the pink from Ollie's gifted polish long gone, as well as the acrylic extensions. She was torn between being glad she wouldn't be there to witness what was sure to be an epic tantrum and sad she would be the one to destroy her family once and for all. It might be just a house, but it was the only thing holding them all together.

She frowned. It probably had been for a very long time.

CHAPTER
Seventeen

JERRY SHOWED UP like clockwork every two weeks for visitation.

Without intending to, Olivia used those visits as a marker from which to chart her time in jail.

He was her only contact from the real world. She had to wait to see him so she could get any information he brought from her outside life again. Her twice-a-week, thirty-minute tech breaks felt like a long-ago dream. She'd hardly know how to handle herself once she had free access to the internet again.

Six am wake-up call, off to a shower with terrible flow and cold water with at least a dozen of her closest cellmates and guards. Some breakfast before going back to her little box to do some more thinking. Repeat for two more meals with some recreation time mixed in.

She'd done more introspection and evaluation of her life in a few short weeks than she'd ever been able to do before. There was never complete silence inside the jail, but it was quiet enough the noise inside her own head was too loud to ignore.

It was terrifying at first, but she started to get used to it with the help of a few of the tricks she'd picked up at Sunrise.

The irony wasn't lost on her about it, either. There wasn't a day that passed where she didn't want to go back and shake some sense into the version of her who made such a stupid, impulsive choice. Jerry would have talked her out of signing for the show, she was sure of it. Which was why she'd sent it on without his approval, if she was being honest with herself.

Most days were spent on a rotation from cell to dining hall and back again, but there were times she was allowed to visit the little common room for a little bit of TV. They all loved the high drama shows or the gossip station, and Olivia quickly got tired of seeing the clip of herself being arrested pop up on the screen.

They were able to borrow books from a little library room, and use pen and paper. She sat at the little slab of countertop in the cell and stared at a blank page lots of times, though there were days when all of her thoughts about who she might actually be under the big entitled attitude and fake hair, nails and makeup spilled out onto the page. Dr. Clay would have been proud, she thought.

Jerry was busy between their visits. He coordinated the eviction of her parents, the sale of the house, and the payments for the back taxes with the help of her parents' accountant. After the debacle with the taxes, Olivia would not be retaining his services after these dealings were done, but she was glad Jerry had someone who could help him get checks cut.

On the third visit, he brought good news.

"How are you?" Jerry asked, as usual, when he took his seat on the other side of the glass.

"I'm fine, Jerry."

He scrutinized her. "I'm not going to insult you by mentioning you look like you could use a few hearty meals and a solid night's rest." His mouth twitched into a grin.

"Thanks for not bringing it up."

"My pleasure. I want to start by saying congratulations on selling your house."

Olivia brightened. The sale price had made her choke when he'd first reported the listing. Nearly two million dollars for her little childhood home seemed outrageous, but the real estate agent was confident it was appropriate.

"It sold?"

"Yes, we got an offer last week, and it looks as though all the paperwork should go through. There's always a chance something will happen, but it's looking as though everything will process as expected."

"That's great news."

"It is. I'll get the payments all sorted out and bring the paperwork as soon as I can so you can sign off."

"And my parents?"

Jerry's mouth twitched. "They're not happy, but I couldn't care less about that. Your offer to pay them what they'd invested plus interest was generous. They'll be fine."

"Are they going to have to be… removed? Or do you think they'll go on their own?"

"Time will tell, but don't worry about it. We'll get it taken care of."

She had learned the hard way not to trust those words from her own mother, but from him, they were as reliable as ever.

Jerry steepled his hands. "I also have a new hearing with the judge."

Olivia's breath stalled. She'd resigned herself to being stuck for the full sentence at this point. "Oh?"

"I'm afraid it won't save you much time, but it's still worth a shot. Your fines have all been paid at this point, and you haven't caused any trouble."

"I appreciate everything you're doing, Jerry."

"I believe you, Olivia. And you're welcome."

His visits were never long enough, but she knew as each one passed, she was two weeks closer to her getting out and going… somewhere.

There was no home to go back to, and she foolishly had purchased her car with her mom, so it was unlikely she'd see her wheels any time soon.

She didn't have anything left of her old life, except a few items she'd made sure to ask Jerry to retrieve and put somewhere safe. He'd opened a small storage unit for the items she'd asked for, but there really hadn't been much.

More often than she'd have liked, her thoughts drifted to Ollie.

She wondered what he was doing now that he was out of Sunrise. Whether his return to *Destiny Falls* had been successful, and even though it was selfish, she wondered if he was thinking of her.

Olivia had written him a few notes, but never had any intention of mailing them. Even if she had wanted to, she didn't have his address. But they were helpful for her to process what she thought had occurred between them.

If she ever saw him again, she'd apologize in person for so many things.

With the hope Jerry might get another chance to plead her case for early release, she went back to her cell, trying to focus on how her life was moving forward rather than how she'd allowed it to crumble out from underneath her.

CHAPTER
Eighteen

ON DAY SEVENTY-NINE, after lunch and a short walk around the exercise yard, a guard came to her cell, said her name, and told her she was going home.

"Are… are you sure?" Olivia had asked, glancing at the calendar, then back at her cell mates as she followed the burly man through the block. Mags smiled at her, but Joan just looked surprised. Olivia gave a stilted wave to the ladies she'd lived with for the last couple of months, unsure what the protocol was for saying goodbye.

"That's what they said out front."

"Oh." Olivia did the math again, still coming up well short of her expected ninety days. It was the Wednesday before a visitation weekend. She'd been prepared for Jerry to come on Sunday to talk with her like he normally did. Last they'd spoken, there'd been no further word on her getting a shorter sentence.

They walked through the corridor at a steady pace, the noise increasing the closer they got to the main part of the station.

"I don't have my phone or purse. My attorney kept it all. Will I be able to contact him?"

"I'm sure there's a phone you could use in a pinch. They'll let you hang around a few hours, probably. After that, you'll have to start walking."

He seemed unsettled by the idea, his mouth drawn into a tight line as he guided her to the front desk.

"Hey, Clarence. We got a vacancy, I see?" The receptionist gave Olivia a genuine smile. "Glad to see it, honey."

Whether she was addressing Olivia or Clarence with the endearment was unclear.

"Ms. Black is headed out today, Brenda. She's going to sit up here for a bit, waiting for her ride. Alright?"

Brenda nodded. "Of course. You just have a seat. I'm not expecting any trouble, am I?" Her head lowered, a sly grin on her mouth as she looked at Olivia through her lashes.

"No, ma'am."

"Perfect. I got it from here, Clarence."

"I appreciate it. You take care of yourself, young lady. Okay?"

"I will."

Olivia's humbled heart warmed at his concern. After a quick pat on her shoulder, he made his way back into the depths of the building, leaving her standing awkwardly at Brenda's desk.

"Go on and have a sit down. You need a drink or any-thing? Water?"

Olivia shook her head. "I'm okay, thanks though."

"Well, you let me know. They send people out here all the time and only about half have any kind of money on them. I'm guessing you're one of the broke kind." Brenda winked and Olivia blushed, dipping her head.

"You'd be right."

"It's too bad, but I got a feeling you won't stay that way for long. You get thirsty or need a quick snack, I got a stash back here."

"Thank you."

Olivia took a seat in one of the leatherette chairs near the front windows. There were magazines on a nearby table, but none from the last few years.

Her phone was in her purse, which was locked up safely somewhere with Jerry. She had no immediate access to any money, no friends. If nobody showed up to get her, she'd be in for one hell of a walk across the city to Jerry's office. It wasn't her favorite option, but she wasn't sure where else to go and at least she was free to leave.

Boredom set in after half an hour. Panic took root when the first hour passed. Brenda looked over every so often, giving her a reassuring smile. After a quick trip to the restroom, Olivia finally took her up on her water offer.

"If you need to make a call, you just let me know," Brenda said. She pushed a cell phone on top of the counter where Olivia could see it. "Clarence might have kittens, but he's not the boss of me." Her kindness was impressive, especially considering the people she saw pass by her desk on a daily basis.

"I appreciate it. I'm going to wait a little bit longer. I'm sure my attorney was notified. Thanks, though." He had to have been told she was getting out. Nothing else made sense. Plus, if she had to make a phone call, the kind receptionist would need to look up a number for her first. She didn't have anything memorized except their old home landline, and it didn't exist anymore.

"You bet."

She'd flipped through each one of the dated magazines when a familiar car pulled up out front.

"Oh my God." Tears stung the back of her eyes, relief mixing with a new wave of anxiety because this was a complication she hadn't even dreamed of.

It took everything she had not to jump to her feet and run out the door to meet him. Instead, she forced herself to remain seated and waited for him to come inside.

He pushed open the heavy glass door, looking around before approaching Brenda.

"Well, how about that. Not every day we get actual celebrities up in my office. How can I help you, young man?"

"I'm here to pick someone up."

Brenda's eyes shifted to Olivia, who had lost the battle with her excitement and was standing in front of the chair she'd been occupying.

"*This* someone, by chance?"

Ollie's head turned and intense relief washed through Olivia. His expression was unreadable, but still, he'd come.

"Yes, she's the one." His aqua eyes scanned her up and down, but he didn't take a single step towards her.

Olivia's heart was galloping in her chest.

"You ready to go?" he said, still giving nothing away.

"Yes."

Brenda cleared her throat, offering a piece of paper and a pen. "Sign here, if you don't mind. This form states the former prisoner has been remanded into your custody and you agree that when you picked her up, she was in possession of..." Brenda paused, taking in Olivia and her lack of belongings. "Nothing but herself."

Ollie read over the document, hesitating with the pen in his grasp before signing his name at the bottom.

"That's all I need. It was nice to meet you both, but I hope to never see you here again." Brenda gave a gentle smile and a wink.

"Thank you for the water."

"My pleasure, honey. You take care, okay?"

"I will."

The acrid smell of downtown Los Angeles was refreshing, despite the lingering layer of exhaust and bitter sunshine hanging over it.

"I appreciate you coming," Olivia said quietly once they'd both gotten into his metallic blue Tesla.

"It was against my better judgement." His fingers flexed around the steering wheel and a muscle popped as he clenched his jaw.

"I don't understand, though. The only person I expected was Jerry. What are you doing here?"

"He got caught up with a family situation. He asked me to come instead."

"Oh." A dozen new questions cropped up at his answer, how the two of them knew each other first and foremost.

"Where am I headed?" He asked, interrupting her train of thought.

Olivia dipped her head. "I don't know, honestly. I thought I had a couple more weeks inside and at least one more visit from Jerry to work that part out. I... I don't have anywhere to go."

"You don't?" His brows were pulled together and his mouth pressed into a line.

"My parents' apartment probably isn't an option. My old house is... well, it's not mine anymore. Jerry's office probably isn't far, but if you're here instead of him, he won't be there anyway, right?"

Ollie squeezed his eyes shut as he breathed in a long, purposeful breath. Olivia held the door handle so hard her knuckles turned white, afraid he might kick her right back out of the car. She wasn't sure if he was trying to restrain frustration aimed at her, or just at the general situation, but it was a side of him she wasn't familiar with.

Instead, he shocked her by asking, "When was the last time you had a decent meal? Are you hungry?"

His words sent an electric thrill through her veins. They gave her hope.

Her stomach answered for her, letting out a deep growl in the silence of the car.

"Guess so," he said, angling the car away from the police station and navigating them further into downtown.

"My last decent meal was breakfast at Sunrise a few months ago," she admitted. He didn't reply, just quirked an eyebrow at the information.

Olivia would normally have been worried about her state of dress and lack of makeup, but today she didn't care. She was on the outside of the cold concrete walls that had been her residence for seventy-nine days and she was ready for her fresh start. It didn't matter if she was wearing dirty clothes—if nothing else, at least they were *hers* and not another scratchy jumpsuit.

"I…" Her throat was thick, so she had to try again. "I don't have any way to get to my money right now." She showed him her hands like a blackjack dealer checking out of their shift at the table.

Ollie pulled up to a red light and swung his face in her direction. His expression was still closed off, maybe one degree friendlier than it had been when he walked into the station.

"What the hell does that have to do with anything?"

"I thought… well, I'm just saying, for the moment, I'm broke, Ollie. I'm not expecting you to take me to dinner, though I am hungrier than I can ever remember being. I just don't have any way to pay for it."

He scoffed before cracking the first sign of a grin she'd seen since he showed up.

"Are you being serious? Pretty sure I can handle taking you out for a cheeseburger, Princess."

Warmth surged through her, the nickname giving her more hope than she probably had any right to claim. "Still, it's worth mentioning. Realistic expectations and all."

He turned away, focus back on the road. "You're still something else, but I have a feeling the brand of your outrageousness has changed a bit."

"Brand?"

He pinched his lips together, as though the conversation was going a direction he wasn't quite ready for.

"Before you were all piss and vinegar, someone who thought they'd been wronged by the whole world and who was owed something. Your spoiled bitchiness was your brand. I can already see a difference in you. You're quieter. More… at peace. It's weird. Could be since you're fresh out of jail, but I'm hoping it's more. I half expected you to fling yourself at me with some dramatic sob story the second I walked into the station. I almost didn't come because of it. But you didn't. You just stood there. You were even polite to the woman behind the counter."

Pride surged in Olivia's chest. Of all the things she'd been worried about, that had been the most troubling. Once she truly hit rock bottom and all the layers of her had been scraped back, she'd been concerned she was beyond saving. How even jail wouldn't correct her crash course toward shitty humanity. She knew if anyone understood, it was him.

"Oh. Thanks, I think." Her lips curled up in a soft grin, and his face brightened when he saw it.

"You're welcome. Let's get you some food, okay? We can talk about where you're going to sleep tonight later."

"Okay."

Silence filled the car back up, but the weight of it had passed. It was peaceful now, companionable. As though sensing she was completely touch starved, he reached over and gently took her hand in his.

Tears threatened again, but this time in a good way. Relief coursed through her again, and she began to breathe a little easier.

She hadn't lost him, not completely. For now, it was enough.

Nineteen

OLLIE PULLED INTO a packed parking lot, carefully maneuvering around some badly parked cars and other people who also stalking an available space.

"Must be good if it's this busy," Olivia muttered, a sudden case of nervousness settling in, making her stomach twist.

She was going from the most isolated she'd ever been, directly into a very densely crowded space and had anxiety about it she wasn't really prepared for.

"This place has the best onion rings around."

They had to drive around a couple more times before they finally got lucky and caught someone leaving. As she got out of the car, Olivia curled in on herself, feeling over-exposed.

Ollie waited by the front of the car, brow furrowing as he looked her over.

"You alright?"

She forced a smile. "Sure. A little unsure how to act out in the world, I guess."

His arm twitched as if he'd been about to put it around her shoulders, but it remained at his side.

"This place is my best kept secret. Nobody will bother us here."

Olivia nodded, the irony not lost on her how before, she'd have been making a spectacle of herself specifically to be the center of attention. Now, she wanted to request the most out of the way booth in the darkest corner of the barn-wood paneled restaurant.

The hostess brightened when she saw them walk in.

"Well, look who the cat dragged in! Want your usual spot?" She gathered two menus and glanced at Olivia, but her attention was faithful to Ollie.

"Yes, please. Appreciate it, Molly."

Olivia's gut tightened further. They were clearly on friendly terms and he knew her by name. Jealousy should have been the furthest thing from her mind at the moment, but she felt the cold tendrils wrap around her chest regardless.

As luck would have it, Ollie's 'usual' was indeed a far, dark corner of the dining room.

"Can I get you something to drink?" The waitress asked, turning her attention to Olivia first.

"Just water, thanks."

"Plain in a cup, okay? We don't keep anything bottled on hand."

"Yes, that's fine."

"And you?" She turned her attention to Ollie, pen poised over her order pad.

"Iced tea."

"You got it. I'll be back in a sec with those and to get your order."

As she dashed away, Olivia caught Ollie staring at her. "What?"

"Nothing. I just can't get over the fact you learned how to say thank you. I'm certain I've never heard you say it before."

Olivia relaxed when his lopsided smirk appeared, realizing he was being funny, not poking an insult at her.

"Shush."

He chuckled, scanning the menu for less than five seconds before setting it at the edge of the table.

"What are you getting?" she asked. There were many options, from the basic burger to vegan options. Olivia was a bit overwhelmed, if she was being honest. Having genuinely free options for food was a novelty.

"The mushroom and Swiss burger with a side of onion rings."

"Sounds delicious, but I'm not big on mushrooms."

"There's not a single bad choice here, not even the chili. Please get whatever you want." He placed one of his hands over the top of hers, meeting her eye with a serious expression. "Whatever you want, Olivia. Okay?"

She bobbed her head, skimming the options. What caught her eye happened to be a chicken sandwich with grilled pineapple and teriyaki sauce. It was something she wouldn't have been caught dead eating not too long ago, but now it sounded positively heavenly.

Growing into a wholly different person brought fresh challenges and surprises every time she turned around.

Molly delivered their drinks and efficiently took their orders before vanishing back into the crowd. The restaurant was super busy, the ambient noise constant but not so loud she couldn't comfortably hear Ollie over it.

"So?" He said, pushing his cup back and forth between his index fingers. "What's new?"

Olivia stared at him. "What's new?" she parroted.

He shrugged. "I'm not sure what else to ask. How was your stay in jail? Better?" He laughed, taking a drink of his tea before pushing it off to the side. She felt the full weight of his attention as he speared her with a solid gaze.

"It honestly wasn't all bad. I mean..." She tilted her head off to the side, opening her hands on the tabletop in a gesture of 'you know'. "It wasn't anything like Sunrise, but it could have been a whole lot worse. They said I wasn't getting any favors, and for most things I wasn't, but I was in a pretty tame group of women in an area that was more likely to see fights over the TV channel than anything else."

"Well, to be fair, you weren't sent to the area where they keep violent criminals."

"Right. It was… good for me."

Ollie's eyebrows went up. "You're still full of surprises, Princess."

"Not really." She took a deep breath. "I'm sorry, Ollie. I didn't mean—"

He put his hand over hers and squeezed. A muscle in his jaw ticked a few times before he spoke.

"I accept your apology, Olivia. I believe you." His head nodded sharply once before he retracted his hand as though he were physically accepting his own statement.

"Thank you." Olivia glanced around at the other patrons, unsure of where to direct the conversation. "What have you been doing? Did you finish out your show?"

Ollie nodded. "I did. It only went on for a couple of weeks. After that, they paid me and sent me on my merry way. The tabloids had a field day with you, by the way. Took two solid weeks for them to find something else to talk about. You definitely made a statement getting hauled away from the set the way you did."

Olivia shrank in on herself in embarrassment. "I know. They always had on the freaking gossip channel at the guard station. It was so bad a couple of ladies felt kind of sorry for me."

Ollie chuckled, their discussion interrupted as Molly returned with their food.

"Enjoy," she said, dropping the plates.

Everything about the food overwhelmed Olivia's senses.

She'd been surviving on industrial slop and pre-packaged snacks, but this was hot, fresh and delicious.

Ollie didn't hesitate for a moment, just bent his elbows and grabbed his burger with both hands, leaning over the plate to catch the drips. Olivia opted for cutting her sandwich in half, but it was still a messy affair. It was a delight, though.

He dipped a crispy onion ring in ketchup and offered it to her. She grasped it in her fingers, breathing in the scent before taking an enthusiastic bite.

"This place is amazing," she muttered over her full mouth.

"It's my favorite."

They ate in companionable silence, assuring Molly when she stopped by everything was wonderful.

Olivia was one step beyond comfortable when she finally took the last bite of her sandwich, sagging back in the seat.

"Thank you so much." She groaned. "I needed that."

"I bet." His grin slipped as he meticulously stacked up their plates. "Where's your mom's place?"

Olivia resisted the urge to cringe. She'd known the conversation was coming, but she wasn't ready to deal with her mom quite yet.

"Toluca Lake."

"Burbank area, yeah? That's not too far. She glad you're out?" He dug around in his pocket, ready with his card as Molly swung by for the plates with the check in her hand.

"No idea," Olivia replied, the honesty stinging. "I don't know if she was informed I was released. The last time I spoke with her, she was really upset how I'd had my assets transferred into an account under my name only and was selling the house. I'm pretty sure she has me blocked."

He blinked slowly a few times. "Come again? I'm not sure I got all that."

"Jerry helped me sell the house, so I didn't lose everything while I was in jail. It's complicated, but there were some issues with late bills. Anyway, I'm guessing she's still beyond pissed."

Ollie's mouth pinched. "Sounds logical. Okay. Well, is there… a friend you'd like to call?"

She met his eye and snorted a laugh. "You know as well as I do I don't have any of those."

His expression was mildly sympathetic, his eyes and mouth soft as he watched her.

"It went against my better judgement initially, but I'm glad I picked you up. I hate to think you'd still be sitting in the jail lobby, or worse, out front."

"I'd probably have started walking to Jerry's office, eventually." She frowned. "I would have gotten lost, I have no doubt. Is this the part where you tell me how you know my lawyer and why you were the one who came to pick me up?"

Ollie's gaze shifted from her to the table, then back again, embarrassment or something close making him fidgety.

"I guess. The short version is I tracked him down. You'll have to ask him why he decided to take a chance on talking to me, but he did. It turns out we were both concerned for you."

A floaty sensation buoyed Olivia at those words. "That's… thank you. I'm sorry I worried you."

Ollie laced his fingers together. "He's a solid guy. Cares about you a lot."

"He's been around a long time. He's pretty great." She smiled, and Ollie's face brightened as well.

"Which brings us to where you're going to sleep," Ollie said, changing the subject.

Olivia's mood took a nosedive at the words. She didn't have anywhere to go.

"I can either put you up in a hotel for the night or you can take my guest room. Your choice."

Olivia froze. He was giving her an option? The fact that he might trust her enough to let her into his house wasn't unappreciated.

"Won't your…" she stopped, cutting off the manipulative question old Olivia would use. "Do you have a roommate? Or a girlfriend?" The last word tried to stick in her throat. "Anyone who would be bothered by you inviting me over? I don't want to be the reason anyone is upset with you."

Ollie's mouth slowly ticked upwards. "I live alone. Well, except for Jenkins." The shock must have been plain on her face because he started laughing. "My cat."

"Oh." Olivia blushed, giggling at herself for jumping to the wrong conclusion. "You named a cat Jenkins? He sounds like he's your butler."

Ollie snorted. "If anything, I'm his, but no, he came from the rescue that way."

"I'd appreciate a place to stay for the night. Very much." She hesitated, still wondering if it was the right decision to go to his home, no matter how much she wanted to. "But I don't want it to be weird, Ollie. Are you sure it's okay?"

Ollie sat back, a proud expression on his face.

"I'll be damned. You really are a whole new you, aren't you?" His question did not require a response. "If you're uncomfortable, I'm happy to get you a hotel room. But I..." He shook his head, looking off to the side as if he were worried about saying something he would regret. "I don't mind you taking up some of my space. I'm doing pretty well, honestly."

"Then your guest room sounds incredibly appealing. I'm glad to hear the transition back hasn't been too rough." She fidgeted with the butter knife she hadn't used, spinning it on the tabletop. "I can find a hotel room in the next couple of days. I just have to get my ID and credit card situation sorted out. In order to do that, I need to get in touch with Jerry."

There was a warm current in his words. He was thawing, and her heart raced as she considered the possibilities of what that meant.

"I can help there. All of it, actually. Sounds like we have a plan."

Ollie collected the receipt from the envelope Molly dropped off with a smile, her gratitude obvious in her wide smile.

"You come on back soon, okay?"

Olivia's nerves set back in as she slid out of the booth, following Ollie across the busy restaurant.

She knew things were going to get messy when he reached a hand back for her, but she took it anyway.

CHAPTER
Twenty

OLLIE MANEUVERED HIS way through the busy lot once again before finding quieter side streets to take them back to his house.

Olivia watched out the window as they passed strip malls and tiny old bungalows crowded between apartment buildings. Los Angeles had always held a certain charm she couldn't quite find the words to describe. There was something special about the little postage stamp lots with their houses from the fifties and sixties, all easily identifiable by era and the somehow obvious *California* style.

She lost track of the turns as he tapped the steering wheel with his fingers, conversation lacking but the silence comfortable.

He paused at a metal gate fifteen minutes or so after they'd left the restaurant, using a button on his sun visor to open it.

"Home sweet home," he muttered, pulling through to a parking space underneath the apartment building.

"Where are we, exactly?" Olivia asked, following him as he made his way across to the stairs.

"Not far from Griffith Park," Ollie answered, gesturing for her to precede him up the stairs.

"I wouldn't have guessed we could get over here so fast. I always liked this area, it's nice."

He gestured down the hall. "I agree. I'm the second to last on the left."

"Then again," she added, "my sense of direction is generally terrible, so I usually don't know where I'm at in this city. I have no idea what people did before using GPS."

Ollie's grin was wide as he unlocked the door to his apartment.

"Come on in. It's not much, but it's home."

Olivia took in the modestly furnished apartment. *Cozy* was the first word that popped into her head. There were none of the gaudy decorations her mother loved to spend money on, for starters. Everything seemed to have a function, but was also loved. The furniture looked comfortable, and the general vibe was a cared for, nicely lived in place.

"This is super cute," she said, surprised by the heartfelt compliment even as it came from her mouth. Ollie looked similarly stunned by her venomless words, a slight blush rising to his cheeks.

"It's still weird," he said, shaking his head.

"What is?"

"This *nice* version of you." He gestured to the couch. "Make yourself at home. Want a water or something? I need to feed Jenkins."

"Sure."

Olivia sat on the couch, and it was even more comfortable than she predicted. She would sleep perfectly right there if she had to. As the thought passed across her mind, exhaustion set in and she felt herself melting into the seat.

She heard distant meowing, but no cat ever appeared where she could see it. Animals weren't usually very quick to warm up to her, though she had a special soft spot for cats.

Ollie came back with a bottle of water. As he handed it to her, he said, "You look wiped."

"I'm way more tired than I thought I was. This couch is amazing." She allowed her head to drop back against the fluffy cushion.

Ollie chuckled. "Yeah, this couch has seen an incredible amount of naps. Come on. We can talk tomorrow. I imagine sleep in a real bed is something you've been looking forward to."

"You have no idea."

Olivia hauled herself up out of the embrace of the sofa and followed him down a short hall. He flipped on a light in a bathroom before walking into the room directly across the hall from it.

"Mattress is pretty nice and the sheets are clean."

"It's perfect."

Ollie nodded, the energy between them shifting from companionable to awkward. "Let me go see if I have a spare toothbrush. I'm sure I have a shirt or something you could wear, too." He scanned her, Olivia feeling momentarily self-conscious. "You probably want to take a shower."

"Do I smell?" She joked, straining not to sniff at herself.

"No, not at all. I just thought…" Ollie shrugged, and while it was clear what he was implying, she let him flounder for a moment. It was adorable.

"A shower would be a dream actually. Unlimited hot water? Real shampoo and soap? No audience or guards? I might not know how to handle myself."

Olivia could see the moment Ollie realized she was poking a bit of fun at him.

"Let me go put a few things together," he said, winking at her as he left the room.

There were sparse decorations in the room, but the comforter on the bed looked as though he might have inherited from his grandmother. There were a couple of generic floral prints hanging on the wall, each perfectly placed next to a smaller painting of a butterfly. A small table with a lamp next to the bed reminded her of the one she'd had as a child.

It was perfect.

Staying here was a much more appealing option than setting up camp in a hotel for a week or more while she sorted out the fragments of her former life, but she didn't want to push her luck.

As she was mentally going over the list of phone calls she had to make in the morning, Ollie returned with his arms full.

"What's all this?" She asked as he set the pile on the bed.

There was a large fluffy towel and matching washcloth, travel sized everything for her shower plus a tube of toothpaste and a new toothbrush. He'd also found a well-loved concert t-shirt and pair of shorts for her to wear.

"I don't have guests often, but I do travel sometimes. I take everything I can get my hands on from the nice hotels so the bathroom is stocked up." His hand scratched nervously at the back of his neck.

Olivia found herself overwhelmed. Tears sprang to her eyes. She felt silly, but his gesture was very, very sweet. "Thank you."

"Hey," he said, a look of worry tugging at his features. "It's nothing. Really. It's okay, Princess. Please don't cry."

Olivia had started to sob in earnest, and Ollie pulled her gently into a hug. "Is this okay?" He asked, loosening his hold.

"Yes, it's fine, thank you. I could really use the hug."

He banded his arms tighter around her as she fought to still the flow of tears.

"I'm okay," she muttered into his shoulder, regrettably prompting him to drop his arms.

"No problem. I'll get out of your way. If you need anything, I'll be watching TV for a bit in my room. I'll leave the door open in case you need something. I'll see you in the morning, okay? Sweet dreams."

He gave a little wave as he left the room. Olivia took in a few slow breaths before gathering up the supplies. She took the longest, hottest shower she could stand, thankful beyond words for the luxurious spa brand shampoo and conditioner he'd given her. The soap wasn't the dry cake she'd been using for the last few weeks either, and when she got out, there was lotion.

It was heavenly.

Warm, clean and safe, she slid into his t-shirt and giant basketball shorts and all but fell into the bed, deep sleep claiming her the moment her eyes closed.

IN THE MORNING, Olivia woke up at six am, as she'd gotten accustomed to doing in jail. Not hearing the sounds she was familiar with, she sat straight up, heart pounding as she scrambled to figure out how late she was for roll call. She'd tossed the blankets off of her and was halfway to her feet before she realized the scenery was all wrong.

Once she got a long look at the room and remembered where she was, she'd lay back down and languished gratefully under the comforter, dozing until her bladder demanded she get up.

After freshening up in the bathroom, she padded into the kitchen where she found Ollie sipping at a mug of steaming coffee.

"Pot's fresh," he said, voice still gravelly from sleep.

"Thanks."

"How'd you sleep?"

A smile crept across her face as she poured her coffee. He'd left a cup and a couple of options for creamer on the counter. Ollie was proving time and again to be one of the most thoughtful people she'd ever met.

"Amazingly, thank you. I guess I have some catching up to do because I'm still exhausted, but it was wonderful. I appreciate you letting me stay last night."

"No problem."

She sat at the small dining set across from him, an appreciative noise rumbling through her throat as the coffee made its way down.

"Oh my god. Real coffee."

Ollie chuckled. "I'm guessing most of the simple pleasures are going to seem super fantastic for a while."

"Definitely. I hope more than a while, actually." Her brows pinched.

"Making an effort to enjoy the little things and all?" Ollie guessed.

"Yes. It's a little weird for me to want that, right? I mean, you know me. Who I was. I had everything I could have wanted before and it was never enough. So I feel like

I should make an effort to try to see everything for what it's worth now."

"I don't think it's weird. You just went through a pretty significant identity crisis, I'm guessing." Ollie nodded knowingly. "You need to see your therapist, asap." He was teasing, but it wasn't a joke.

"I don't have one. I was seeing the one provided by the jail once a week. After Sunrise, well, it was… an experience."

"I'll bet. You can call Dr. Clay and get a referral."

"I should. Hopefully she'll still talk to me." The humorous fact she was proactively seeking a therapist out after a lifetime of refusing any idea of needing one was not lost on her. "I'm sorry to ask for more favors, but I need to make a bunch of phone calls, starting with Jerry. If nothing else, I need my ID and my keys. He should have my purse."

Ollie picked his phone up from the table. "Of course. I messaged him last night to let him know what was going on. Let me see if he's answering yet. He's had his phone off quite a bit."

This ominous news had Olivia concerned. "Is he okay?"

Ollie already had the phone up to his ear.

"Good morning. Sorry to call so early, but Olivia was hoping to get her belongings so she can get some things taken care of. Are you back in the city?"

Olivia held her mug in both hands as she took a drink, thrown for a loop by the comfortable conversation happening between the two of them. It was fascinating to watch.

Ollie's aqua eyes met and held hers, and she squirmed under the intensity. She hadn't realized eye contact from him was something she'd missed.

"Sure, hold on." He extended the phone toward her. "He wants to speak to you."

"Thanks. Hi, Jerry."

"Olivia! I'm glad to hear you're back in the outside world. Sorry for the surprise yesterday, I've been visiting with my granddaughter and couldn't get back in time for your release. The judge surprised us all by putting through your paperwork."

"It's alright, Jerry. As far as surprises go, it was definitely a good one. Is everyone okay?"

"Yes, yes. My daughter needed some help, so I went to Arizona for a few days. I'm on my way back now, and should be at the office soon. If for some reason we miss each other, I'll have everything waiting for you up at the front desk with Maggie, but I should be there."

"I appreciate it."

"I hope you learned what you needed to, kid." His tone was soft. Kind. The gravity of his sincerity hit Olivia right in the chest. She found herself battling a lump in her throat again.

"I did. I think I did, anyway."

"I'm glad to hear it. Truly, Olivia."

"Thanks, Jerry."

"We can go whenever you're ready," Ollie offered.

Olivia nodded, but looked down at herself, frowning.

Ollie pushed his chair back, gesturing with his empty mug as he crossed the kitchen.

"We'll stop and get you something to wear on the way. Do we need to buy you some things, or do you have stuff somewhere?"

"Until I get my purse, I don't have anything, unfortunately. My phone, bank cards, keys… it's all there. It seemed like a good idea at the time for him to take it all, but I probably should have at least brought my purse with me."

Ollie grinned as he bent over to grab some items for breakfast out of the fridge. "You need to make that a chapter heading for your memoir."

"What, 'seemed like a good idea at the time'?"

"Yeah. We could label almost every chapter some version of that, to be honest."

"Definitely." Olivia looked at her hands before giving voice to the question racing across her mind. "Why are you being so nice to me?"

He froze, eggs and a block of cheese in hand. "Should I not be?"

"I was pretty terrible to you, Ollie. A horrible, venomous bitch, more than once. You would have been well within your rights to leave me sitting in the waiting room until Jerry got back. But you're feeding me, giving me a place to sleep. Making sure I can get my stuff, offering to take me shopping." He didn't jump in to defend his behavior, just gave her a sympathetic look which only compounded her complicated feelings. "Don't get me wrong, I really appreciate it, but I don't deserve it."

Those sneaky tears were creeping in again. She absolutely needed to make an appointment to see Dr. Clay. Her thoughts and emotions were a mess, all over the place, overreacting. She gulped at the hot coffee, hoping it would melt the lump forming in her throat and disguise her mini-breakdown.

Then, he said something that made her heart completely implode.

"Everyone deserves redemption, Olivia. Even you."

CHAPTER

Twenty-One

OLIVIA KNEW HOW much power those words held, especially for him.

They kept finding a way to run across her thoughts through the omelets he cooked for breakfast, then around the store she dashed through to find something to wear other than his t-shirt for at least a couple of days.

If Ollie had decided *everyone* deserved redemption, maybe he was finally including himself. She hoped he was, at least.

On the off chance he didn't send her on her way the moment she got her purse back, perhaps they could have a conversation about it.

Ollie parked in the small lot adjacent to the law firm, surprising her when he got out of the car at the same time she did.

"You don't have to come in if you don't want to," she said.

"I know."

She stared at him over the roof of the car, unsure what else to say. His neutral expression shifted to something more along the lines of confusion.

"Unless you don't want me to? Would you rather I wait out here?"

Olivia shook her head firmly, sorry she'd given him the wrong impression with her commentary.

"I just didn't want you to feel uncomfortable. This is my deal. I thought…" She shrugged a shoulder. "Going into what feels like the principal's office has never been one of my favorite things. You've already done so much for me, I didn't want this to be one more if you didn't want to go."

Ollie's chin dipped to his chest. "I see. Well, lucky for us both, I don't have any issue with attorneys, Jerry in particular."

Olivia rounded the back of the car and tucked her arm through his. "Wonderful news. I could use the moral support."

On the way up the elevator, Ollie tousled his hair with his fingers in the reflection of the metal wall.

"You look great," she teased him.

"I know." He grinned back at her. "You look different, Princess."

"Different how?"

He squinted at her, eyes roaming from her hair to her toes. "I'm not sure. Your natural hair color suits you, though."

"Thanks?" She laughed. "No makeup, in need of a salon and fresh out of the system does it for you, huh?"

She was teasing, through and through, but something slid across his face that made her heart trip over itself.

He didn't answer, but the slight incline of his head to the side as though he couldn't deny it was enough.

Olivia's heart was lighter, as though he were personally responsible for all of the positive emotions she was feeling.

When they arrived at the floor and the doors slid open, Olivia's gut tightened. There had been dozens of tense meetings in this office. After dissecting and analyzing every moment of her life in jail, she could admit most of them were her fault. They were always for her benefit as well, but she'd never been very receptive before.

As she approached the desk, the receptionist's eyes widened. "Ms. Black. Is he expecting you?"

"Hi, Maggie. Yes, he should be. He said he might leave some things with you for me though, if he wasn't here."

The woman blinked quickly a few times, as though expecting a verbal slap for the question. Surprise dawned in her dark eyes when Olivia didn't say anything further. On the inside, Olivia was cringing. She had been so awful to this poor woman. How she ever could've believed it was okay to behave the way she had for so long was a mystery.

"He arrived a few minutes ago. I'll let him know you're here." She tapped a message into her keyboard, eyeing the pair of them warily.

"Thank you. I'm sorry, by the way. For the last time I was here. And every time before that."

The whites of Maggie's eyes grew impossibly large. "Oh. Thank you, Ms. Black."

To prevent the woman from having a heart attack from the shock, Olivia turned toward the small seating area. She didn't have any time to choose a chair, however, as Jerry came through the door at the end of the room right away.

"Come on back, Olivia. Nice to see you again, Oliver."

Olivia followed Jerry, walking double-time to keep up with the older gentleman's long stride.

"Thanks again for making yourself available yesterday," he said over his shoulder to Ollie.

"No problem. It worked out well."

They followed him into an expansive corner office with windows overlooking the city.

The large mahogany desk was, as always, situated in the middle of the corner office. Windows graced two full walls, the bright late morning sun warming the space. The only thing missing was any evidence of a person inhabiting the space. None of Jerry's credentials or photographs remained.

Jerry gestured to the two open chairs in front of the desk as he smoothed the front of his button-down shirt. After taking a seat himself, he reached into one of the desk drawers.

"You look well, Olivia."

"I feel... different. Thanks."

Jerry raised an eyebrow, glancing at Oliver before

offering her favorite small Marc Jacobs bag, placing it reverently in her hands.

"Everything should be there. It's been locked in the drawer since I brought it up."

Olivia pulled it into her lap, riffling through the contents. "I'm not sure I remember what all was in here, but it looks right to me. Thanks."

He rose and went to another locked cabinet at the back of the room. He pulled out the two bags she'd packed for Sunrise. Ollie got up to claim them.

"I left these as they were. I had to wrestle your mother for them." Jerry returned to the desk and produced an envelope from his jacket pocket before sitting down. "This is for your storage unit. Address, gate code and key."

"What all is in storage?"

"Not much, to be honest. The things you asked me to get from your room, mostly. Your mother wasn't keen to part with things." He steepled his fingers, leaning forward against the furniture. "For what it's worth, I always thought of you as more than just a client, Olivia. I couldn't continue, though. It was time for me to be done." He heaved a sigh, eyes soft.

"I know, Jerry. It's okay. Really. You did everything you could. For years. I hope you get a chance to enjoy your retirement. Is your daughter okay?"

"Yes, she's fine. Had a minor surgery and needed some help chasing around my granddaughter."

The smile that broke out on his face was positively beatific. Olivia's chest squeezed. She'd nearly given this man a heart attack a million times over. He deserved a chance to hang around playing grandpa.

He opened his mouth but closed it before voicing whatever he'd been considering saying. His face hardened.

"Your mother…" he trailed off, concern tugging at his features.

"What about her?"

"She'll want to fight you over what happened. Now that you're out, I think she'll try to start a war. Are you ready to fight, if it happens?"

Olivia's heart throbbed in her chest, an ache beginning to form in the shape of her mother. "I think so. If she does… I don't think she'll win."

"Doesn't mean she won't exhaust you both in the process. She'll go after you in the media if she doesn't get what she wants. I can imagine she has quite a bit of ammo?"

Olivia swallowed thickly, flashes of her misdeeds crossing behind her eyes. Ollie reached out and squeezed her hand.

"I'm honestly not sure what more she can do. After all this, my image is pretty well destroyed. And it's my own fault, no matter how much I'd love to blame her."

"Be that as it may… just be cautious."

"I will," she promised.

Jerry shuffled through multiple drawers, looking for something. Finally, he pulled out a business card. "Call this firm if it goes wrong. They can help."

Olivia took it from his fingers, the melancholy sensation she was closing the door on their relationship potent. "Thanks."

As if he could hear her thoughts, he said, "I promise to take your calls within reason. If you need me. I'm not using my office number anymore. Ollie can give you the better one to use," he said, tone even softer than it had already been. Jerry seemed to be taking it hard things were ending, too.

"I appreciate it," she murmured, offering a weak smile.

"Well…" Jerry got to his feet, reaching out to shake Ollie's hand. "Take care."

"We will." Ollie assured him.

"He's a wonderful young man, Olivia. Might be wise to keep him around." He raised an eyebrow as if asking if she were listening.

Olivia couldn't help blushing. "I'm well aware, but thanks."

He pulled Olivia in for a brief, tight squeeze. She realized he wasn't exaggerating how he'd felt about her. She'd always thought of him as an annoying uncle, or overbearing father figure, but it never occurred to her until things went totally sideways he might actually see her as his daughter or niece as well. Guilt compounded on itself, bringing the lump back to her throat.

Once they'd said their goodbyes, Ollie shouldered the bags and pressed his hand gently into the small of her back to guide her out of the office. Maggie was just still wide-eyed, totally unused to Olivia outside of her temper-tantrum diva self.

There were so many people she owed apologies to.

They sat there for several long minutes with the windows down as the air conditioning cooled the boiling interior off. Olivia compartmentalized her emotions as she sorted out the belongings in her bag.

Her wallet was still full of cash, her license and cards all accounted for. Functional was another story, but she could figure it out with the help of any local bank branch.

"Got everything you need?" Ollie asked quietly as she refilled the purse.

"I think so."

"Where to?"

"I have money now. If you have something else to do, I can call an Uber or something."

He heaved a deep sigh, his gaze intense as he pinned her with it. "There's nowhere else I'd rather be, Princess. Quit trying to get rid of me, okay? You're not a burden. I don't mind helping you out. Where to?"

She listed off her most urgent requests, and without a word, he put the car in gear.

Her debt to him kept growing, perfectly proportionate to her gratitude.

ONCE BACK AT Ollie's apartment after running around town getting things straightened out, Olivia's exhaustion settled into her bones again. She sank into the wooden dining room chair, unenthusiastically pushing around the green seafood curry he'd picked up at his favorite Thai restaurant.

"Does it not taste good?" Ollie asked, noticing her malaise as he paused for breath. He, on the other hand, couldn't seem to eat his selections fast enough.

"No, it's great, I'm just tired."

"Been a busy day for sure." He expertly scooped noodles into his mouth with chopsticks.

"Thank you again."

He preened under the gratitude, smiling broadly over his full mouth of food.

"No big deal. You'd do it for me."

"Would I?" She asked, doubt coating her words. For a brief moment she sounded like her old self, and it made her shiver. To cover her discomfort with the odd personality discrepancy, Olivia speared a chunk of fish with her fork, scooping some rice and sauce as well so she could have a perfect bite.

When she glanced up, Ollie was staring at her.

"What?" She wiped her face with her hands, thinking she had something smeared across her cheek.

"You would."

"I would what?"

"Do the same thing for me." There was no hesitation in his tone, no doubt.

Olivia stared back, caught by the intensity of his expression. His bright eyes looked right through her.

"I would," she admitted, the truth of the words lifting a weight from her shoulders. "If I could, I would."

"If you could?" He asked.

She set her fork down, appetite sadly diminished.

"Well, right now I don't have a car or a house, so how I could help you would look pretty different. Thanks to you, I now have access to my money and a functional phone, so things are looking up."

"You're welcome," he teased.

Olivia drank some of her sweet green tea. "I'll call some hotels tomorrow. I need somewhere to stay while I figure out where I should go."

Ollie stopped cold, his eyes snapping back to hers from his plate. "Oh."

"I appreciate everything. So much. I just don't want to overstay my welcome, you know?"

Ollie nodded slowly, wiping his mouth on a napkin. "Sure."

They finished the meal in silence, Olivia feeling guilty over ruining what had been a bizarre but nice day.

He'd gone quiet, and Olivia didn't know what to think, let alone do about it. She busied herself with putting away the leftovers while he showered.

Jenkins appeared as she was loading their silverware into the dishwasher. He was a regal black and white tuxedo cat with the most adorable perfect white mustache on his black face.

"Hello," she said, immobilized by the cat's full attention.

He meowed at her a single time before he came forward to sniff at her toes. Olivia stood still, allowing him to get familiar.

"I'm sorry, but I don't know what you can and can't eat."

Jenkins regarded her thoughtfully, then ducked his head, rubbing against her legs. Getting approval in the form of affection from the feline brought her endless joy.

"You're very sweet. Can I pet you?" She reached down, and he bumped her hand with his head as well.

"I see you've met my roommate," Ollie said with a smile.

He was freshly showered, his hair still wet as he stood over her. Olivia was sitting cross-legged on the kitchen floor with Jenkins walking around and over her as he got his fill of attention.

"He seems nice enough," she said, her smile wide as the cat rubbed his face on her fingertips.

"Looks like he's taken to you."

"Animals were never my biggest fan before."

"Huh," Ollie said neutrally. "Feel up to watching a movie? I bet Jenkins will snuggle with you on the sofa."

Olivia couldn't picture anything better. "Sure."

"Great. You go get comfortable, I'll get supplies."

She got up, careful not to disturb the cat too much.

"Coming, Jenkins?" She asked, heart fluttering when he followed her out of the kitchen and through the living room, tail up in a happy flag.

The night was looking up again, after all.

Twenty-Two

THE NEXT MORNING, Olivia got in touch with Sunrise and set up a call with Dr. Clay. She was sweating bullets the whole time leading up to the appointed time, rehearsing in her head what she wanted to say to the therapist she'd given such a hard time to not so long before.

Ollie left her in the apartment alone so he could run a few errands and attend a business meeting of his own.

Stuck in waiting mode while anticipating the phone call, Olivia was both useless and restless.

She used Ollie's computer to scan through some apartment listings and skim through the gossip pages.

As she worked, Jenkins watched her from the back of the couch. He seemed just as relieved as Olivia was when her phone finally rang for the meeting. She'd started pacing and he couldn't seem to help but watch her.

"Olivia, I'm so pleased you reached out. How can I help you?"

She continued to walk in circles through the living room, unable to stop moving in an effort to help quell her nerves. "I'm not sure, honestly. I need help finding a therapist in my area, I guess."

"I'm glad to help if I can. What cities should I look in?"

Olivia hesitated. She still wasn't sure where she'd be living. "Um…"

"If you don't know yet, I can go broad. I have quite a few for the greater Los Angeles area. I assume L.A.'s where you'll be?"

"Yes. I think so, anyway."

"Alright. I'll go through my lists and see if I can find you a match. I have your email too. In the meantime, do you want to set up a Telehealth video call?"

Olivia was confused by the relief her simple offer sent through her body. "I would. Thank you, Dr. Clay."

There was a pause, likely because she was processing the new, humble tone of Olivia's voice.

"You sound different, Olivia. A good different."

A thought flitted across her mind and she spoke it into existence before it could escape. "Dr. Clay, do you think there would be any benefit to me repeating the program at Sunrise?"

"Oh. Well, the inpatient program here has benefits for sure. Do you want to come back? Do you feel like it's a reasonable choice for you right now?"

Olivia thought about how to answer. She'd lain awake for a while the night before, trying to pin down something she wanted for herself. A house, a job, a hobby… anything. There was no time in her life where she hadn't had some kind of next goal as far as her career, and having nothing but freedom was somehow terrifying.

"I'm not sure what I need, Dr. Clay. While I think my time in jail helped me, I don't feel as though I have much of anywhere to go from here."

"Are you somewhere safe, Olivia?" With a tiny shift in tone, Dr. Clay's concern levels went from minor to code red. Olivia was touched by her concern.

"Yes, I'm fine. A… friend has been kind enough to let me stay with him, but I can't stay much longer. I sold my house and haven't found an apartment yet for obvious reasons. I'm not sure I'm ready to commit to anything if I'm being honest. I don't have a direction right now."

"I see. Well, the program is always here for you. Your situation has changed, so the restrictions would be different, of course, but if you feel it's the right place for you and you'd benefit from the program, I'm happy to put in a note on your application to return."

"I…" Olivia looked over at Jenkins who had fallen asleep in a beam of sunshine coming through the slats of the blinds. "I need to do a little more thinking, but I'd appreciate it."

"Of course. I'll still collect some recommendations, just in case. The next cycle starts in a few days, so if you're ready, we'd be here for you. You'll need to call Pauline to make the arrangements, but I can't imagine it would be a problem. Are you sure you're alright, Olivia?"

"Yes, I'm sure I'm okay, thank you."

They talked for a few more minutes and when she hung up, Olivia was both exhilarated by the idea that she might have a next step and exhausted by the thought of what it might entail.

First, she wanted to talk to Ollie about it, get his thoughts about things.

"I appreciate the support, Jenkins," she told the cat, who had come down from his perch when she sat down on the couch.

He yawned and curled up next to her, his back snuggled up to her thigh.

She was taking that as a good sign.

OLLIE BLINKED A few times, frozen mid-bite.

He'd returned a couple of hours after her calls, bearing a bright smile, an audition prospect, and an early dinner of brick oven pizza.

"Back to Sunrise? Are you sure?"

Olivia nodded. The more she'd thought about it, the more sense it made.

"I looked it up and I think the intensive thirty-day program would work. I need help." She breathed in deeply after the admission crossed her lips.

"I'm really glad you're reaching out for what you need," Ollie said genuinely, dusting the crumbs off his fingers as he continued to stare at her.

"You're looking at me funny, though."

"Not funny. Impressed."

"Why?"

"Because the Olivia I met at Sunrise a few short months ago didn't even believe she'd done anything wrong. She certainly didn't think she needed therapy. You've come a long way. You should be proud of it."

A warm pulse bloomed in her chest. "I am."

"Good. I'm one thousand percent here for you. You can stay here until you're ready to check in, if you want. I just want to put the offer out there. If you're ready for a hotel, I support that too, though. When were you thinking of going?"

Her face twisted, anticipating some kind of shock from him, but it never came.

"Monday. I talked to Pauline after I got off the phone with Dr. Clay. If I can get there, I can start with this cycle. If not, I have to wait until next month."

"Okay. I'll drive you."

Instead, Olivia was the one left in shock. "No, Ollie, I can't ask you to. You've already done so much. I can Uber or something, it's no big—"

"You're not asking, Princess. I'm offering. I don't have anything else going on. I'll drive you. I wouldn't mind checking in with Dr. C, anyway. I have some questions for a few people, in fact. No biggie."

"Are you sure?" Heavy emotion weighed on Olivia's chest. The kindness continued to pour from this man, and she felt like she was taking advantage even though it was offered freely.

"Of course." He gave her his signature lopsided grin and reached for another slice of pizza. "Go get your head right, Princess."

They ate in silence for a few minutes, Olivia's head spinning with the things she needed to do before disappearing into rehab for another month.

"Well, that gives us the whole weekend together. What do you want to do?"

She hadn't had a full weekend to plan in quite a long time.

"Um, I'm not sure. Did you have anything you wanted to do?"

He looked at her with his head cocked to one side. "I asked because I don't want you to pick what I want. I want you to pick what *you* want."

"I don't know what I want."

"Well… think about it. We have some time."

"Okay. What if it's nothing? I mean, I sat around in a cell for a while, but it wasn't super restful."

"Then we rest. Who doesn't love weekends in, doing a movie marathon or something? It's fine. This isn't a test, Princess. It could be something as simple as going to your favorite coffee place or taking a walk in the park. Nothing extravagant. Unless you want to hit a theme park or something, in which case… we can do that too."

Having so many options open was paralyzing in its own way. Having to choose what she wanted to do for the weekend was a smaller version of trying to figure out where she was headed in her life. There were so many open doors to walk through, yet she couldn't move her feet to choose one.

"Okay, I'll think about it."

"Good." Ollie smiled at her and got to his feet, dropping the faintest of kisses on her hair as he passed her on his way to the sink.

"Are you sure staying here is—"

"*Olivia*," he growled, before starting to chuckle. The timbre of his voice as he said her name had her body warm for a whole host of reasons. "It's fine. I'd love it if you could stay. Stop worrying about it."

"Sorry."

He raised an eyebrow briefly before turning his attention back to washing his hands. He dried them on an old tea-towel, leaning his hip against the counter.

Her heart pounded at the tension forming between them, and that worried her, too. It was excitement she was feeling, and at the moment, she didn't trust it at all.

She could feel the heat of a blush creeping into her chest and cheeks. Olivia took a bite of her pizza to cover any wayward emotions from being too obvious.

"I've already explained it, but I like this new version of you."

"You do?" She muttered over her bite.

"Yeah, I do. I shouldn't have liked you nearly as much as I did when we were there together."

"I was… manipulative and mean. I was my whole life, honestly."

Ollie laughed. Olivia tossed her paper plate and picked up the pizza box so she could put it in the fridge.

"You weren't as bad as all that. Not all the time. When you let your guard down, you were pretty likable. I get it though, we all have our reasons. Besides, I had my share of cruel responses to your bitchy moments. I feel like we're even."

He opened the fridge for her, crowding her body with his as she maneuvered the box onto a shelf.

She straightened, their faces mere breaths apart.

"Ollie, I…" Her words faltered as he reached a hand up and cupped her cheek.

"I wish I trusted myself more, Princess. Things could be so different between us."

Emotion surged, Olivia felt torn between crying and relief. She'd used her body plenty to get what she wanted. She'd always given consent, enthusiastically even, but it had been a tool nonetheless. She could understand his hesitation, not only because of his history, but hers as well.

His tortured expression made her gut twist. His eyes locked on hers and she could practically hear the noise in his head as he debated with himself about what he could or should do in this situation.

"Hey. It's okay. I'm fine. We're fine. I understand." She wasn't sure the words meant anything at all, but she had to say something.

His lips brushed hers, a faint warm sensation traveling from where they touched to her stomach, where butterflies swarmed. He never completed the kiss, despite how desperately she wanted him to. It was a simple pass, enough to promise something more, then it was gone. She sighed shallowly as he closed his eyes and leaned forward, pressing his forehead to hers.

"I trust you," she said softly.

There was no mistaking the hitch in his breath.

"You're not the problem, Princess."

They stood there for long minutes, simply breathing together, his palm cradling her face. Olivia's pulse was rioting, pounding in her throat as she breathed in his citrusy scent. She wanted nothing more than to kiss him, but she just gave him space to take whatever he needed. She had to believe they would get their chance to be more once they were both ready.

When he finally pulled away, they were both breathing tensely, the energy between them ready to spark at the slightest provocation.

"I'm going to go take a shower." He grinned slowly, the innuendo clear in his smirk.

"Okay."

He disappeared down the short hall toward his bedroom.

Olivia breathed out heavily as his door shut, need cascading through every part of her body and yet no relief in sight.

"Shower," she said, glancing up to find Jenkins watching her from the back of the sofa again. "A cool shower all the way around, right?" After the cat yawned, stretching out one paw in her direction, she added, "We're okay."

Whether she was reassuring the cat or herself was a mystery, but hearing the words out loud still helped.

ONCE SHE HEARD the water shut off in his bathroom, she went into the one in the hallway.

As she stood under the spray, she considered what she might want to do over the weekend.

Old Olivia would have planned a full schedule, ensuring she got her face in front of as many paparazzi cameras as possible. She grimaced at the thought as she rinsed out the shampoo. Nothing about being photographed, shouted at or otherwise treated like a commodity held any appeal now.

"Might be time for a full-on career change," she muttered to herself, applying a generous layer of conditioner to her hair.

As she massaged the thick mask into the strands, she decided she could use a decent haircut and style. Something that suited her instead of whatever her mother thought was on trend at the moment. There was something unique and powerful about reinventing yourself with a fresh look.

She added it to the list.

As she washed her body, she continued to dig into what it was she really wanted. To the new hairstyle, she added shopping for some clothes to match the person she'd become.

She could envision Ollie's face for every step of the excursion in her mind. In each of the visions, he was smiling. Reaching out for bags. Complimentary. Kind.

Olivia's pulse began to pound in her throat as her thoughts trailed off in that direction. It wasn't fair how he was so sweet and generous. She didn't have any defenses against those traits at all. In truth, those were some of the things she'd fallen hardest for in Maxwell.

She turned the water off, taking her time getting dried and dressed.

The list in her mind kept expanding, but also kept coming back to some very quiet moments. She wanted to do the makeover things, but also didn't want to be away from the apartment for long. Getting some kind of takeout and lounging on the couch held as much appeal as anything else.

Old Olivia would have been planning to hit every hot spot in town; clubs, bars, restaurants, secret pop-up parties. The thought of those things now just gave her a headache and made her tired.

As she swiped on some moisturizer, she found herself smiling.

Maturity was one hell of a thing.

She knew more than anything else that when her weekend with Ollie was over, the memories of it would keep her going through whatever came next.

Twenty-Three

OLIVIA DECLARED HER wish list for the weekend the next morning.

In response, Ollie enthusiastically got out his phone and started looking up where they should go and in what order so they were being efficient in their route.

The first stop was for coffee. It wasn't until they pulled into the lot Olivia realized where he'd taken them.

"This place?" Olivia shrank into the leather seat, anxiety spiking.

The lot for the coffee shop was tiny, but he'd gotten lucky. Usually, there was plenty of circling to find one, though there was also a garage not far as a backup.

"Absolutely. This is my favorite coffee place, though I don't come over to this side of the city very often any more. Best pastries in town. Why?"

She looked at him, a grimace on her face. "Bad memories."

"Oh." He tapped the steering wheel, clearly torn between his need for caffeine and her hesitancy. "*Oh*," he said the word again, meaning pressed into it. "This is where… shit. I'm sorry, Princess, I wasn't thinking. We can go somewhere else—"

"No, no. It's okay."

He was reaching to turn the car on again, so she opened her door to prevent him from doing so. She waited by her side of the car while he followed her lead, gratefully accepting the casual press of fingertips into her spine as they walked toward the building.

The last time she'd come, she had flung her overpriced car into the handicapped space. She'd been wearing a fluorescent pink romper and bad hair extensions to go with her manic, entitled attitude.

There was no part of that day she would ever forget.

The memory alone had her running her hands over her shortened locks to reassure herself the woman who had done those things wasn't still hanging around.

Ollie led them inside, waiting in the short line to place their orders at the counter while Olivia claimed a small table near the front windows.

She laughed out loud when he turned away from the counter with a full box of pastries as well as their cups. "How many did you get?"

"One of every kind I could get in this box. Don't tell Jean-Pierre, but I think these are better than his."

Olivia gasped dramatically, hand at her throat as though clutching at pearls. "Better than JP's? How dare you!"

"I know." He chuckled, passing over her coffee and napkins. "It sounds crazy. But hear me out. Try the chocolate croissant and this fruit tart thing, then tell me I'm wrong."

He cut the two items and placed halves of them both on the napkin in front of her. Ollie smiled, plopping his whole croissant half in his mouth.

She reached for the tart first, the glossy coating on the fresh fruit making it look like art instead of something edible. The tang of the custard and the buttery crust were a perfect match for the sweet glaze on the fruit topping.

"Wow," she breathed out, licking some of the jam off her fingertips. "Your secret is safe with me. As long as we can get these once in a while. Like one of everything." She reached for the chocolate croissant. "Is it all this buttery?"

Ollie smiled. "I'm not sure, but I'd love to find out." Eating real food, regularly, had truly become Olivia's favorite thing about separating herself from her mother's management.

"We can work through the box a few at a time. That actually sounds like the best idea—" Olivia stopped short, the flaky pastry sticking in her throat.

If they'd come inside to get drinks, she hadn't seen them, but there was no mistaking the couple sitting at the metal table on the other side of the glass. It was Maxwell and Nora.

Her heart thudded to her feet. Bile rose, and she hated how the beautiful tart was now swimming in a vat of churning acid.

"Is that…" Ollie peered to the side, seeing Olivia's stunned expression. "Oh, shit."

"I should apologize, right? Make amends? Or should I just ignore them? I don't know the right thing to do." Her breath was coming rapidly and she started to feel lightheaded.

"Hey, calm down. Don't give yourself a panic attack. What about the restraining order?"

"Oh." The urge to speak to them, if only to say she was sorry for all the terrible things she'd done, was electrifying her body. She wanted to jump up, run out, spew the words, then race away in Ollie's car. "Yes, I'm sure it's still in place."

"Okay, we need to be careful, right? If they're still there when we're ready to leave, maybe you can say something quickly on our way to the car? I honestly don't know the right move here, either. I did have a chance to talk to Nora when I shot those last few episodes. I apologized again, for what I'd done the last time we were on set together, but mostly just tried to keep my distance. It seemed okay."

Olivia couldn't peel her attention away from the window. Nora's wheat-blonde hair was tied back in a braid, some stray strands flying around her face on the breeze. Maxwell had gotten quite a tan since she'd seen him last, his hair now at least two shades lighter. He was still handsome in his own laid-back way, but she didn't feel the magnetic pull to him she expected, nor did his smile take her breath away the way it used to.

"Hey, are you okay?" Ollie asked, bringing her back from staring.

She nodded, shifting her attention from the couple on the patio to the man across the table from her. His eyes were rounded as he watched her, his mouth tensely bracketed by lines.

Olivia realized he was braced to see how she'd react to Maxwell. Whether she'd jump up and race to her ex. Guilt rushed in. She couldn't blame him for feeling discomfited by the situation. It was strange on a number of levels.

She reached across the table, giving his hand a squeeze.

"I'm okay. But I owe them an apology. I had a lot of time to think about it and I think... I may not have really loved him?" The lilt to her words made them into a question. "I thought I did at the time, but I think it was more the idea of someone like him and not actually him as a person."

Ollie nodded. He'd said as much to her when they'd argued back at Sunrise. It had just taken some extra time for her to really accept the truth.

Her eyes wandered again. Maxwell and Nora were seated similarly to how she and Ollie were sitting. One hand touching, enjoying a morning with coffee and pastries.

Maxwell had always loved these pastries. It was convenient for him, too. His father's law firm was close by.

"I don't feel the same for him as I used to. I promise."

"I believe you." One corner of his mouth lifted, the worry easing as his face relaxed.

"Can we… can we go?" She asked. "I feel like I'm not actually here with you while I'm worried about them. Honestly, I don't really feel totally in my body at all right now."

"Sure." Ollie gathered their trash and tossed it into the closest can. "Are you going to approach them?"

Olivia finished her coffee, wiping a drip with the back of her hand. "I think I have to."

"I get it. I absolutely do. But be quick and then we have to go. I don't want you getting arrested again."

"Me neither, trust me."

Her nerves went into overdrive as they left the building. As she moved in what felt like slow motion, they didn't see her approaching their table. When they did, the panic on their faces made her voice not work properly.

"Hi." It was not the greeting she'd planned or hoped for, but it would have to do. She held up a hand, indicating she wasn't a threat. Ollie hung back a step or two, but also raised a hand. His was a friendly wave. Nora's gaze shifted nervously between them.

"Olivia," Maxwell bit out the syllables as if they tasted bad.

Olivia knew in his mouth, they probably did.

"We're leaving. I promise I didn't know you were here, we just came to get coffee…" She shook her head, trying to clear her thoughts as she started to ramble. "I wanted to say I'm sorry. I know it's not ever going to be enough, but I need to apologize, anyway. I am really, really sorry."

"For?" Maxwell prompted, body stiff as he prepared for confrontation.

Regret dug deep furrows in her heart as she watched him transform from the joyous, laid-back man she knew him to be to a fierce protector. His hand had grabbed Nora's under the table, and with the other, Nora was casually pulling something up on her phone. Something that looked like an emergency services app. Olivia knew her time was running out.

"Everything. Sleeping with James. Getting back in touch with David and setting up the blackmail. Breaking into your apartment. Destroying your things… trying to destroy your life. I understand if you can never forgive me for it. You probably shouldn't. But I am genuinely sorry. I wish I could go back and do things very differently. I apologize."

"Thank you," Nora's gentle voice surprised Olivia. Before today, she would have bet Nora wouldn't have any-thing at all to say to her. At least not anything that didn't involve threats or swearing. Certainly not gratitude.

Maxwell turned away from Olivia to look at Nora. Nora had turned her attention to Ollie. She said nothing, but they shared a meaningful nod between them.

"Sorry. Again." Olivia gave an awkward bow and backed away from the table, all too aware of how their eyes followed her across the small patio and into Ollie's car.

"That went well." Ollie blew a breath out between his lips as he started the engine.

"If 'well' is what that was, sure."

"It was. Nobody got arrested, nobody yelled… it was a success. How do you feel?"

Olivia took stock of her body. "A little bit lighter."

"Good. You need to tell Dr. Clay what happened. And you need to remember apologizing was for you, not for them."

"That's…" She wasn't sure what it was, but the revelation shook her.

"Apologies are like that, especially for unforgivable things. They may never feel better about any part of it. But it was for you to move on, not them."

He stared at her long enough someone waiting for the parking spot got impatient and honked.

Olivia looked back at the patio as Ollie backed out of the space, finding Maxwell and Nora still staring after them. Their mouths were moving, so they were discussing something, but they looked stunned.

She raised her hand in an awkward wave and told herself she was letting them go. She'd done enough damage, and it was time to move on.

"I'm sorry I ruined our morning."

Ollie tsked at her. "You didn't. That wasn't anything you did, just an odd occurrence. It's not a big deal."

"But now every time we get pastries, you'll think about it."

"So what? Those kinds of things are pieces of you, Princess. And me. We both have a lot of shit to sift through. It's bound to happen. Would you be mad, or upset, if things were the other way around?"

"No."

"There you have it. Some things are going to happen that way. Especially with us."

Olivia shook her head, astounded by his boundless capacity for understanding and forgiveness.

"Us?" She asked.

He grinned back, looking at her over the top of his sunglasses before pulling out into traffic. "You bet. Unless you've got someone else already?" He teased.

"Ha, ha."

"Then maybe you're ready to get rid of *me* already?"

"You really are something else," she said. "Thank you."

He grinned back at her, and her heart thudded in her chest. What had happened back at the coffee shop was her past. She had a suspicion whatever her future held, it had something to do with the man in the driver's seat.

CHAPTER
Twenty-Four

AFTER THE STRESSFUL experience at the coffee shop, Olivia had been on edge, but Ollie still wanted her to do everything on her list if she was up for it.

As they drove under the brilliant California sun, palm tree lined streets gave way to older architecture mixed with modern injections of strip malls.

She found a few more outfits to bolster her wardrobe at a department store. How the store had sprung up on a busy street between a bank and a church was a mystery.

After clothes were bought, he delivered her to his own personal hair stylist. The thoughtful gesture made Olivia's heart grow three sizes in her chest, like The Grinch. Once she was well pampered and finally looked like the version of herself she felt she was in her heart, he took her back to his apartment so they could relax.

They spent the afternoon binging a Netflix show she'd

been wanting to see, and while they lounged, they gradually moved closer and closer to one another.

By the end of the last episode, Olivia was drowsily lying on a pillow propped in his lap, his hands alternating between playing with her freshly cut hair and rubbing soft circles on her arm or hip.

He was fidgety when it came to his hands, no less so now than he had been at Sunrise. She didn't mind one bit; she'd take all the affectionate caresses he wanted to give.

As the credits rolled, he looked down at her, a soft smile gracing his mouth. The air between them was charged with something potent as they held eye contact.

"I… can I kiss you, Princess?"

"I wish you would." She punctuated the request with a slow smile, blood rushing in her ears as Ollie lowered his mouth to hers. His fingertips stroked at the line of her jaw, his lips warm and soft as he learned the shape of her mouth.

After a long, chaste press, she parted her lips, inviting him to deepen the kiss like she was craving.

He made a noise deep in his chest and bent his upper body closer to her, fingers twining in her hair as his tongue swept into her mouth.

Olivia met him need for need as he sampled and nipped. The pressure that had been building between them since they'd been matched up at Sunrise finally had an outlet, and it was all rushing to escape at once.

She reached a hand up, locking her fingers around his neck. Breath didn't matter, nor did time. They could have been kissing for a minute or an hour by the time he pulled back. He tipped his head back, eyes closed as his chest heaved.

Olivia was all tingles and sparks, craving his hands on her body.

"I knew..." he muttered. He sat up, eyes locking on hers as they opened. "I knew you would be dangerous."

The words were not a condemnation, though they held an edge of tension to balance the lust.

Olivia whispered, "I'll sign a waiver if I need to, but I really need you to touch me right now."

Ollie's panicked expression cut through the haze. He looked genuinely terrified.

"Sorry," she said, dialing down her tone and sitting up so he could have some space. "It's okay. I mean, I still definitely want you to, but... I'm sorry."

The moment between them broke, and Olivia mourned the loss, cursing herself for saying anything at all.

A breath leaked slowly from between his tight lips as he relaxed. "My fault."

"No, it's mine. I should have thought more before saying what I said."

The silence wrapped itself around them, the prickles of danger retracting.

"I definitely enjoyed kissing you. For the record."

Ollie cracked a grin. "Noted. I really am sorry. I just can't... yet."

"I know." Olivia rested her head on his shoulder, the simple gesture was a comfort for them both.

The sigh he heaved was deep and full of regret. "I think… I *know* I want you, Princess. But I still have some shit to sort out. I'm getting there though."

After some prolonged eye contact, he carefully reached out for her hand, lacing his fingers through hers.

"I need a little more time. I'm functioning in my life and feeling better than I have in years, but I'm not recovered. I'm not even totally sure what 'recovered' means. I may never be. I'll be better, absolutely better, but I don't know what true recovery looks like. I don't want either of us to end up back where we started, you know? I'm not using, but… I don't want to end up using *you*."

His words hit hard. "You wouldn't," she tried to reassure him.

"I wouldn't mean to. Absolutely not. But I also can't trade one obsession for another. I need to be sure when I touch you, there's no lingering fear of acting how I used to. Of being who I used to be." He took a deep breath. "In fact, I'm trying to figure out if I want to go back to acting at all because it's such an unhealthy place to be. I could feel the same heavy bullshit when I did those last episodes. I didn't run to any of my coping mechanisms except calling my therapist, but I couldn't help but feel the same blackness that always made me want to take something so I couldn't feel at all. It's tainted. I hate it."

Olivia swallowed her ego and tried to listen to what he was saying. While she didn't enjoy denying herself some of the more enjoyable physical pleasures, she knew he was right.

"Me, too. I get it."

He squeezed her hand reassuringly, reaching up to cup her face with his other hand. Drawing her forward, he leaned his forehead on hers, closing his eyes and breathing in deeply. Olivia felt all of her sour feelings warm as she allowed herself to relax into his intimate gesture. She smiled, realizing in her new, topsy-turvy world, Ollie Parkinson had become the voice of reason. It was too amusing not to enjoy for a moment.

"I want you too," she said quietly, not wanting to break the spell wrapped around them. "For the record. And we can work up to… other things."

He pulled his head away from hers, running the pad of his thumb over her swollen bottom lip before dropping his hand.

"I know." His smirk was back, the tension evaporating as he stared at her adoringly.

"Have you given any more thought to what you might do if you don't go back to acting?" She asked, feeling a familiar pull to explore something outside the familiar but awful machine that was Hollywood.

Ollie settled back into the couch, fiddling with the edges of a fleece blanket as he considered his answer. "I don't know. Something to help people like us, like we talked about before. I'm no therapist, but some kind of peer support for someone with the same struggles as me sounds possible."

Olivia nodded, sitting forward. The suggestion was interesting for a number of reasons.

"You're good at it. I can write a testimonial, if you need one."

He blushed when he grinned, making her heart thud in her chest. She could think of several exciting ways to punish the people who had manipulated this kind soul into the monster he had been well on his way to becoming. The monster he still thought he was.

"You could always go back to school."

"Yeah…" he shook his head. "I don't think that's the answer. But maybe. I've seriously considered going somewhere out of state even. Get a little space. You can get a whole lot more for a whole lot less in other places."

Olivia didn't know what to say, but she made a thoughtful noise in her throat.

"Anyway, it's something I've been thinking about since I got out of Sunrise. The mentor thing is great, but I could afford a real house somewhere. Start a camp or something maybe…" he looked off across the room, but she could tell he was a million miles away. She loved seeing him enthusiastic and dreamy about some kind of future. "I don't know. It's like playing the 'what I'll do when I win the lottery'. Lots of daydreaming."

"Daydreams are healthy."

His head tilted to the side and he smirked at her. "What do you daydream about, Butterfly?"

Olivia blinked, mouth open to give a response that never came.

She didn't know.

For the last few months, she'd dreamed about food, comfort, anything but the cage she was in. She'd thought about everything she'd do differently if she had a chance to do it all over, and all the people she'd hurt. The things her mother had done *to* her, under the guise of doing things *for* her. But there'd been no thoughts about what was next, at least not beyond getting out of rehab or jail.

"I'm not sure."

"It's okay." Ollie grinned at her, reassurance in his features. "I can help you figure it out."

Her heart did a hollow thumping thing again, and she realized she was in deep trouble when it came to this man. He was her friend. Her only one, and he was a thousand percent correct, she needed to get her head on straight before she did something she couldn't take back.

Something crazy, like falling in love with him.

CHAPTER
Twenty-Five

OLIVIA SPENT HER Sunday getting familiar with the washer and dryer in the hall closet of Ollie's apartment.

She'd done her fair share of laundry in her lifetime, but for some reason, going through the luggage she'd filled so recklessly before leaving her parents' house for Sunrise the last time around was extra cumbersome.

As things dried, she folded them and made a decision about whether they were traveling with her again or staying behind.

"I can take what's left to my storage unit, too" she was mumbling to herself, but Ollie had been hovering close, offering a hand with whatever she needed.

"You can always leave it here," he suggested.

The idea felt extra… personal. Leaving clothing behind was a step beyond a spare toothbrush in the drawer in her book.

He saw the startled look on her face and dipped in, kissing her temple as she froze in the middle of folding a shirt.

"It's not a big deal, Princess. Stop overthinking things. I'm only trying to help."

"I'll consider it. But Jerry got me a storage unit for a reason."

"True, but it's just some clothes. And who knows what kind of bugs or critters might be trolling around the storage."

Olivia cringed. "Fair point."

"Come on," he said, pulling her to the couch where he'd set up a bunch of snacks and a movie.

Ollie had been warming up throughout the day, having come to some kind of understanding with himself after they went their separate ways the night before. He was quick to touch her, and they'd shared a handful of soul-melting kisses throughout the day, but he always pulled back before things got too heated.

The way they came together left her wanting so much more, but she wouldn't push. They were on his clock.

About a third of the way through, Ollie's normal caresses developed an edge of intent. Instead of a feather-light brush against her clothing, his fingertips were pressing into her skin. Everything in her body heated up at the subtle change, an ache for something more growing between her legs.

"Ollie," she sighed, leaning her head into the cushion back so she could look at him.

He stilled, turning his attention from the TV to her. There was no mistaking the lust in his eyes; she recognized it well.

"When you left..." He shook his head, a muscle in his jaw ticking as he gritted his teeth together. "I was so angry with you for making the decision you did. For being so impulsive." His chin dropped to his chest, regret tempering the heat. "And I was angry with myself. For saying what I said."

"You weren't wrong though." Olivia gave an impish grin. If she had it to do again, she wouldn't have left. She wouldn't have taken the reality show and things could have been very different. But she also knew she'd needed to make those decisions the way she did to get to where she'd ended up, and she didn't regret where she'd landed.

"Even if I wasn't wrong, it was an awful thing to say. I was frustrated, because I could feel this... *thing* between us, and even though I wasn't ready to act on it, I wanted to hang on to it. To you."

Olivia's chest ached at his sweet admission. "I needed the reality check. You know as much as I do how much I did."

He tilted his head to the side in agreement. "It didn't have to be quite so harsh though."

"I think it did. I had to do it that way to see how my mom was pulling the strings behind the curtain. I needed nothing but time to sit and think about who I wanted to be and all the ways I'd spent my life *not* being the same person. I needed it. I hated it at times, but it was necessary."

He twined his fingers through hers on one hand, using the other to play with her hair.

"I hunted Jerry down after about a week. I was worried about you."

"That's really sweet," Olivia murmured. "My parents never once checked on me."

Those words made him frown. "Jerry put me through my paces. He protected your privacy completely. I just wanted you to know."

"I didn't doubt it." And she hadn't. It never crossed her mind that her lawyer would have been anything but one hundred percent professional and protective of her as his client.

"I think he was relieved to find someone else who truly cared for you. Not just another leech trying to get something from you."

Olivia shivered. The words struck deep with their truth. "I don't think my dad is anything worse than apathetic. But that's been bad enough."

"Whatever the case, I was pretty motivated to make sure you were okay, and Jerry was hoping to find someone he could rely on. We spoke quite a few times. I was shocked when he called to ask me to pick you up. I was genuinely scared I'd built everything up all wrong in my head."

"I was the one to try and kiss you, remember?" She teased.

"I remember." He smiled, and the tone of their conversation made a shift.

He lowered his mouth to hers again, starting with the soft brushes along the contours of her mouth, then pressing in before getting teeth and tongue involved. Olivia dove into the embrace enthusiastically, moving his fingers from between hers to over her hand on her breast. She knew he needed small steps, but she needed touch.

"I'm always going to be an addict, Princess." His hands moved down her body, squeezing her hips, and he drew her closer to him across his lap, the heat of their bodies mingling between them. "I see multiple people every week who keep me on the straight and narrow. It's possible…" He dipped his head, breathing in her scent as he moved her hair away from her shoulder and grazed her skin from earlobe to collar bone with his nose. "It's possible I'm trading all those addictions for a new one. This one though? This one might actually be good for me. I know I could be good for it. For you."

She gasped, both from the sensations rioting under her skin and from his admission. The last thing she needed was to be obsessed about a man, but at the moment, she couldn't think of anything more attractive. Everything about him made her body pay full attention.

She'd been naked, or nearly so, in front of men since she was a teenager. But him looking at her like she was the embodiment of beauty while still fully clothed was different from any other time before.

Fire chased along the places he grazed her with his gaze, desire mounting the more he resisted the pull of their attraction.

It was thrilling. It made her feel young and beautiful.

The last thing she needed was to have a torrid love affair with him. But maybe… maybe it could be more. Maybe it already was.

"What are you thinking, Princess?"

"Nothing," she lied.

"Yeah?" His breath was warm on her shoulder as he continued to map her flesh with his fingertips. "Doesn't seem like nothing."

Her eyes slid closed, a moan she tried to suppress rumbling gently through her throat.

"This is dangerous," she gasped as the backs of his fingers grazed her breasts.

"Yes."

Just the fact that he wasn't disagreeing had her opening her eyes to gauge his expression. "Yes?"

"It is. You make me feel everything, and that scares the shit out of me. The last time I fell in love with that sensation I dove face first into an addiction to pills." She stiffened. "But it doesn't mean it's wrong. We've been chasing this thing between us for a while. I'm tired of fighting it, Olivia. Aren't you?"

"Yes," she breathed the word, ready to devour him at the first sign he was ready for that too.

"What if it's the right thing? What if I'm worried for nothing?"

"Is there a right thing?" Her hands gripped his forearms as he rested his hands on her shoulders.

"I think there is. I feel like I've been looking right at her since she arrived at Sunrise ready to give me nothing but attitude." He grinned and she felt the desire in her body turn everything to liquid.

"I don't know her," she teased.

"Me neither," he agreed. "At least, not anymore. This Olivia is the new and improved version. I like her a lot."

"She likes you too."

The words felt too shallow, but she enjoyed this game they were playing. She hadn't flirted with someone this way in a very long time. Perhaps since the last time they'd gone down this road.

Olivia pushed those thoughts away, desperate to cling to the magic being stirred between them instead of sliding back into memories that may not be quite what she remembered.

"Maybe we can stop doing this push and pull thing. I feel like I'm in a good place. Do you?"

"Yes," Olivia repeated.

"Then I'm going to kiss you, Princess. And I'm going to really mean it."

"You'd better."

Olivia's nerves suddenly kicked in, but any worries she had were firmly dispelled the moment his mouth touched hers. Soft lips met her mouth gently, becoming more insistent as his hands made their way around her back. One broad palm pressed her closer to his body from between her shoulder blades as another cupped her hip. His tongue gently licked at her bottom lip, and she opened her mouth, every nerve center in her body singing.

They sat this way for several long minutes, trading breath and exploring one another with their hands and mouths. Ollie kissed her like he might never get another chance, hesitating to break contact even for a moment. Every time she pulled back a little, thinking they were going to separate, he pulled her closer.

By the time he did finally press some final soft kisses to her mouth and pull far enough away to look at her, she was certain she looked drunk. She certainly felt like a starry-eyed girl who had just discovered what hormones were for.

"Slow," he said quietly. She could feel the rumble of his words through his chest.

"Slow," she repeated.

"But more of that."

She pulled back, hand over her mouth and face warm from embarrassment and the massive rush of endorphins she'd gotten from being close to him. "Yes, please."

His hands didn't stop moving. They traced the lines of her waist before moving to her arms and legs.

"Can I touch you, Princess?"

"Please. Can I touch you back?"

He grunted permission, and one of her hands slid down his chest and into his lap. Her hand grazed the evidence of his arousal, and she decided a better tactic was to climb in his lap.

He made a noise deep in his throat before consuming her again, his hands grasping her ass cheeks as she rocked herself over him, their clothing causing a delicious friction.

Sparks of intense arousal flared in her core, the heat of his palms infuriatingly far from where she needed his touch.

"I need more," she breathed against his lips and after a moment of hesitation, he shifted a bit. Her pulse pounded in her throat as she lifted up, allowing both of them access to the others' pants.

"Olivia. I…" he groaned as she grasped him firmly in her hand, the heated flesh pulsing under her palm.

"I know," she replied, pressing her mouth back to his as one of his hands pressed into her thigh as he moved toward her center.

She slid her hand up and down his shaft as he sank two fingers into her heat. She shifted until pressure was exactly where she needed it most. Ollie responded to her cues, pressing the heel of his hand against her clit as she rocked against his fingers. She moaned, struggling to focus on what she was doing to him through the heady fog of her own pleasure.

They nipped at one another's mouths as they settled into a rhythm that had every sensation spiraling out of control. The slide of his hand against her body, the feel of his hot flesh in her palm, everything was heightened as she panted for breath against his mouth.

"Princess," he groaned, "I can't—" he cursed as he stiffened under her touch, muscles locking up throughout his body as his release spilled warmly over her hand.

Olivia scrunched her eyes closed as his focus returned wholly to her, one hand manipulating her nipple into a tightened peak, the other plunging in and out as she adjusted her angle to chase the orgasm building low in her gut.

"Don't stop," she begged, rocking her hips at the speed she needed. As the climax sped through her body, she cried out, body shuddering.

He removed his hand from her slowly, making her sweat as he placed them in his mouth.

"Well worth the wait," he sighed, dreamy expression on his face.

Olivia giggled nervously, no part of her feeling her true age. She felt like a giddy schoolgirl who had finally gotten to make out with the popular boy at school on her parents' sofa.

She buried her face in his shoulder. He wrapped his arms around her, cradling her body to his instead of being put off by her reaction.

"Movie cuddles are going to be much more interesting, for sure."

Olivia laughed in earnest, picturing them snuggled up on his couch, blankets flying every direction with them underneath.

"Jenkins is going to be very jealous."

Ollie tilted his head. "Or pleased that there's basically one giant lap to curl up on instead of two."

"True."

As the moment faded, reality flooded back in over the top of their lust.

"I'll need to talk to my therapist about all this. Is that alright?" He asked.

"Of course. I will too."

He nodded knowingly. "It's not bad, though. This is healthy, right? Talking through major life changes with your trusted team of professionals?"

"Healthy, yes. Normal? Probably not. I don't think everyone has a team of professionals helping with their lives to start with." Olivia pulled herself off of him, much to their mutual regret.

"Too bad. I need my team to function."

Olivia collected their dirty dishes, dropping them on the breakfast bar before heading down the hallway.

"Me too."

The words surprised her, and she wondered how long it would take before her new normal was no longer shocking.

Ollie was barely half a step behind her, running directly into her back as she stopped at the bathroom doorway.

"Sorry," he muttered.

"It's okay. Did you want to…"

"A thousand percent. More than anything in the world. But that's not slow."

She felt the smile spread across her face. "I was going to ask if you wanted to shower first, or if you wanted me to."

"Oh." His eyes went wide, the rosy hue of his cheeks highlighting the aqua sparkle of them. "You can."

Olivia winked at him. "Me too, for the record. Maybe we can try just sleeping one night soon. See how it goes?"

"Okay."

"Okay."

Ollie kissed her cheek softly before moving down the hallway to his room. Olivia basked in the moment as long as she could, reliving the best parts of the evening every time she closed her eyes under the spray.

CHAPTER
Twenty-Six

THE DRIVE TO Malibu the next morning was quiet. The passage of time had moved in an odd way since she'd gone to jail. Getting out and going immediately into a hormonally charged reality warp with Ollie had thrown her perspective completely off.

Both of them had been somber as they gathered her things. Conversation was sparse as they drank their coffee and moved through their routines. All too soon, her things were loaded in his car and it was time to go.

He kept one hand on her knee as he drove, the miles passing all too quickly.

Now that she'd had multiple days with Ollie, uninterrupted, a whole month with nothing more than a couple of thirty-minute calls a week between them would be a challenge.

When they pulled into the lot, there was a lot of hesitating and delaying before she finally got out of the car.

He unloaded her bag, setting it at her feet.

"I'm not going in with you. You need to do this on your own."

"I know. Will you at least kiss me?"

"For the record, I don't think it's the best idea." His smirk disagreed with his words.

"That's not a no."

He sighed, dropping his chin to his chest. "You're killing me here, Princess. You know they're watching, right?"

"Who cares? Let them watch. Come on, one little kiss." The tip of her tongue poked out, teasing her upper lip. "A *good* kiss, though."

His expression grew serious, pupils enlarging as he narrowed the distance between their faces.

"If it's too good…" he started to argue, but the words never fully formed.

"We'll be alright."

His hand cupped her cheek, and he closed the gap between them, first pressing his warm lips to hers and then tilting his head to deepen it. Olivia held his hand in place with hers, teasing at his closed mouth with the tip of her tongue, eager to taste him.

Finally, he parted his lips enough for her to lick along his full bottom lip.

He groaned, the sound was all the encouragement she needed.

She leaned into his body and he pulled her as close as she could get with his arms. One hand pressed between her shoulder blades, the other lingering just over her hip. Their heads tilted the opposite way as they nipped and licked at one another, tracing the curves and planes of each other's mouths as they swapped breath.

Olivia was heaving one breath after another through her nose as he worked her mouth with his, eager for the next step but all too aware this was going to end soon and he was going to go home without her.

"Olivia," Ollie gasped, panting for breath. He pressed his forehead to hers, eyes closed. "We have to stop."

"I know." She mourned the loss of her connection with him, their shared breath, the moment.

"You drive me crazy. What the hell am I supposed to do with this raging hard-on?"

Olivia beamed. "I'm sure I could think of a few things."

"I'm positive you could. But it'll have to wait." He took a deep breath, an obvious bid at trying to calm himself. "How did I do?"

"Perfectly," she admitted.

"No notes for my next take?" He teased.

"I'll get back to you."

"Do that," he said, shy grin overtaking his face. He lifted her fingers to his mouth, brushing a kiss against her knuckles. "Definitely do that."

After a moment, he let her go, giving her a brusque kiss on the forehead before pushing her toward the building.

"Go on. Get started so you can get finished."

Reluctantly, she grabbed her bag and headed in. She looked back to find him leaning up against his car in a casual way, grin pulling on his mouth.

"Like I said before, Princess, go get your head on straight. I'll be here when you get done."

She kissed the tips of her fingers and gestured his direction. On a deep inhale, she pulled open the door, ready to begin what came next, riding the wave of her endorphins the whole way.

IF POSSIBLE, PAULINE was even more welcoming the second time Olivia showed up in the lobby of Sunrise.

The receptionist did her normal name-taking and nod, and Pauline was as fast to open the door as the first time.

"Olivia! Welcome back. Come on through."

They walked into the main visitation room with the solid-molded plastic tables and chairs, but Pauline didn't pause.

"I thought we'd stop in the dining room for a quick cup of coffee or something while we go over things. If that's alright? You don't need the formality of the group room." She paused, glancing over her shoulder to confirm Olivia was following.

"Sounds great. I missed the dining room."

Pauline laughed, the keys on her lanyard jingling as she walked. "Oh, I know. It's never the same, even when I eat at home. There's something special about the food here."

Pauline left Olivia at one of the smaller tables as she placed her order with one of the few cooks on shift between meals.

"They'll bring it all over." Pauline sat across from Olivia, hands folded. She wore a kind, open expression. "So. Tell me what it is you hope to get out of your stay with us this time."

Olivia had known the question was coming, but still felt awkward saying the words out loud. "I need help."

"Mmm."

"I didn't work the program last time… obviously. I went to jail. It was… enlightening. But I have no idea how to move forward."

"Yes, well." Pauline paused, allowing some space for the coffee service, complete with an assortment of cookies and pastries, to be delivered. "We were quite disappointed with how things went last time. I did worry we could've done something differently, so I was very glad when you reached out."

"It wasn't you," Olivia reassured her, making up her cup with cream and sugar. "I… well, to be truthful, I didn't believe I needed to be here. There was no effort on my part to do much of anything except put on a smile and fake it."

Pauline nodded, eyes squinted in thoughtfulness. She gently tapped the spoon against the rim of her cup before setting it down on the saucer.

Olivia squirmed under the scrutiny, though she didn't feel judged or as though she were in a meeting with the principal.

"Dr. Clay worried you weren't getting everything she wanted you to out of her sessions. I feel I can speak for us all when I say we're relieved you're giving this another chance. After… dealing with the consequences of leaving," she hedged, for whatever reason not willing to say the words 'went to jail'. Olivia appreciated her ability to twist the situation into something much prettier than it really was. "We hope we can help."

Olivia laughed. It was the kindest phrasing she'd heard yet for her going to jail and said so.

"Well." Pauline's cheeks turned a warm pink shade and she reached for a cheese danish. "We do try to be discreet."

"I'm sure your clientele appreciates it."

They sat a few minutes longer, sipping coffee and enjoying the flaky pastries. In the lull, Pauline produced the same paperwork as before from a folder she'd been carrying.

"I suppose we should do the important bits. If you don't mind signing these again?"

"Sure." Olivia used Pauline's pen and scribbled her name on all of the documents.

"We've put you back in the same room, if that's okay?"

"Perfect, thanks."

"Well." Pauline pushed away from the table, standing. "Enjoy your stay. We hope you find what you need while you're here. Go on over when you're ready. Nothing on your schedule until tomorrow morning, like before, so you can get settled in."

"Thank you, Pauline. Are there many other residents right now?"

"We're down a few attendees since your last stay. There are a few in your building though. Perhaps you'll meet a new friend."

"Maybe."

Pauline left her alone in the dining room. She considered taking the entire basket of goodies they'd brought to the table for them.

Olivia wasn't holding her breath, but she felt a surge of excitement about it rather than revulsion. How people reacted to being her friend was a totally different story. She honestly wouldn't blame them if they hesitated to get close to her. Her track record was total shit. For the first time in her life, she'd temper the angry reaction to her hurt feelings, however.

In the end, she compromised, taking only the cookies and a chocolate croissant with her as she returned to the room she realized she'd come to miss.

THERE WAS FAR less luggage this time around, but the small desk and bathroom counter looked much the same with her things set up neatly on them.

She relaxed into the cozy hug of the bed, wishing she could text Ollie to let him know how she was getting settled in.

After a few moments of rest, where a nap threatened a bit too stealthily, she sat up and went through the schedule they'd put together for her and the rest of the contents of her folder.

There wasn't much difference in her daily routine as far as she could tell. Group sessions were all the same, yoga and meditation too. Her art and music were switched around, but that was no big deal.

Her shoulders relaxed as the familiar surrounded her.

This room had been more hers than the one at her parents' house, and the realization felt truly tragic. A rented bed in a carefully staged suite intended for rehabilitation was more comforting to her than the bedroom she'd spent literally her entire life living in.

Olivia sat heavily on the coverlet, the weight of the things she needed to discuss with Dr. Clay heavy on her shoulders.

To relieve the strain, she scribbled a few notes in the notebook they'd given her in the folder before lying back down. A nap suddenly didn't seem like such a waste of time. Instead, it felt like a healthy step toward self-care.

CHAPTER
Twenty-Seven

"OFTEN, IT ISN'T until we've lost everything that we truly understand we've hit rock bottom and need to make a change."

Dr. Clay, as usual, seemed as if she was speaking directly to Olivia, despite the fact that she was actually addressing the whole group.

Their circle of chairs was ten strong for the group therapy session the day after she'd arrived, and the young doctor was in her element. Most of the new residents were on the younger side, not a single one on her side of twenty-five if Olivia had any eye for age.

"Sometimes even then, it's difficult to really move from wherever we've become stuck. Would anyone care to talk about their rock bottom moment?" She opened her hands as though inviting someone to volunteer. "It's definitely a difficult subject, so I understand if you aren't comfortable. But as you listen, think about your own, okay?"

Olivia raised her hand.

Dr. Clay smiled in surprise, but her eyes glowed with warm approval. "Olivia, yes. Please, go ahead."

Out of habit, she looked around, trying to find Ollie as an anchor. A familiar tug in her chest when she couldn't find him reminded her for the dozenth time he wasn't there. She was on her own.

"Hi, I'm Olivia. This is my second stay at Sunrise. My first time, I didn't take it seriously. I left even though I'd been made well aware that leaving before my program was complete would mean I'd be arrested." She gave a smile to some of the wide-eyed newbies, hoping the ones who seemed bored heard what she was saying. She could see herself in them and didn't want anyone to repeat her mistake. "I decided I knew better than all the professionals trying to help me and I left for a job. Naturally, I was arrested. I went to jail." There was a long silence as she puzzled together the words she wanted to use. "Realizing I was being hired basically to be the punchline of a joke and learning some things about my parents were my rock bottom. I know it sounds strange, since going to jail is kind of the worst, but the thing is… I needed to go to jail to see all the moving parts of my life clearly. I'm not upset it happened. I'm upset it had to happen in order for me to change."

Dr. Clay was beaming by the time she finished speaking. There was a gentle round of applause, and Olivia was pleased to see at least two of the young women that reminded her of herself were paying attention.

"Lovely, Olivia, thank you for sharing. Anyone else?"

There were some half-hearted confessions of stealing money to purchase drugs and the like, which honestly left Olivia relieved. She'd gladly be the worst-case scenario.

As group broke up, one of the women hung back, drawing Olivia's attention with a quiet comment.

"I saw the video of you being arrested. What they did to you was shitty."

"Oh. Thanks."

The girl was painfully thin, even for the model she'd claimed to be. Her hair was stringy and the dark eye makeup around her eyes smudged.

"I'm Shari."

"Olivia. Nice to meet you."

"See you around?"

She was acting uncomfortable, so Olivia let her go, but called after, "I'm nearly always by myself in the dining room. You're always welcome to join me, if you want. I wouldn't mind the company."

Shari's mouth twitched. There was a slight nod before she dropped her chin to her chest and loped out of the room.

"That was a wonderful session." Dr. Clay approached her, rearranging the awful plastic chairs as she went.

"Yeah. Lots of new residents. Young ones."

Dr. Clay grinned. "You noticed? They do come in waves. How are you doing today?"

Olivia did a quick internal assessment. "Pretty well. I'm feeling much… lighter?"

"I'm glad to hear it, Olivia, truly. I'm looking forward to our one-on-one. I'm happy to see you back."

Dr. Clay patted her shoulder and left the room, leaving Olivia to bask in the rush of pride for a few minutes before she headed off to her next session.

OLIVIA FOUND A nervous Shari hanging back just inside the dining room doors when she went over for dinner.

She looked relieved when Olivia walked in, then dropped any and all expression from her face, trying to appear bored.

Olivia knew all too well the mental gymnastics the poor girl was putting herself through. You had to be pretty, but in a unique way. Thin, but not so willowy you lost your hips and breasts. Disinterest in everything was highly desirable, but be sure to pout and bat your eyelashes at the menfolk.

Garbage and lies, the lot of it. Never going back to any of the industries involving a camera was more and more attractive every day.

"Come sit with me, Shari. Have you had the chance to eat in here yet? When did you arrive?" Olivia took control of the conversation, knowing the girl would likely follow along out of deeply ingrained habit of politeness.

"Yeah, I had dinner last night. I got here yesterday afternoon," Shari said, slumping into one of the chairs across the table.

"What suite did you get?"

"Orange Blossom."

Olivia paused at the familiar name, a broad smile painting her mouth. "That's a lucky one. A… friend of mine who graduated out not long ago was in your room."

"Yeah?" A hopeful sparkle lit up Shari's amber-colored eyes.

"Yep. He's doing great, too. He's a lot of the reason I decided to come back, actually."

The waiter stopped by to drop off their menus. Shari visibly shrank back from it.

"I can make recommendations if you like. There's nothing bad here, but I do have some favorites. Do you have any allergies or things you don't care for?"

Shari's hands disappeared into her lap. "I'm allergic to pine nuts."

Olivia tried to school the twitch in her mouth. "That's pretty workable. Did you report it when you got here? Chef Jean-Pierre is stellar about accommodating allergies and preferences."

"Yeah, it's in bold letters all over my paperwork."

"You'll be well taken care of, then. Anything stand out when you look at the menu?"

Olivia would wager a large amount of money this decadent display had the girl terrified.

"I haven't had potato soup in a long time."

"It's delicious. I've had it a couple of times. It pairs perfectly with the roast chicken. My favorite dessert is the tiramisu, but if you ask nicely, he'll let you have one of each." She winked at Shari, hoping what she was saying was encouraging.

"Okay."

"See there? Easy."

When the waiter came back, they made their requests before being plunged into awkward silence for a few minutes. Shari used a fingertip to trace patterns in the condensation of her water glass while Olivia tried to find another conversation starter.

"Is there anything you want to know? About this place or... me?"

Shari met her eye, surprise in her light brown orbs. "Really? You'll just tell me?"

Olivia laughed. "Well, kind of depends what it is, but probably."

"Did you really come back because you wanted to?"

Olivia was relieved the question she asked wasn't something difficult right off the bat.

"Yep. I know it sounds bizarre, but the decision was one hundred percent mine."

Shari's face screwed up and at Olivia's encouragement by example, she reached for the basket of rolls the waiter had delivered.

"Why?"

"Because I needed help. And while I'm not rolling in wads of cash, I knew I could afford to come back here to get it. I already knew Dr. Clay would help me. I already knew I felt comfortable here, even if I never wanted to admit that's how I felt the first time around. So it seemed like the logical choice."

The girl accepted this as she methodically shredded the roll into infinitesimal bites.

"Why did you take the show if you didn't need the money?" Confusion pulled her mouth into a frown as she asked.

"Well, at the time, I *did* need the money. Pretty much everything in my life changed when I decided to leave here before my program was over to take that show." Olivia paused, seeing a rapid replay in her mind of everyone laughing at her as she realized she was the butt of the joke. She flashed through the conversation with her mother, the arrival of Jerry, the arrest.

"Was it terrible?" Shari was staring intently at Olivia now, and she couldn't help but wonder if the next destination for this girl was jail. She was giving Olivia every ounce of her rapt attention.

"Jail?"

"Yeah."

"It wasn't *fun*." Olivia chuckled. "It was hard. It's supposed to be, though. And I still got super lucky. I was in a cell block with mostly non-violent inmates. My cellmates weren't interested in battling it out for power. Everyone mostly left me alone and I got to do a whole lot of thinking. What I discovered is I didn't like anything about who I was or how I'd acted and I needed to change."

Shari nodded, and they both sat back as their soup arrived.

"I don't think I want to go to jail," Shari said, spooning up some soup, then tilting her spoon so it would fall back into the bowl. Olivia wondered how long it would take her to actually eat some. She hadn't consumed any of the roll she'd destroyed; it was all a pile of mangled crumbs on the bread plate.

"I don't think you want to go to jail, either," Olivia parroted. "Are you worried that might happen?"

Shari nodded again, slowly. "Yes. If I don't do well here."

"Then do well here," Olivia said, taking a bite of her roll dipped in the soup, hoping it encouraged Shari to do the same. She was pleased when the girl sipped a shallow spoonful, discovered she liked it, and went back for more.

"How do I do that?"

"Participate in your therapy sessions. It's going to seem weird and dumb sometimes, but answer the questions. Be honest. Don't blow off Dr. Clay or whoever is assigned to you. They really are trying to help. It's not just a put-on."

Shari stared at Olivia for a long moment, as though trying to detect a lie in her words. Eventually, she nodded and took a bite of her food.

"This is good," she muttered.

"*Definitely* eat as much as you can, as often as you can. It's integral to working the program." Olivia winked at the skeptical girl, who released a slow smile in response.

"Okay." The word was barely above a whisper, but it preceded her digging in with what was likely her version of gusto.

Olivia kept up small talk as they made their way through the courses, pleased when Shari finished at least half of everything, including each dessert.

"Come find me if you need anything," Olivia invited, pausing at the bottom of the stairs as she'd done so many times with Ollie. "I'm up in Juniper. I'm sure I'll be around. And you're always welcome to eat with me if you want. Like I said, I'm probably going to be by myself. I make friends easier than I used to, but I'm not popular. People recognize me, just like you did."

Shari still appeared shy, but much more warmed up than she had when dinner had started.

"Okay. Thanks, Olivia."

"No problem. Goodnight."

"'Night."

As the girl wandered down the hall, Olivia wondered if the surge of happy feelings was the reason Dr. Clay did her job.

And she found herself wanting to see the information on mentoring. If she could help the Sharis who came through the doors at Sunrise, she wanted to. All she'd done was eat dinner with someone, and it seemed to have changed their whole day. That was easy, especially when it was Jean-Claude's food.

As she washed her face, she considered how the rush of endorphins from helping someone was just another high to chase, but maybe it wasn't one of the dangerous ones.

Maybe.

As the perfect cap to her night, it was tech day, so she got to talk to Ollie via text. He was so close, yet so far away, and she realized she was anxious to see him again despite how recently she'd been with him.

> **OLLIE:** How are you settling in? Have you braced yourself for ALL THE THERAPY?
> **OLIVIA:** Had a group session already today. I'm actually glad to have some time to talk with Dr. Clay. Who am I?
> **OLLIE:** I'm proud of you, Princess.

The simple words hit her straight in the heart. She took a deep breath as the wave of emotion washed over her, threatening tears.

> **OLIVIA:** Thanks. I ate some dinner for you. And I already got some cookies.
> **OLLIE:** I'm so jealous. Tell Jean-Pierre I miss him desperately and when I get filthy rich I'm going to lure him away from there to be my private chef. On my yacht.

She laughed, drawing the attention of the helper who was wandering around behind them.

OLLIVIA: Will do.

She set the phone down on the counter next to her, smiling. She missed him already, and she'd only been gone a few days. While adorable, she also realized the attachment she was forming with Ollie needed to be treated with caution and probably examined with Dr. Clay.

The phone buzzed again and she lifted it finding another message.

OLLIE: Do great things, little butterfly. I'll see you
soon. Text whenever you can, okay?
OLIVIA: I will. Thank you again. For all you did.

He sent back a wink-face emotion, and she turned the screen off.

Between that revelation and her pride at having impressed Dr. Clay, she laughed at how full circle everything had come for her where Sunrise was involved.

"You're ridiculous," she chided herself before opening one of the laptops to take care of her email.

She watched a few minutes of TV in the living area before heading to bed.

Tomorrow was another day, and for a change, she was looking forward to it and its possibilities.

OLIVIA WAS PLEASED to find Shari waiting at the table she considered hers the following morning for breakfast.

The girl was still rotating between glaring daggers at anyone who happened to look her way, acting bored by all the goings on of the busy room, and anxiously seeking attention from the very people she was actively trying to push away with her angry or bored faces.

Olivia considered her approach carefully as she poured them both a coffee, deciding instead of her usual pastries and eggs, it needed to be a full, luxuriously filling breakfast day.

"How did you sleep?"

"Okay, I guess."

Olivia found herself biting her tongue to stop herself from asking what the bed smelled like. She knew it was completely inappropriate and not at all realistic to hope the bedding, which was meticulously cared for and cleaned, would retain any of Ollie's cedar scent.

"I'm glad to hear it." Olivia accepted the basket of pastries the waiter offered, scanning the contents quickly. After making her selection, she placed it in the center of the table.

"Do you just go ask them to make whatever eggs you want?" Shari asked, eyes wide as she took in the omelet bar and buffet at the end of the room. "Or do you just do coffee with a pastry?"

Olivia laughed. "There's no meal or snack here I don't allow myself to enjoy. I know it's a hard adjustment, but you need the energy. Therapy is draining, even when it's something like painting or listening to different colors of noise or yoga."

"Different colors of noise?"

"Yeah. White, pink, red… there's a bunch. The static is all different frequencies."

"Huh. Who knew?"

Oliva nodded sympathetically. Who indeed?

Shari grimaced as she glanced over at the buffet tables. "I guess I could do the oatmeal."

"Oh for sure. It's just the right texture. The waffles are to die for too. They will cook them fresh right there while you wait."

Horror returned to the younger woman's face. Olivia could almost see the calorie and fat gram calculations crossing over her features.

"If you're set on the oatmeal, by all means. You can get cute little sides of milk or this amazing homemade jam, applesauce… whatever you like, it's delicious. But I'm probably having the blueberry pancakes with some bacon and a couple of eggs."

Shari shifted around before reaching for the coffeepot and pouring herself a cup.

"Don't you worry about gaining weight?" Her voice was quiet, the tone somewhere between shame and shock.

Olivia shrugged. "I used to. Before I came here, I was on a very strict meal and exercise plan so I was always camera ready, but I was beyond tired. I didn't even know how hungry I really was until I started eating regularly. My stomach rebelled for a few days, but adjusted fine. I gained a few pounds, but I actually like my body better a little bigger. And it likes me back for giving it some decadent food."

Shari stirred a packet of sweetener into her cup, the clang of the spoon on the side of the mug loud in the quiet space between them, but said nothing. Olivia could see her computing what she was saying, though, and it clearly wasn't the only time she'd thought about it.

"The ideas of what you should eat, look like, act like, all that? It's bullshit for the most part. If you can, in all honestly, you have to let some of it go. Do you want to go back to what you were doing before you got sent here?"

"No, not really. I mean, I'd love to model, but what I was doing before wasn't even fun. It was mostly a lot of 'never do these things' and 'you can't do this' and hearing I wasn't good enough or skinny enough or pretty enough…" Shari scrubbed her cheeks with her palms, trying to chase away the tears before they fell.

Olivia's heart squeezed for the young woman.

"Exactly. So, some fat and carbs won't hurt. Besides, you can swim them off, or do some yoga or kickboxing… there are lots of choices. Sometimes healing comes in the form of food." She punctuated her statement by taking a bite of the fruit danish. A relieved grin cracked Shari's pensive face again.

"If you say so."

Pleased, Olivia smiled widely at the girl, and they enjoyed some small talk over their cups of coffee as Shari geared up to collect some food.

Olivia learned Shari was barely twenty-one and had been trying to break into modeling since she was freshly sixteen. She'd been sent to Sunrise as a last stop before jail for getting involved with an illegal operation dealing in prescription meds. While Olivia didn't know anything about that in particular, she related to the girl and her story.

Pauline came around to give her normal speech about the mentor system shortly after Shari sat back down, and Olivia saw her eyes linger on the pair of them sitting together more than once.

While she never would have predicted she could be a positive influence or support system for anyone, she would be more than happy to take up the mantle for Shari. She could understand now why Ollie wanted to do the things he'd talked about before she signed back in. Now that she was outside her own head, it was something she could see herself being fulfilled by.

Life was nothing but one big surprise lately.

PAULINE WAS HANGING around during the group therapy session, and Olivia flagged her down as the session broke up.

"Hi, Olivia. Everything okay?"

"Yes, everything's fine. I just wanted to talk to you about the mentor and mentee thing? I have someone I've been talking to already so I wanted to get my vote in. If that's a thing. I know usually people on the thirty-day track don't participate."

Pauline smiled. "How wonderful. I'm sure we can figure something out. Come with me for a moment, we can chat."

Pauline strode with purpose toward the dining room. She tucked them into a quiet corner table and jotted down some notes on her trusty clipboard notebook as she nibbled on a cookie.

"Alright. Go ahead and tell me what's been going on, Olivia. I'm all yours."

Olivia recounted the easy friendship she'd fallen into with Shari and how a partnership seemed like a logical match.

Pauline nodded, scribbling down notes.

"How wonderful, Olivia. I appreciate you reaching out to Shari like you have and appreciate that you thought to come to me. This makes things much simpler when the group gets to the mentor stage of the program. You're right, it's usually exclusive to residents on the intensive program, but I'm betting we can find a way to adjust things. You're doing well?"

"Yes, I believe so."

"Glad to hear it. Dr. Clay reports positive things as well. I don't get specifics, but she's mentioned you are much more enthusiastically involved this time."

"I am. I feel different this time."

"I'm so happy to hear it." Pauline grabbed a second cookie from the basket on the table and leaned back.

Olivia noticed dark smudges under the director's eyes. Pauline never let on when she was tired or overwhelmed. She always had time to have a word or get you something if you needed it. Olivia realized it must be an exhausting endeavor to do such a job, no matter the cushy trappings or cost of the treatment.

"Are you alright?" Olivia asked.

Stunned, Pauline's face went blank. She quickly recovered, sitting up in her seat and chuckling. "Yes, yes, of course. Just a bit tired, you know how it goes."

"Sure."

"Well. I'd better get back to my paperwork." She stood, rapping her knuckles on the table, before turning to leave. "Thanks again."

"Sure," Olivia repeated, her insides swirling uncomfortably.

Never before had she been so aware of other people and their emotions. It simply hadn't been something that occurred to her or was expected of her. Gauging how casting directors were responding to her performance? Sure. Feeling out the emotions and moods of everyone in a room? Absolutely. But individual empathy wasn't one of her skills. Not until recently, anyway.

It was very disconcerting while also being quite thrilling. It was evidence of growth. Change. Maturity.

Beaming, Olivia left the dining hall, two cookies in hand. She crossed the courtyard to the residence hall, giving a longing glance at the shimmering pool. Sunday couldn't come soon enough. She wanted to spend an entire day lounging on a chair or floating around in the water.

On auto-pilot, she went right to the Orange Blossom suite and knocked on the door.

When a disgruntled-looking Shari answered, Olivia was thrown for a momentary loop, even though she'd known going in it wouldn't be Ollie behind the door.

"I stopped off for a snack. Want one?"

Shari examined the treats.

"Sure." She selected the one with extra chocolate chunks, leaving the white chip one for Olivia.

"Sorry, you're not also allergic to macadamias, are you? They touched."

A gentle smile spread across Shari's mouth. "No, just pine nuts. Thanks though."

"No problem. See you at yoga?"

"Yeah."

Olivia waved, feet already carrying her down the hall so she could climb the stairs to her room.

She was going to have a very different kind of stay at Sunrise this time around, if only through sheer force of will.

"LISTEN, I KNOW you're here for a month, but have you given any thought to what you'll do after your time at Sunrise is up?" Dr. Clay asked at the end of their next session.

Olivia shook her head, a rough snort coming out as a laugh. Dr. Clay had no idea how lost she was about anything to do with her life after Sunrise.

"I don't have any plans. Well, aside from reassembling my entire life, but no specifics. Why?"

"I think you might have a knack for being a mentor, is all. We'll, of course, continue to evaluate as you go through your program. Something to keep in mind if you're interested. We talked to Ollie about something similar. You two have a particular… knowledge base, let's call it. It's exceptionally useful for the clientele who seeks out Sunrise."

Olivia knew she was talking about all the ugly shit that came along with the fame business.

"What does it entail, exactly?"

Dr. Clay leaned a hip against one of the folding tables where they set up the coffee bar and snacks for the meeting.

"As you know, we have mentors who are residents getting ready to graduate out, but we also have mentors who have successfully completed their programs and come in to give extra help upon request. Some are seeking training in the healing arts or as therapists, others are graduates who have returned to their regular lives but come back to help on and off. We always need more of both kinds."

"I…" The idea settled on Olivia's shoulders with a comforting weight. Something about it felt like a good fit, but she wasn't sure quite what. She wasn't a people person, but she did feel compelled to put her hand out for people like Shari. "I'll think about it. Do you have something I can look over? I just want to be sure I know what I'm committing to."

"Of course. I'll pull together some paperwork before our next one-on-one." Dr Clay rested her hand on Olivia's shoulder. "I'm proud of you. I'll see you tomorrow, okay?"

"Okay."

Pride surged through Olivia's chest. Getting such praise from a woman she'd hated a few short months ago conjured an interesting combination of emotions.

Still smiling, she went off toward the patio, ready to celebrate with some time on a floaty in the pool.

OLIVIA'S DAYS AT Sunrise raced by at break-neck speeds.

Suddenly, three weeks and a couple of days didn't seem like nearly enough time to work on herself and help Shari along, though they managed to fall into a comfortable partnership quickly. She went to her sessions, made sure to take advantage of the pool as often as she could manage, and shared all the secrets of the facility as she could with her new mentee.

Olivia made sure Shari ate as much as possible, encouraged her to talk to Dr. Collins openly in her one-on-ones, and share in group often if she wanted to. As she'd expected, the modeling industry and all the bullshit rules around it had ground the poor girl up and spit her out. She'd had to navigate some things Olivia never had because of the pills she'd gotten used to having around, but for the most part, they were a perfect match. Shari was like the sweet little sister Olivia had never had.

She watched her brighten every single day and loved their after-hours conversations the same way she'd loved the ones with Ollie. They met at the same seating area in the evenings to discuss their day, drink some seltzer, and sometimes, eat the cookies Jean-Pierre put out in little baskets for them.

On tech nights, Olivia talked to Ollie, their phone conversations threaded with heavy flirtation that frustratingly, had no real place to go since she was being monitored. More than once, he had her blushing from what he said, knowing she couldn't respond in kind.

She went from meal to meal, session to session, and it all blurred together. Peace found her, and it was just as surprising as everything else along the journey had been.

BEFORE SHE KNEW it, her thirty days were already coming to an end.

Ollie was planning to pick her up and she couldn't wait to see him in person. They had regularly used her tech time talking on the phone or texting, but she couldn't wait to hug him.

Shari was doing well, but Olivia was still sad to leave her. She knew Shari would be okay, but she loved getting to see her blossom as she progressed through her treatment.

In her last one on one with Dr. Clay, there were genuine tears.

"I'm really pleased with your progress, Olivia. I'm so glad you came back."

"Me too."

"Did you have a chance to look at the recommendations for doctors to see once you leave?"

The truth was she'd scanned through them, but still wasn't sure where she'd be living when she left. Olivia said as much.

Dr. Clay nodded in understanding. "As we talked about once before, that's totally okay. We simply want to arm you with good choices so you can continue with your progress once you leave Sunrise grounds." She folded her arms at the wrist over the top of her notebook. "As for the mentor program… have you made a decision?"

"I think so. I've loved having that kind of dynamic with Shari, like I've mentioned. I think… I think I would be really happy to sign on. Besides, it gives me something to look forward to. I don't have anything else going on."

"How wonderful! I'll make sure Pauline knows you made a decision, so she can start getting the paperwork rolling." She chuckled. "That part of her job never ends, poor thing."

Olivia felt buoyant. Her head was clear, she was well-fed and ready to start the next part of her life. It had been one hell of a year, but she was coming out of it a brand-new person.

A *whole* person. Perhaps for the first time ever. And on her own terms, which was definitely a novel situation as well.

Dr. Clay asked Olivia a number of questions as she went down a lengthy check-sheet. Smiling, she got out a rubber stamp and applied it to the bottom of the last page.

"You're all clear to check out of the inpatient program of Sunrise, Malibu, Olivia. We're so proud of you, and hope you find your best life outside those gates."

Immediately, Olivia's throat clogged with emotion and hot tears formed in her eyes. Having someone like Dr. Clay be proud of her was a much bigger deal than she'd ever imagined. More than that, she was proud of herself.

"Thank you so much."

Olivia stood, and Dr. Clay reached out her arms.

"Only if you want," she said quietly.

Without hesitation, Olivia held out her own arms, sharing a hug with the doctor she had hated on sight when she'd first arrived, and now owed a huge debt of gratitude to.

"Thank you," Olivia repeated.

"You're so welcome. Now…" Dr. Clay swiped her fingertips under her eyes, removing the moisture there. "Go pack up. Tell Chef Jean-Pierre you want one of every single one of your favorite dishes before you leave and get ready to start your life."

Olivia gave a sharp nod, not trusting herself to speak again.

As she moved through the building, everything seemed just as it should be, but also very distant. She wondered if her mind was already trying to claim some separation so leaving wouldn't hurt quite so much.

At that, Olivia snorted a laugh.

Leaving rehab was hard? Emotional? She didn't even recognize herself.

Meditation and yoga were definitely something she'd have to find a way to integrate into her daily routine at home. Surely, there was a video online that could coach her through the poses a lot like instructor Jay.

It was too hopeful, and probably not healthy to plan on anything with Ollie, but when she pictured herself on a yoga mat, it was next to him. Jenkins was there too, throwing bored, judgmental glances from the back of the sofa.

Olivia smiled as she stretched out her muscles and focused on her breathing.

When she got back to her room, she took a quick shower before heading over to the dining hall. She might miss the meals from the kitchen at Sunrise more after leaving the second time.

She'd gotten completely spoiled, especially after Shari became her dining companion and she was overly enthusiastic in order to encourage her hesitant table mate.

As had become their routine, Shari was waiting at their usual table with a basket of bread and their drinks in front of her.

"How was yoga?" She asked.

"I'm all loosened up and ready to chow," Olivia smiled. "And you? How was music therapy?"

Shari smeared the whipped honey butter on a yeast roll. "Really fun, actually. We're still working through the full Beatles catalogue with interpretive dance."

"Ooh, nice."

Olivia took a piece of the dark bread she loved. Shari had put on a few pounds, but more importantly, seemed to be thriving under the help Sunrise provided.

"It's almost leaving day," Shari said, looking at Olivia with glassy eyes.

Olivia wouldn't have believed it if someone had told her everyone would be crying because she was leaving, herself included. From joy maybe, to be rid of her finally, but this was an unexpected turn of events.

"It is. But I'll be back."

Shari's face pinched. "You will? Why?"

"I don't know what the details are yet, but I agreed to be a special circs mentor."

"Oh!" Shari brightened. "I love that for you. I don't know what would have happened to me if you hadn't invited me to sit with you on my first day."

"You helped me too. You keep telling me I have all my shit together and how I'm doing so much for you, but it goes both ways." Olivia stopped to fan her eyes. "I don't want to cry through dinner."

Shari nodded, her laugh subdued. "I'm not used to having this many feelings, it's fucking weird."

They enjoyed as much food as they could, then sat for a while with their feet in the pool, watching the stars come out before going their separate ways.

"Goodnight, Olivia."

"'Night, Shari. See you in the morning."

"Last morning." She sighed.

"Yeah."

Unsure what else to say, they drifted their own ways.

In her room, Olivia double checked all the drawers and cabinets to be sure she had everything packed up. It felt as though she'd just arrived. This was the only bedroom she'd ever had any positive attachment to, and it felt strange to be preparing to leave it.

Ollie called as usual during their last tech time.

"Hey. You ready to blow that pop stand?" He teased.

"Actually, I'm kind of sad to go," she said, dropping onto the bed.

"I get it. You sound happy, O. You feeling ready for the world?"

She smiled, the concern in his voice making her heart squeeze.

"I'm great. Better than great, even. I agreed to be a special circumstance mentor. You signed up for it too, right?"

"Yeah, I did. I know the girl you've been helping probably could use someone to call. I think it's great."

"Dr. Clay was pretty excited. Me too, honestly."

"I can't wait to see you, O."

"Me too. Are we going back to your place after?"

Ollie got a devious tone to his voice. "Actually, I thought we might spend a night or two at the beach. We're right there, and you keep saying how all you want to do is lay in the sand for a while. I thought it was the perfect opportunity."

Olivia's heart thudded. This man. He was so considerate.

"Really?"

"Really."

"Sounds perfect." The tears she'd done so well tamping down returned with a vengeance.

"Hey now. None of that. Unless those are tears of joy?"

Olivia chuckled through the thickness in her throat. "They are. I think."

"You think?" Ollie laughed with her. "I guess I'll take it. Sweet dreams, okay? I'll see you tomorrow?"

"Okay." The words neither of them had yet dared to say lingered right at the back of her tongue. "Good night, Ollie."

"'Bye, Princess."

She knew it was dangerous to be thinking about love. But she didn't have any other word for what this might be.

Later, as she tucked herself under the blankets, she tried to memorize the sounds she'd miss when she was in another bed the following night.

CHAPTER *Thirty*

SUNRISE'S OFFICIAL GRADUATION ceremony was essentially a short group therapy session.

The graduates sat in the uncomfortable plastic chairs in the massive living room of the main building, their normal circle two half-moons, one behind the other. The staff was gathered at the front of the chairs, standing and smiling back at the residents.

Instead of the normal breakfast, there were tables full of special treats set up under shady canopies in the grassy area of the yard. After the ceremony was complete, family members would be invited in to help celebrate, walk around the grounds at which point... the graduates could leave. Go home. Go shopping. Go to the beach. Whatever they wanted.

It was still odd to Olivia, but she was beyond excited to see Ollie and get to the ocean.

"We are all so very proud of what you've accomplished during your stays here at Sunrise," Pauline said, hands clasped together near her chest. "Now it's time to go out into the real world and apply what you've learned to your everyday life. Remember, we're always here if you need us." She stepped back, looking a bit teary-eyed.

Altogether, there were eight residents graduating out. Olivia had a fleeting thought campus would look rather empty once they were gone.

"Today is the end of this journey, but the beginning of the next," Dr. Clay said, giving a bright smile that matched Pauline's. "To confirm your completion of your programs, we have a little certificate and token you can keep with you as a reminder of what you've accomplished."

One by one they went up to the front, accepting a piece of paper and a little metal coin with a sun stamped on it from the staff. When they'd all finished, there were a few hugs shared around before Pauline basically shooed them out the door.

"Go! Hug your loved ones and get something to eat."

Olivia was buoyant as she exited the building, the pool, as always, a welcome sight. She was looking for Ollie in the sprinkling of people milling around between the food tents and the seats, but her heart stuttered to a stop when she recognized the older gentleman in a tie walking her direction.

"Dad?"

"Hi, Liv."

"What… what are you doing here?"

He looked at the ground, then off to the side. "This is quite the place, isn't it?" Olivia knew him well enough to see his discomfort disguised as distraction.

"Yeah, it's really gorgeous."

"Let's get something to eat and sit, yeah?"

"Okay," Olivia dragged the syllables out, heart pounding against her ribs. Her dad had come to her graduation. Pulse already jumping, her stomach pitched at her next thought. "Is… is Mom here?"

He had already turned and was loping toward the food line. He glanced over his shoulder. "No. She… she didn't come."

"Oh. That's okay." Disappointment was in Olivia's tone, surprising even her. She and her mother had, in no uncertain terms, parted ways for the foreseeable future, but there was still part of her seeking her parents' approval. Both of them. "I was expecting someone else, too." She glanced around, but Ollie was nowhere to be seen. "But I don't see him yet."

They made their way through the buffet line, Olivia piling her plate with every extravagant item she wanted. Her father, who had only seen her eat the carefully measured, pre-portioned items approved by her mother, chuckled.

"That's the spirit."

"You have no idea. I'm going to miss this food so, so much."

They shared a laugh, the sound of it making Olivia's chest ache. How long had she waited to speak more than two words to her father, let alone laugh with him? There was tension between them, no doubt, but he was looking her in the face for the first time in years. Talking to her in full sentences.

He'd *shown up* for her.

They took a seat at one of the long picnic tables they'd brought out for the occasion.

"So…" he said, after tucking into the omelet and bacon on his plate. "What's next?"

"I don't know for sure, honestly. But I agreed to come back as a special circumstances mentor, so at least some of the time I'll be here."

"Oh?" Her father's eyes were the kind, blue orbs she remembered from her childhood. "Listen, Olivia." His mouth drew tight as he set his fork down. He laced his fingers together, elbows on the table. "I owe you an apology."

Impulse rode her to say something along the lines of it being okay, he didn't, but she held her tongue. She held his gaze instead, encouraging him to continue.

"I…" He shook his head, unable to keep up the eye contact. "I'm sorry, honey. When you turned eighteen and decided to do the films you did, I didn't know what to do. You were my little girl, and you were filming… well." He couldn't even form the words, clearly still struggling with some of the choices she'd made. Choices her mother had pushed on her more than she'd realized at the time.

"You were doing it for money, which I could understand, but you were still my baby. And I just, I couldn't get my mind around my daughter being a young woman doing that kind of job. Inevitably, the guys on the crew would find out, and…"

"I know it wasn't easy to deal with, Dad." She offered no apology. There wasn't one to give. For better or worse, she'd made the choice and it had led to a path she'd followed for her career for years. She'd heard all about the teasing he'd gotten from the guys on his crew, especially early on. He'd fired quite a few people before they all figured out not to bring it up. She'd heard her parents talking about it once, and someone had been bold enough to start watching one of her movies on his phone on the job site.

"It wasn't, but you didn't deserve how I continued to react. When you were in jail, I realized I was responsible for allowing a lot of what happened to take place. I didn't realize you were carrying as much as you were. Your mother…" He grimaced and shook his head. "After you sold the house, a lot of things came to light I should have known about. I should have been paying closer attention to say the least. I'm sorry. Maybe if I'd done things differently, you wouldn't have ended up here. You wouldn't have done those things. I should have said something, I was trying to keep my head in the sand because your mother had everything handle I was angry when Jerry showed up to tell us you were selling the house, but I think now it was the right thing to do."

The lump in Olivia's throat grew impossible to ignore. Hot tears burned in her eyes and it was only a matter of time before they started streaming down her face. He was giving her the apology she'd craved for years. Validation. Actual attention.

"Dad, I'm sorry about the house—"

"No, no," He cleared his throat, moisture gathering in his eyes too. "Please don't be. I didn't know about the taxes. I should have known everything. I just put my head down and went to work. I messed up."

Breakfast was forgotten as they built the foundational planks of a bridge between them.

He nodded, grunting over the lump in his throat. "I'm proud of you, Olivia. I love you. And I hate how I wasted so many opportunities to tell you so."

"I love you too, Dad."

Those words were all it took to push her emotions completely over the edge. She buried her face in her hands and sobbed, not caring who might see. Graduating was one thing, but this? This was a gift she couldn't quantify a value for.

When she finally stopped the flow of tears, she looked at her dad, who was not so casually wiping his face with one of the cloth napkins.

Unsure how to proceed, Olivia picked up her fork and picked at her food.

"I really appreciate you coming today."

Her father nodded, taking a bite of some fruit, before pushing his plate away. "I should have been here for you a lot sooner."

Her heart couldn't take any more. Her soft-spoken, often silent father had spilled his guts and continued to say all the right things.

"We can't go back, Dad. Just be here now."

He scanned her face, as though finally seeing her clearly.

"Solid advice. I think I'll take it. Here." He dug in his pocket. "This is yours."

Olivia took the familiar car key from his hand. She had her copy back at Ollie's apartment.

"My car?"

Her dad nodded. "It was always yours. For your mom to try and keep it… wasn't right. I talked her into surrendering her key. You can switch over all the paperwork into your name, too. It's ready for you to pick up whenever you want. Just let me know when you're ready."

"Thanks, Dad." Olivia smiled broadly, burning bright from the inside out with joy.

And that was before she spotted the handsome actor making his way across the lawn with his intense focus set on her.

Thirty-One

OLIVIA BEAMED AT Ollie as he approached the table. From the corner of her eye, she saw her father assess the man headed directly toward them, but he said nothing. At least not yet.

"Mind if I interrupt?" Ollie gestured to Olivia.

"Of course," her dad said, standing up. "I'll take care of these plates. Might find a little something else, too."

"Dad," Olivia said, seeing the question on Ollie's face. "This is Oliver. Ollie, this is my dad."

Ollie stuck his hand out. "Nice to meet you, sir."

Her dad gripped Ollie's hand, giving it a firm shake. "Likewise. I'll be back," he said, taking the plates away.

Ollie pulled Olivia up out of her seat and into his arms. "I'm so proud of you, Princess." The words caressed her ear and neck warmly, sending tingles down her spine.

"Thank you. I'm proud of me too."

He grinned down at her, arms lashed around her for a moment longer before letting go.

"Your dad, huh?"

"Yeah." She blew out a breath, eyes landing on her father who had indeed picked up another plate and was collecting finger foods at the tents. "How about that."

"You doing alright?"

Olivia turned a smile at him. "I'm wonderful."

"Good to hear. You mind?" He waved a hand at the food tables.

"Of course not. I know you miss the food."

"So much." He chuckled, wandering away while rubbing his stomach.

The three of them had a stilted conversation when both Olivia's dad and Ollie returned to the table. Lots of questions about work dominated as the main topic of the conversation. Ollie no doubt learned more about concrete than he'd ever wanted to know. Olivia was pretty sure her dad was about to ask Ollie what his intentions were with his daughter, but he never did.

She increased the awkwardness between them shortly after when she slipped off to the ladies' room. On her way back, she got detoured by Pauline who stopped her to give her congratulations once again and a celebratory hug.

When Olivia got back to the table, Ollie and her dad were sitting in companionable silence. It was as though they'd simply depleted the pointless small talk already and were enjoying the quiet.

"Well, I think I'll make my way back," her dad said quietly.

"Already?" Disappointment flooded Olivia's body.

"I'm sure you're ready to get out of here and I've got a long drive ahead of me."

"Okay. Thanks again for coming, Dad. This was nice."

"It was."

They stood, embracing for a long moment. Olivia's heart thudded behind her ribs, desire to lock away this memory forever making her grasp for every possible descriptor of the moment. She could smell his familiar cologne, the rasp of his stubble on her cheek.

"I'll see you soon, okay? Maybe we can plan to get together one day soon."

"I'd like that."

He turned his attention to Ollie. "Pleasure to meet you, young man."

"Sir. The honor was mine."

Another quick hug, and her dad ambled off across the grass, disappearing into the main building.

"Wow," Olivia breathed.

"Yeah. It was definitely something, and I'm not even involved."

Olivia sat back down, the weight of their relationship no longer bogging her down.

"Hey," Ollie said, reaching across the table to take her hand. "You want to get out of here? I know a spot on the beach with your name on it."

"Absolutely. I just have to say goodbye to someone."

"Of course."

Olivia waved and said goodbye to people as they crossed the grass toward the resident building. If her guess was right, Shari would be between sessions.

Ollie hung back a bit as she entered the building, before walking confidently toward the Orange Blossom suite.

When she knocked on the door, Ollie smiled. "Excellent room."

"The best."

The door opened, and Shari peered out. "Are you leaving now?" She asked, voice small.

"I am. But I'll be back. Mentor program, remember?"

"Yeah."

Olivia glanced from Shari to Ollie, whom Shari was openly staring at.

"This is my friend Oliver. He was the one who stayed in this room the last time I was here."

"Really?" Shari appeared to be blushing.

"It's a great room. Nice to meet you, Shari."

"Hi." Her hands twisted together as she blinked at him for another moment or two. "I'll miss you at meals," she said quietly, darting forward for the world's fastest hug.

"Me too," Olivia said. "Remember what I told you, eat everything you can for as long as you can."

"I heard you. Eat and work the program. I got it."

"No jail."

Shari chuckled. "No jail. Go on, get out of here."

Olivia offered her number to the girl, just in case. She was still on the restricted tech privileges, but Olivia felt better having it in case of an emergency.

As they crossed the patio, she said a silent goodbye to the pool. Once they were on the other side of the front doors, she breathed deeply. Something had shifted. She could feel the change in her bones.

If anyone had told her the same thing a few short months ago, she'd have rolled her eyes, called them an idiot, and gone along with her day after flipping her hair. But now? Now, she understood.

She caught Ollie's hand as they crossed the parking lot toward his car. "Thanks for coming to get me."

"Anytime, Princess. Are you glad you finally worked the program?"

She clucked her tongue at him, teasing as he unlocked and opened the passenger side door. "You know I am."

"Well then, that's the best possible outcome." He winked, waiting for her to drop into the seat before closing her door and sprinting around to the other side so he could get in.

She really was on the other side, and ready to tackle whatever came next.

Lucky for her, up next was a little casita on the beach.

DESPITE HER ENTHUSIASM at seeing him, and the way everything felt right when they were together, there was still a layer of tension separating them.

"So…" she started, but couldn't think of a single way to continue the sentence.

"So?" He chuckled, glancing over at her as he pulled up to a stoplight. "I picked a place up past the main part of town. Should be pretty private."

"Sounds great. Thanks for taking care of things. I do feel a little bougie taking a vacation after my month-long stay at Sunrise."

"Can you even imagine a day with no therapy sessions?"

Olivia shook her head, considering the thought as they passed by a shopping strip with an upscale grocery store and coffee shop. Part of her wanted to ask him to pull in, but the other part wasn't quite ready.

As though interpreting the way her fingertips went to her lips, he said, "We can come back out later. Things are pretty busy now, I figured we'd stop after we had a chance to get checked in and maybe had lunch. Okay?"

"Sure." She turned a smile on him, and he returned it, but the tension remained. "You feel it, right?" She asked.

"Yeah, I do. But we'll be okay. We weren't officially a couple before you went back in, and we're still finding our footing. I want to be very clear—I don't have any expectations." He turned his eyes her way and stress flashed in the depths.

"I know. Of course not." Olivia blushed. "I don't have any either. Well, I mean, aside from getting too much sun in my bikini and maybe having a cocktail."

Traffic lightened up as they passed the lagoon parking lot and most of the major shopping centers.

"Wait, is a cocktail okay? I don't want to drink in front of you if I shouldn't."

Ollie reached a hand over and patted her knee. Olivia would have been perfectly okay with him leaving it there, but he retracted it after the brief touch.

"Alcohol was never something I struggled with. Pills? Those would be a problem. Booze I indulged in too much for too long, but I could care less about most of the time. It was a good vehicle for pills. I still tend to avoid it, but you indulging once in a while is fine."

After a quiet moment, Ollie turned the car into a shallow driveway which led to a series of small houses, each at a decent distance along the rocky shore. He turned into the one labeled with a number six.

"Here we are."

She got her door open and out of the car before he could make it around, mostly because he paused to open the trunk.

"That's cheating," he teased as she circled around to help with the luggage.

"Once in a while won't hurt. Though I appreciate the chivalry." She tossed him a wink as she pulled the smaller bag from the trunk. "Thanks for bringing me some stuff. And for keeping all my junk while I was at Sunrise."

"Of course."

He left her on the tiny patio with the luggage and walked over to the office to retrieve the key. Olivia sat on one of the iron chairs, the warm sun soaking into her skin in a pleasant way as she turned her face upward.

The sound of the waves crashing only yards away mixed with the salt heavy on the air spoke to her soul.

After being able to see the water from the patio at Sunrise, the tease was finally over.

And if she had it guessed right, the ocean wasn't the only thing she'd been anticipating that was about to be fulfilled.

CHAPTER
Thirty-Two

OLLIE RETURNED WITH a key and some paperwork. He unlocked the door, gesturing for Olivia to go in first.

The beach front cabin was small, but felt airy thanks to the windows that ran both wide and high, giving nearly every room an immaculate view of the water.

Olivia paused at the compact chef-quality kitchen, then turned to the living area with comfortable chairs and sofa while Ollie brought in their bags.

As she was making her way down the hall, she paused. They hadn't discussed sleeping arrangements, but she shouldn't have doubted his forethought.

"Two bedrooms?"

Ollie rubbed the back of his neck, coming toward her, a lopsided grin on his mouth.

"We don't make assumptions, especially about things like that. Right, Princess?"

She returned his levity, smiling as he dipped close to

her face only to turn at the last moment and duck his head into the bathroom.

"Never."

"Pick whichever one you prefer. Doesn't matter one bit to me."

"Alright."

Olivia examined the rooms, which were nearly identical except for the direction the beach view faced and the paint color.

"I'll take peach."

"Perfect, guess that leaves me with yellow."

Ollie delivered their luggage accordingly, then they both stood there, staring at one another. After a moment, Olivia burst out laughing.

"Why is this so awkward?"

Ollie chuckled. "I don't know, but let's un-awkward it, yeah?" His lopsided grin transformed as he lowered his face toward hers, one of his hands reaching up to hold her face along the jawline.

The places his skin met hers burned as her body immediately reacted to his touch.

"I missed you," he breathed the words.

"Yes," she agreed, closing the little distance between them, pressing her lips to his.

Ollie made a noise in his throat, the littlest grumble that sent sparks to all of her extremities.

They reoriented themselves to one another, standing in the little beach house living room, pressed up against one another as they kissed long and slow. Ollie used his hand to guide her face, taking ownership of the moment and making Olivia melt into a puddle right there.

When he pulled away, she was breathless. Had he not been anchoring her to the ground, she might have floated straight to the ceiling.

"Come on, Princess. Let's hit the beach."

Words evaded her for a moment, his eyes peering into her soul as his thumb stroked her jaw.

"Sounds perfect."

Olivia pulled away from him and changed into one of the suits she'd found during their shopping expedition. She grabbed a beach towel from a stack near the sliding glass door leading from the living room out onto a small deck. Ollie wasn't far behind her, a tube of sunscreen in his hands and a pair of brightly colored trunks on.

"Safety first," he said, applying a thick layer to her back, neck, and arms. She helped him as well, then they stepped off the deck into the hot sand.

"I needed this," Olivia said, her toes reaching the cooler sand just under the heated top layer.

"I don't get to the ocean very often, but I always enjoy it when I do."

Olivia took a deep breath, the salty tang of the air coating her tongue.

They found a spot in the soft white sand to leave their towels, anchoring the corners with some rocks they dug out of the wet sand a few steps closer to the water.

Ollie was shading his eyes with one hand, watching her as though waiting for her to set an example for what came next.

There was a conversation they needed to have, and the urgency with which it pressed at her refused to be ignored. If they were going to go to the next step, she had to be sure he knew where she stood about their past.

"Listen, Ollie... I..." Her brows pulled together as she reconsidered where to start. The words wanted out, but they were disjointed.

Ollie turned, expression dropping as he took in her pensive features. "Everything okay?"

"Fine. It's fine. I just... I wanted to be sure you knew what happened between us a long time ago? It wasn't your fault." Ollie took a deep breath, nostrils flaring as he sucked in air. Olivia continued on, "I know I explained it before, but I instigated what happened. I just need to be very clear on that. Dr. Clay and I talked about it... about a lot of things, you know how it goes, and I'm guessing when I dropped the bomb about what happened between us that night in the club, you only heard part of what I said."

"No," he said with the slightest of grins. "I heard everything you said, Olivia. Every word. I appreciate you trying to clarify, though. I understand—it wasn't anyone's fault. You were there at the right place at the right time—"

"And I took advantage of the situation as it was presented to me, Ollie. I'm sorry for doing that. Truly."

He shook his head. "Maybe you did, but I don't blame you, Princess. Neither should you."

"But do you blame *you*? Because you shouldn't. That's all I'm trying to say. I bribed my way in, snuck past security, and maneuvered my way into your presence. I did all of those things on purpose, including heavy flirting, drinking, and dancing. I'm at least as much to blame for what happened as you are. If there's any blame at all."

Ollie nodded, gaze wandering momentarily out to the surf. "I did blame myself, at first. But I don't anymore. I don't blame you either. It's just a thing that happened. An important thing, but one event of a million I could get hung up on if I chose to. If you remember it fondly, then I can't be too upset about anything other than the fact that I can't remember it at all."

"Okay. Okay?" Her chest felt lighter, a weight she hadn't realized she was still carrying lifted.

"More than okay, Butterfly. I promise. Come on, let's go." He waved her along as he dashed into the surf. The day was hot, but the water was crisp and cool. She waded out to about waist deep, Ollie not far away in the water.

As the waves embraced her, she smiled.

"I'm glad you're happy here, Princess. If only I'd known it was this easy. We could have skipped all the shopping." Olivia flattened her palm and pushed a spray of water in his direction. "Kidding, only kidding."

She turned her face to the sun again, soaking in the rays as the waves rocked gently at her body.

"You're gorgeous, Olivia," Ollie rumbled, an easy grin

on his mouth as he allowed his body to roll with the water a few feet away.

The absolute sincerity of his words made her blush. "Not so bad yourself, handsome. Thanks for this. It's perfect."

"We aim to please."

To break up the heavy moment, Ollie ducked under the waves, yanking her legs out from under her. She surged back to the surface, sputtered the mouthful of saltwater she'd gotten, but laughing the whole time.

"So much for hair and makeup," she said, laughing too hard to put any venom into the words.

"Who needs 'em?" He asked playfully, dodging the water she was using her flattened hand to push his way.

They played in the water until she was too tired to continue battling the waves and her sunscreen was giving out along the back of her neck.

The sand was warm under her feet as she made her way across the beach to her towel, and the sun took care of drying her off in short order.

Ollie helped her reapply the cream so she didn't get burned, but it wasn't long before they had to make their way back to the house.

Anticipation built as they padded back across the scorching sand.

"You can shower first," Ollie offered as they used the outdoor shower to rinse off as much sand as possible.

What Olivia wanted to say was, "You could join me," but she held her tongue. It wouldn't do to rush into things at this point in the game. Or ever, really. As much as she wanted to move to the next phase of intimacy with Ollie, his comfort trumped anything else.

She washed quickly, forgoing anything but moisturizer on her face when she was done.

Ollie was on his phone when she came into the living room. Without looking up, he said, "I'm ordering a few groceries and dinner. Any requests?"

Relief swamped her. So much for being ready to go out into public and do normal things like shop for food.

"I'm sure you have it covered." She looked over his shoulder anyway, selecting some of the alcoholic seltzers as her boozy treat before he sent the order all the way through.

He went off to shower and she made her way around the room, looking through the cute decor they'd used, seeing what books were on the shelves, just admiring the space for all it was. She wasn't much of a cook, but the kitchen was similarly well appointed, so she took herself on a tour through there as well before heading off to her bedroom.

"You're killing time," she scolded herself as she pulled out a few outfits and hung them up so they wouldn't be quite so wrinkled.

She heard the water turn off in the bathroom, forcing herself to go out into the living room and relax while he got dressed. Olivia was like a nervous teenager. The threat of them having sex looming over her made her fidgety which made her feel ridiculous.

Ollie joined her a few minutes later, hair still wet as he sank into the cushion next to her.

"Food should be here soon."

"I'm fine," she said, picking at her nails as he flipped channels. On a whim, she told Ollie she'd be back in a minute and went into the bathroom.

The pink nail polish he'd bought her still resided in her makeup kit. She'd used it with Shari, but it had all worn off since they'd had a mini spa evening together.

It went on like a dream, so she painted a quick coat on her fingers, waving her hands around so it would dry faster.

He gave her a quizzical look when she came back, but a knock at the door interrupted any question he might have wanted to ask.

Ollie tipped the delivery driver, quickly loading the groceries into the fridge as quickly as Olivia could take things out of the bags and set them on the counter.

"Hey," he said with a grin, noticing her nails. "That's a pretty color on you."

"This amazing friend of mine gifted it to me a while back. It was a really impressionable moment, to be honest."

"Yeah?" His gaze heated as he lifted her knuckles to his lips. "Sounds like a good guy."

"I never said it was a guy," she teased.

"Mmm. My mistake."

Ollie pulled her close again, her chest pressed up against his as he slow-danced her in place.

"Are you hungry?" He asked. The rumble of his chest pressed against hers made her pulse spike. She couldn't help but wonder if he was actually talking about food. He tucked his face into her neck, teasing up and down with his nose.

"Starving," she replied, a burn starting in her blood.

His eyes drifted from hers down to her mouth, his lips parting slowly as he exhaled. "Me too, Butterfly. Me. Too."

"Ollie…" she sighed, desire pulsing through her body.

He heard the invitation she was giving and devoured her mouth, hands roving up and down her back as he walked them out of the kitchen and toward the sofa.

"Bedroom," she muttered around his lips, and he grunted, changing their course as he tugged at her shirt.

"Which one?" He panted, shucking his own shirt and flinging it somewhere down the hall.

"Doesn't matter."

He placed his hands on her ass and braced. Olivia took the cue and lifted her legs, locking them around his waist as he walked them into his room.

They fell together onto the comforter, his hardness pressed into the V of her legs as they bounced on the mattress.

"Yes," she gasped as he pulled her shirt over her head. "Yes, yes, yes…" She chanted it as he divested her of her pants, his not far behind.

He stopped suddenly, panting as he gazed down at her in nothing but her underwear.

"Everything okay?" She asked, the haze parting at the serious expression on his face.

"Perfect." He grinned, reaching for her once again as he lay himself gently on top of her, resuming the kiss they'd briefly broken.

Olivia ran her fingernails down his back, teasing the waistband of his boxer briefs where she could reach it.

She could feel him throbbing against her, right where her panties were already damp.

Ollie slid backward off the edge of the mattress, pulling her with him. He knelt down, dragging her panties down her legs and propping her feet on his shoulders.

"I need to taste you, Princess."

"Please." She could hear herself moaning, the anticipation of him touching her left her feeling as though she might burst out of her skin.

Ollie kissed his way up the inside of her left leg, stopping just before reaching her center. Then, torturously, he started over with the right ankle.

She channeled every ounce of patience she could muster, knowing it would be worth the wait... if she survived.

When he finally swiped his tongue along her, pausing to suckle at her sensitive nub, she arched her back off the bed. Encouraged by her reaction, he dove in with unmatched enthusiasm, feasting on her as though he'd been starving for years.

After she warned him she was careening her way to climax, he slowed his ministrations, much to her frustration.

He pressed a finger to her entrance, her wetness allowing it to slide easily inside. Frustratingly, he took his sweet time, moving one knuckle at a time.

"*Please*," she begged, an edge to her tone she didn't recognize.

Ollie grunted, and she looked down the length of her body to find his eyes on hers, a grin on his mouth as he added another finger and increased his speed once more.

She gasped as the orgasm whipped through her body, the contractions making her twitch against his mouth and press into his hand.

"Fuck, Princess. That might be the most beautiful thing I've ever seen."

Olivia was too drunk on sensation to respond properly. She used every bit of energy she had to slide her body backward on the bed, watching as he stood and stripped off his underwear.

He watched her with drowsy eyes for a moment before leaning to one side. Olivia's eyes were closed, blood still crashing in her ears, but she heard the wrapper open.

"Implant," she managed to mutter. When she opened her eyes, she saw he'd frozen with his hand on his cock.

He blinked slowly, twice.

"We can talk about that later. Safety first and always, yeah?"

"Whatever you're comfortable with." She gave him a smile she hoped was encouraging.

He crawled over her, bracing his weight on his forearms. "Okay, Princess?"

"Perfect," she confirmed.

Ollie pressed a kiss to her mouth as he pushed inside her body. She felt him gasp, and it was undoubtedly one of the sexiest sounds she'd ever heard.

"Fuck," he swore, fully seated inside her. She agreed one thousand percent.

Olivia lifted her hips, trying to get the friction she needed to go along with the fullness. Ollie slid one hand under her hips, lifting her body into his as he started to move.

She nipped at his full bottom lip, a second climax already building low in her abdomen.

"Yes," she moaned into his mouth as he began to find a rhythm, the thrusts progressing from gentle and cautious to intentional and punishing.

Olivia wondered how long it might have been since he truly let himself go. How long he might have held himself hostage from enjoying this kind of pleasure.

"I can't… you feel too good." He groaned and slowed down nearly to a stop. He drew himself out of her body excruciatingly slowly before pressing back in, one millimeter at a time.

Olivia grumbled a complaint, trying to chase his body with hers, clinging to the frantic energy that had been building. He was having none of it and when she moved toward him, he moved back.

"Patience, Princess. I don't want to embarrass myself again." The grin on his mouth made her melt, despite her frustration.

She smirked, dropping one hand to where they met and rubbing in drowsy, slick circles over her clit.

He made a pained noise. "Killing me." He plunged as deep as he could go, then proceeded to build a slow, intentional rhythm. He replaced his hand with the pad of his thumb after pressing it to her lips and having her suckle on it for a moment.

She could feel him pulse inside her walls in direct response to how close she was getting to climaxing again. As she moaned out, thighs trembling as she teetered on the edge of release, he pulled her as close as he could get her, turning his head and biting lightly into her shoulder. She grasped along his back with her fingernails as sparks went off behind her eyes. He drove into her, shuddering with his own climax as her body tensed from her toes to the roots of her hair.

There was no time or space, only sensation as they lay there together.

"Thank you, Olivia," Ollie breathed, planting a sweet kiss on her temple.

Overwhelmed, a tear sprang to her eye, but she never stopped smiling.

CHAPTER
Thirty-Three

EVENTUALLY, THEY DISENTANGLED themselves and Ollie went off to get cleaned up. Olivia managed to find the ability to move again while he was gone and went off to take care of some things herself once he got back.

She came back to the bedroom to find him sitting on the edge of the bed in some sweats. He looked up at her, adoration in his eyes as she lingered in the doorway. She was still naked, the way he was drinking her in resolving any internalized issues she might have had about her body.

Still, as she crossed the room, Olivia grabbed her t-shirt. She pulled it on before sitting beside him.

"You okay?" She asked.

He nodded, pulling her in for another brief kiss. "I'm great. I knew it would be worth the wait, but holy shit. You nearly killed me, Princess."

"I could say the same. Come on, let's find something to eat."

Olivia got up, reaching a hand behind her. He took it and followed her into the kitchen.

"I got lots of things we could graze on," he said, pulling trays of cut fruit and cheese out of the fridge.

"Perfect." She glanced down at herself. "I'm going to go find some pants."

"No need for formality on my account." He winked at her.

"Not my couch," she laughed. In her room, she dug a pair of panties and some yoga pants out of her bag and pulled them on. By the time she got back, he had a full spread on the coffee table.

"Movie?"

"Sure."

They piled onto the couch to eat and watch, replicating a pattern they'd loved at his apartment.

"Where's Jenkins?" She asked, the idea of the sweet cat being home alone for multiple days was bothersome.

"My dad is cat-sitting."

"The whole time?" Olivia selected a piece of ham to go with her cheese and chunk of cantaloupe.

"Nah. He'll stop by every day for a few hours."

"Poor guy. He's probably lonely."

Ollie chuckled. "Jenkins is okay alone most of the time. He'll be fine. Besides, he lived at their house while I was at Sunrise. They're best buds. I'll be surprised if Dad hasn't just carted him back to their house, to be honest."

They ate in silence, brushing one another's knees and hands every so often. About halfway through the movie, Ollie seemed pensive.

"What's wrong?" Olivia asked, seeing his frown when she reached for her drink.

"It's silly," he said, shaking his head.

"What is?"

He paused the movie, turning a very serious look to her way.

"It's ridiculous, but I want to know how that compares to your memory."

The question took Olivia by surprise, but she didn't hesitate to give her answer.

"No comparison. This was a thousand times better than my memories. It was at least that much better than any of my other… experiences." A furious blush overtook her face as she admitted so. Right on the heels of embarrassment was doubt about whether he'd believe her, especially considering her career—no matter how short—in adult films.

Instead, he smiled warmly at her. "High praise indeed. I should be so lucky. I appreciate the vote of confidence, Princess."

She shrugged. "All true."

He grunted, turning the movie back on. They slumped together under a blanket for the rest of the movie, Olivia's head pillowed on his shoulder. He rubbed slow circles into her flesh all along her shoulder and arm.

It was the most relaxed and at peace Olivia had ever been.

THEY SPENT TWO more days rollicking in the waves and learning how each other's body responded to touch. Nothing else existed.

It was the perfect little bubble.

They'd taken a picnic dinner out to the deck, enjoying the last of the sun for the day and the cool breeze coming off the water.

She'd finally toasted with one of the hard seltzers, complete with a paper umbrella they'd been lucky enough to find in one of the kitchen drawers.

As they were cleaning up, Ollie paused right in the middle of washing a plate and turned her way.

"How exactly did we manage to have sex in that booth?"

Olivia barked a laugh, the question taking her by surprise. "What?"

"At the club. It's been bothering me for weeks. How did we do it?"

Olivia set down her glass, grabbing some ice out of a bag in the freezer. She couldn't help giggling at his thoughtful expression. She could almost see the math equations floating past his face.

"I just can't figure out the logistics. I'm sure I'm missing something."

Olivia filled up her glass with water, taking it with her to the living room. Ollie was right behind her, face still scrunched up. She tucked her legs underneath her as she sank into the cushion.

"I think you were kind of sitting on the table. I had my stomach over the back of the booth…" She gestured with her hands, trying to mime what she was describing. He didn't seem convinced, so she got up on her knees on the couch, pressing her front into the cushions of the backrest. "Like this."

Playing along, Ollie got up and stood behind her, sinking down onto his knees as well.

"Yeah, my ass was probably on the table. I wonder if I knocked over any drinks."

Olivia laughed. "I couldn't say." He sat back down with a sigh. "Was it really bugging you that bad?"

"You have no idea. I pictured you on your back on the seat, but I couldn't figure out where I would put my knee, and you would have been bent into a crescent. I pictured you on all fours, or on top of me, but same problem. How was it I saw your tattoo? Just the fact it was in a booth like…" He shuddered. "How many people had done the same thing? What all were we touching on the tacky velvet fabric? Did I remember to wrap it up? My guys were right outside the curtain too." He grimaced, one eyebrow up. "I clearly spent an unreasonable amount of time thinking over the logistics of our long-ago booth interlude." He sighed, playful expression evaporating. "I want to remember so badly. But I can't."

Olivia took his hand into hers. "It's okay. It's not important that you remember. There's probably a reason you don't."

"My therapists think so too." He shook his head. "None of that. Not while we're here, anyway. No regrets, right?"

"Not one." She smiled warmly at him, an idea percolating. Before she could logic her way out of it, she stripped off her shirt. "Want to grab a towel or something so we don't get cooties from the couch and give it a shot?" She shifted her hips in invitation.

Ollie laughed, but it only took a moment for him to shift from lighthearted to pressing his whole body against her back, his arms caging her in. She could immediately feel a pulse between her legs as he did so, her hormones set to full blast after their last couple of days.

"Are we going to get cooties from the couch or give the couch cooties?" He asked, nipping along the back of her ear and down her neck.

"Does it matter?"

"Not really."

He grunted and peeled himself away, striding with purpose into the bathroom to get said towels.

Olivia stripped down while he was gone, and he groaned upon his return. "Christ, you're gorgeous."

He pulled her into his arms for a thorough kiss before covering the furniture. She helped him find his way out of his clothes, then resumed her position kneeling on the couch, facing the kitchen.

Ollie climbed up behind her, covering her in his heat and weight once more. It took some maneuvering from them both, but he finally managed to press inside her, the angle intense enough Olivia moaned into her forearm.

"That'll do it," he gasped, experimenting with ways to move on the narrow cushion. He tested the waters with a slow thrust, pulling out nearly all the way before pressing back in. Olivia pushed back into him, matching his pace. Together, they found a way to rock that hit all the pleasure points.

The unusual position put pressure on all the right places and it didn't take long for either of them to start spiraling into breathy moans.

"Sorry, I can't…" Ollie's rhythm faltered as her body began to pulse.

"It's fine. I'm close."

He reached one hand around at her waist, rolling his fingertips over her clit to help her along. He pressed his lips to her tattoo, hips hitching as he crested the peak.

Olivia was only seconds behind him, body spasming under his touch. Her eyes squeezed closed, she rested her head on her forearm for a moment as he stood up.

"Huh. That worked pretty well," he said.

"Told you so."

"I'll never doubt you again, Butterfly."

He gave her an exaggerated wink as he went down the hall toward the bathroom.

Olivia laughed as she heard him mutter *who knew?*

"I did," she murmured to herself. "I definitely did."

And now, she had a brand-new memory that was better than the old one to turn to if she ever needed it.

Who knew indeed.

AFTER A FEW days at the beach, days full of nothing but pleasure, returning to the business of real life was a bit of a shock to the system.

Olivia met with a realtor to find her own place. She also had a meeting with two of the three therapists Dr. Clay had suggested. One felt pretty promising, but she wanted to at least speak to the third before making a decision. Besides, she needed to have a place to live nailed down so she wouldn't drive an hour to every appointment.

Pauline had emailed them both the special circumstances mentor details, and unfortunately, they wouldn't have a chance to get started until after Shari had already moved on. Olivia hoped her friend kept working so she would graduate and build a beautiful life. She'd gotten a text from her, a 'here's my number too' message, but it gave her hope. At least she could reach out if she needed something.

She and Ollie were enjoying their temporary cohabitation, but Olivia knew rushing into something like living together was a terrible idea. Even if she only signed a short lease on a place of her own, she felt as though it would give her some time to find her footing as the new, independent person she wanted to be. The realtor was hopeful there was something out there in her price range, but time would tell.

Days were for working and evenings for sharing a meal and relaxing on Ollie's ridiculously comfortable sofa. The nights were for exploring one another in every way they possibly could. She no longer considered the guest room as her place. Ollie's king-sized bed was where she got her best rest, wrapped up in his arms and his scent.

She would miss it when she went to her own place.

"You can sleep over whenever you like," he assured her, nuzzling into the top of her head.

She was lying against his side with her head on his chest, his arm wrapped around her back.

"I didn't mean to say that out loud. But I'm definitely going to take you up on it."

"I hope so. Did the realtor get back to you with any options?"

The moon was bright outside the window, filtering through the blinds even though they were wound shut.

"She found a couple of places. I'm supposed to go see one tomorrow."

"Fun. I'd love to come with you, but I have a reading."

"I know. It's fine, there are some things I should do on my own. I want you to go furniture shopping with me this weekend, though."

"Sounds miserable." He laughed, and she dug her fingers into his ribs, making him squirm. "Seriously though, when is furniture buying ever fun?"

"Never. But I don't plan to do much except say what I want and write a check. I'm not dealing with any negotiating. Point, purchase, leave."

"Wow, you're sexy when you get all tough. Sign me up."

"You're ridiculous."

"You like it, Butterfly."

Olivia didn't respond, because it was true. She just cuddled closer and closed her eyes, letting the sound of his heart beating under her ear lull her to sleep.

Thirty-Four

AFTER WEEKS OF being busier than she could ever recall, Olivia was finally in a place of her own.

She toured no fewer than a dozen apartments before finding one that met all of her needs without being either too far-flung from the part of the city she wanted to be in or costing an arm and a leg.

She had plenty of funds left from the house sale, but with no prospect of full time work, she was trying to be as conservative as possible. Ollie had arranged for them to have dinner with his dad as an introduction to money management and budgeting. It had been a hilarious evening full of puns, jokes, and spreadsheets. She was hopeful about taking what he'd shown her since her history with money was dismal.

Her little one bedroom was small, but had everything she needed. The living area and kitchen were one open space and there was a small balcony she could sit on in the evenings to catch a breeze and watch the sun go down. She even had a private parking space for her car off the street, which was something she'd never dreamed would be such a sought-after amenity.

She'd never been much of a cook, but she was giving it her best shot. Luckily, everything she could want was within either walking or delivery distance if her experimenting went wrong.

And it did, at least half the time.

The best part was she was only a few short minutes' drive from Ollie, something they were both already taking advantage of.

Getting her car had been slightly more dramatic than she'd hoped, however.

Her dad had supplied the gate codes and directions to their apartment, and Ollie had driven her over one afternoon. She'd foolishly expected a simple transaction, especially since he'd said her mom was still upset about the house having been sold, so she was refusing to allow Olivia into the apartment as well as speak to her.

As far as Olivia was concerned, that was just fine. She didn't have anything kind to say to her mother, either, though she did miss her in a twisted trauma-bond kind of way.

Ollie pulled into the parking space her father had indicated would be available, right next to her car. Her dad came down the steps from their unit a moment after they pulled in, a bright smile on his mouth.

Olivia's heart was light as she hugged her dad.

"I'm glad you came," he said.

"Me too," she confirmed. "I'm sorry it won't be a very long visit."

He nodded. "We'll work up to it."

Olivia turned and opened the passenger side door on her car, tossing her purse onto the seat.

Ollie and her dad exchanged a firm handshake and friendly greeting as she got re-acquainted with the vehicle.

When she looked up from her walk around the car, her mother was stalking across the lawn in their direction, arms crossed firmly over her chest. "Come to take that too?"

"Elena, we talked about this—"

"No, *you* talked, James. I told you she wasn't welcome after what she did."

"And I told you she was coming to get *her* car."

Olivia tensed, Ollie maneuvering himself away from her mother and back toward where she stood between their cars.

"Hi, Mom," she said tensely.

"*Hi, Mom,*" Olivia's mother mocked back. "Don't give me that nonsense, Olivia. You took my home, now my car? How can you sleep at night knowing you tore this family apart the way you have?"

Olivia drew in a deep breath, Ollie taking hold of her hand for strength.

"This is *my* car, Mom. I paid for it. Same as the house. I'm sorry it came down to selling. But the taxes and fines—"

"I was working it out! It would have been okay."

Olivia's dad had his hands on his wife's shoulders, tension evident in the firm set of his mouth.

"No, it wouldn't," Olivia said quietly. "You lied to me, Mom. You were about to lose the house and you talked me into taking a job that landed me in jail to cover your ass. It's not okay."

"You ungrateful brat! How dare you. I—"

"*Elena.* No." The words were clipped, but said in a tone that brokered no further argument. Even Ollie tensed from the power in his voice.

"James, how can you defend this? She stole everything from us—"

"Elena," he said, only slightly softer, weariness showing as his eyes pinched shut. Clearly, this was a conversation they'd had more than a few times. "That's not what happened. You know it, I know it, and she knows it. Go back inside."

"But—"

"No but. *Go.*"

Pouting, and clearly not having gotten her say the way she'd hoped, Olivia's mom loped back toward the building.

"I'm sorry," her father sighed.

"It's not your fault, Dad." Olivia reached forward, giving him another hug.

"It kind of is, but I'm working on it. I love you, baby. Maybe we can have lunch soon?"

"I'd like that."

He smiled, glancing ruefully toward the apartment windows where his wife was now glaring down at them.

After another quick hug and a wave, they'd driven off. It hadn't been anything like what Olivia had anticipated, though in hindsight, perhaps she should have.

Ollie was a reliable constant, which Olivia could not have been more grateful for. He'd been by her side every step of the way, including helping her sort through the things Jerry had put into storage for her. There were dishes, cookware, and furniture her mother had kept in the basement, plus whatever had remained in her bedroom. He hadn't been lying about the unit being tiny, but it was everything she could have asked to be saved for her.

Ollie took her to order a couch like his since she liked it so much, and she went out to find her very own little dining room table.

They had returned to Sunrise together over a weekend for orientation as special circumstances mentors. Pauline had walked them through the process with enthusiasm, welcoming them to the other side of rehab with access to the food they would miss when they weren't on campus, along with employee badges and a mountain of paperwork. They were each set to come out to speak to new recruits a few months out. It was a good first step.

Everything was coming together.

As Olivia was rearranging the cabinet with pots and pans, her buzzer rang.

Her blood warmed despite already knowing who it was.

"Let me in, Princess. I have food."

"Who is this?" She teased.

"You wound me, Butterfly."

"I think you'll survive. Come on up, I guess."

"You guess? I ought—"

She cut him off, pressing the security gate button and opening her door.

He was shaking his head as he got off the elevator at the end of the corridor, but a playful smile graced his lips.

"I shouldn't even share this with you now," he threatened, kissing her before following her inside.

"What did you bring?"

"Happy housewarming," Ollie said, handing her a box from the coffee shop across town.

"Pastries?" She *oohed* in delight, finding a huge assortment inside the pink box.

"And… this." He held a cloth bundle in his hands.

Olivia could feel the gravity of the moment change.

"Come show me." She walked the few steps to her couch and sat down. He joined her, sitting so close their legs were touching as he set the cloth bundle on the low coffee table.

"I had these framed. I thought…" he shook his head, at a loss for words as he unwrapped the bundle.

Inside were four small frames, each with a different colored variation of her butterfly tattoo inside it.

"These are beautiful." Olivia ran her fingertips reverently over the glass.

"I found some of my old sketches. I thought… well. Fancied up, they seemed like a nice housewarming gift."

"They're perfect."

Ollie's cheeks glowed pink, whether from her praise or from embarrassment over sharing something vulnerable, she wasn't sure.

She grabbed them up, taking them into her bedroom. The wall her bed faced was bare, and now she had exactly the thing for them.

Olivia got out her little tool kit, holding up the frames in multiple configurations before settling on a diamond pattern right in the middle of the wall.

"You don't have to hang them up right this minute, you know."

"Sure I do." She winked at him, handing the frames back as she hammered in the tiny nails to hang them from.

She played with which color would go where after the nails were set, finally settling on a vaguely rainbow order going clockwise.

"The pink one is my favorite."

"I like this one too." Ollie took her hand, holding it up close to the frame. Her nails were done in the polish he'd given her again, and it was a nearly perfect match for the shade he'd used on the butterfly.

"How long ago did you draw these?"

"The blue and the green are from a couple of years ago. When I started to come off the drugs, I had really vivid dreams. This damned butterfly haunted me." He was smirking, but the words stabbed at Olivia's heart. "The pink and purple I did during art therapy when I got to Sunrise. There was something about it I couldn't shake. It would pop up in my mind at the strangest of times. Then… you showed up." He smiled at her. "I think… I think it was always you, Olivia. We met years ago so you could be my redemption now." His words were soft, wrapping around her in a warm embrace. "We just had to figure our shit out first. Wild how the universe works sometimes, isn't it?"

Olivia nodded, heart exploding out of her chest. She'd gone through a lot to get to this point, but she wouldn't change a thing.

She planted a fierce kiss on his mouth, taking him by such surprise he made a startled noise.

"Come on. Let's go get the box of pastries. We can get crumbs in my new bed." She winked at him, tugging on his hand so he would follow her.

"Or maybe… we can break in your new couch?"

It was the eyebrow wiggle that did it for her. Olivia burst out laughing. He joined in, drawing her into his arms, walking her with him to the couch where he lowered her down first with him on top.

"I'm damn glad you found me again, Olivia."

He kissed her senseless, and she put everything she had into it so he knew just how much she agreed.

Then, with the rest of her body, she showed him.

And she'd keep showing him as long as he'd let her.

Want a little bit more of Ollie & Olivia?

Sign up for Lily's newsletter to get special
bonus scenes and exclusive short stories!

NEWSLETTER:
http://bit.ly/ALANewsletter

If you enjoyed Image Destroyer, please consider leaving
a review on Amazon, Goodreads or BookBub.

Grab the rest of the Image Series on Amazon!

Danielle Keil

Shain Rose

Katherine L Evans

Shannon Myers

Penelope Freed

Kennedy L. Mitchell

LK Farlow

AK Mulford

KK Allen

Molly McLain

Brittainy Cherry

Saffron A Kent

Jillian Graves

Hollee Mands

Eva Chase

Rachel Jonas

Most of my new reads came from TikTok!
So many great new recommendations there!

A NOTE FROM
The Author:

THANKS FOR STICKING with me, dear reader, and I do truly mean that! This book was meant to happen at least a year ago, but I sidetracked into the Hollywood Connections series instead. Ollie and Olivia were a hard story to tell, but I'm so thankful I stuck with them and I hope you enjoy their love story as much as I do!

As always, this book wouldn't have happened without my Write or Die ladies, Shain Rose and Danielle Keil. They are my rocks and I wouldn't be an author without them to talk to, bounce ideas off of and have as friends. Go check out their books if you aren't already fans, they won't disappoint!

Huge thanks to my betas, ARC readers and anyone who shared the promo! I couldn't do this without you EVER. <3

Thanks to my husband for being my first (and last) idea sounding board, editor and often, my hero inspiration. He knows when I need to escape to the she-shed to really pound on the keys and never lets me procrastinate past the point of no return. I love you!

The team I have for cover, edits, proofreading and formatting is unbeatable! Kate, Abby, H.C. and Stephanie— You ladies are so amazing! Thank you for helping make this book the prettiest version of itself. The details you all add to my books brings my stories to life!

ABOUT THE *Author*

LILY IS A Colorado native enjoying the fantastic climate of Southern California with her family and cranky cats after surviving more than a decade in hot, humid places where hurricanes get their own season and Winter is a myth.

The written word is her favorite thing—reading or writing, she doesn't discriminate. That Happily Ever After is a powerful drug!

Go find her online!

FACEBOOK:
https://bit.ly/LilysReaderLounge
INSTAGRAM:
http://bit.ly/ALAInstagram
TIKTOK:
https://bit.ly/ALATikTok